THE WICKED S

L. M. MAGUIRE resides on
lived on the edge of many
religion, penury, prison, wholesome health and marriage.

Previous publications include volumes of poetry, short stories, plays, critiques and other literary artefacts.

ORMOND BOOKS fiction titles in preparation.

ICARUS FLYING.
A novel about Christopher Marlowe's final five years.

THE MARINATED MAN.

THE WICKED STEPCHILDREN

L. M. MAGUIRE

ORMOND BOOKS

Published by ORMOND BOOKS 1992
9 Lower Morden Lane, Morden Park, SM4 4SE

ISBN 0 9520081 0 6

Printed and bound by Intype Ltd, Wimbledon.

The cause is in my will.
William Shakespeare, Julius Caesar

Children begin by loving their parents; after a time they judge them: rarely, if ever, do they forgive them.
Oscar Wilde, A Woman Of No Importance.

Chapter one

The door bell went DONG and merged with Ivan's bad dream of a mile-long airport check-in queue. There rose a murmuring of voices, everybody shuffled forward three paces, the long line snaked into the far white distance, a tall thin man with a cadaverous face (Why, it is my great-great-grandfather from Omsk) stretched out his skeletal hands and cried, "More, more." A burly, masked executioner raised his sickle-blade axe and the bell went DONG. Ivan opened his eyes and stared at the meandering crack across the ceiling.

"Meander, as in Maeander, a river of Phrygia. Roving river. River of no return. From whose bourn no traveller returns. The Rover's Return. I'll drink to that with as big a mouth as Bournemouth. And then there is Eastbourne where another big mouth had borne and bears—"

Sally turned and pushed him towards the edge of the bed. "Either shut up or get up," she said crossly from the swilling depths of her slumber.

He got up, stared between the drapes at the tousled clouds and pulled up his pyjama bottoms to the place where his waist once was.

"And to cap it all," he said as he stumbled against the overflow of cloth at the foot of the bed, "where is Phrygia now?"

"You're going to make coffee then? That's nice." The voice curled up from the mound of coverlets and crumpled blankets. "Fetch the papers when you answer the door. It may be the post."

He could have made a smart-arse reply that as the door did not ask a question, he could not answer it. Instead he let the moment pass along with his passing water and then padded down to the kitchen in his bare feet. (The slippers had disappeared again. Could it have been the burglars?) The cats appeared from their forbidden sleeping places, sniffed his toes and then circled him as if he were a wildebeest – gnu to you – on the African plain. (As seen on television.)

The bell went DONG again. Where was the DING?

A young constable and a policewoman had arrived five minutes after Sally had made the frantic 999 call. The woman, who was surprisingly small, stood quite still, her dark eyes hardly flickering. She seemed to have an air of ennui about her. The constable, on the contrary, was quite keen to investigate the break-in. He asked searching questions about Ivan and Sally's comings and goings. Did they make a habit of visiting historical places on a Saturday afternoon? They did not. He inspected the scarred front door which the intruder/s had failed to open for their exit and declared that the backdoor lock had been forced with a long blade screw-driver.

Then he tried to interview the neighbours. The old dear on the left pretended to be out – he saw her curtain trembling when he came up the path – and the Finnish au pair on the right did not seem to understand a word he said until he asked when she would be free. "Oi om having my doy, how do ooo soy, free tummoroow." The woman in the house next to that exclaimed, "How terrible! The young people of today. Drugs, I wouldn't be surprised. They should bring back whipping." The constable pressed her about her "young people" remark. Yes, she had seen a skinny young man hanging about in a very suspicious manner during the day, in fact she was quite sure she had seen him going up the front path to ring the doorbell. But she became extremely vague when describing this character and hinted that she did not really want to be involved.

Enjoining the victims to make a list of what was missing and not to touch a thing till the Super arrived, the interested policeman and the disinterested policewoman left and were never seen again. Sally and Ivan stared morosely at the pile of books and papers jettisoned from the bureau and drank six cups of coffee each. Three hours later the Super and a bored fingerprint man called in. "Nice of you to come so soon," Ivan said. The sarcasm was lost on the detective. "Been several today. Woman over in Park Drive had thousands of pounds worth of jewellery taken. How much jewellery have you lost?" He became as bored as the fingerprint man when Sally replied that she had better things to do with her money than buy ghastly fripperies. When he heaved himself out of the armchair, he promised to send them home-security leaflets and told them that over the next few days, weeks and months they would discover that more things were missing. Sally and Ivan never heard from him again.

That was three weeks ago. Ivan still grieved over his vanished camera. It was rather bulky, totally mechanical and not in the least state-of-the-photographic-art SLR, but it had a newish lens and he was on the last few frames of à 36-exposure reel. And yes, to use the detective's oxymoronic phrase, they did discover things missing. For example, a brown A4 envelope containing black-and-white snapshots from his earlier marriage and a copy – a collector's item? – of the first and only edition of a literary magazine he had produced.

Then there were his missing slippers. "Velly comfortable, my dears, velly comfortable," Fagin says as he slips them over his bunions. And what about the DING? Eyes stare into the opened sack marked Swag and Fagin screams at the Dodger, "You've got the DING but where's the DONG, the DONG with the luminous nose?"

Ivan filled the perforated metal cup with fine coffee, poured water into the cylinder, switched on the expresso machine and then, ploughing through the importuning cats and clutching his pyjama bottoms to his belly (the elastic had lost its stretch months ago), he went into the hall to look blankly at the mat. "Post? What's she talking about? There's no post on Sunday. And the papers will be piled on the doorstep if they haven't blown away."

The house had become a fortress since the burglary. Ivan fumbled with the three door-keys and coyly reached out to grab the newspapers without indecently exposing himself to any easily frightened horses passing by.

A man and a woman stood on the front path. The man was middle-aged and wore a dull brown suit. A bulging, battered briefcase hung from his right hand and the newspapers were tucked under his left arm. The slightly younger woman had a sharp nose with a scarlet peak, also held a briefcase and was dressed in sad dun colours.

"Good morning, sir, and it is a good morning for the word of God to be broadcast over the land," the man declared.

"Hark then to the word of God," the woman intoned.

They both had the smug smiles of those who knew all the answers and all the questions too.

"Er, good morning, but I'm afraid we're not religious—" Ivan mumbled, hiding his lower regions behind the half-open door. The youngest cat nipped his ankle.

"Ha, when you say you are not religious, you're echoing the confused cry of many who have rejected the false doctrines of man-made religions. Don't be dismayed. We bring you Good News."

"Don't be dismayed. We bring you good news," the woman echoed.

"I know. You have my newspapers. May I have them, please." Ivan held out his hand but the man stepped back out of reach.

"You will not find The Good News within these Satanic screeds but we shall give you copies of the truth." The woman undid the catch of her briefcase.

"Another time perhaps." The phone began to ring and the expresso machine to hiss. "If you'll excuse me, I must answer the—"

"Ah, but have you asked yourself what is the question you must answer?" said the man pertly.

Ivan's pyjamas majestically descended. "Give me my fucking newspapers," he snarled. The phone stopped ringing.

The woman gasped with horror at the sight of his naked dangler and the couple scurried down the path with such haste that they nearly collided with Old Fred from around the corner.

"Hello, Ivan, getting some fresh air then," Old Fred shouted. "Had any good news yet? About your burglary?"

"No, Fred, no good news yet."

On the other side of London a young woman with long pale hair gently replaced the phone in the receiver and looked at herself in the mirror. "You have your father's eyes," she said. She pressed the stop button and removed the CD (The Merry Widow) from the player. "I hate Lehar. He's so unremittingly jolly."

"Here we are again," Ivan called out irritatingly in that unremittingly jolly manner he assumed when he was fully awake and Sally was still sleepy. She lay, eyes fully opened, staring at the meandering track of the ceiling crack. Ivan threw the papers on top of her stomach, nudged aside the clutter of cosmetic jars on the bedside table to make room for her coffee and then trotted round to his side.

"Awake, my beauteous one," he continued as he clambered in between the sheets, "for morning has flung a whacking brick into the bowels of night and given all dozing owls gall-stones."

"It's not funny and it doesn't even scan," she grumbled and then shrieked when he put his hand between her thighs. "Take it away. It's freezing." She sat up, sending half the papers overboard, and rifled through the remainder. "Where's the review section? Don't tell me they're not all here. I did want to read what old so-and-so had to say about the Theatre de Complan mime version of The Three Sisters." She did not seem to be in the best of humour. "Who were you talking to?"

"Well, I had a few stern words for the cats and told them in no uncertain terms that they'll just have to eat the food we give them and not expect us to lash out money—"

"At the door. Who were you talking to at the door?"

"Old Fred from around the corner. Wanted to know if we had any good news about the burglary."

"That windbag! Tramps up and down past our door every half-hour on his way to and from the shops but when asked if he saw anything out of the ordinary on the day of the break-in, oh no, the purblind idiot had to stay indoors because he had a limp. A limp what, I ask? But didn't I hear you talking to a man and a woman?"

"Oh, them. Wait till I tell you. This will make you laugh."

"I'm waiting."

"They were a pair of Witnesses."

Sally leaped out of bed and into her dressing-gown like an agoraphobic flea. "Witnesses! Where are they now? Did you get their names and addresses? I bet you didn't think of that. We must let the police know."

"Hold hard there, me proud beauty. They didn't say they were witnesses."

"But what did they say? My God, you're hopeless when it comes to things like this. How often have I told you to make sure you get people's names, addresses and phone numbers."

"These were Jehovah's Witnesses.They didn't say they were but then they never do, not at first."

"Jehovah's Witnesses? Not the other kind of witness?" She put her right knee on the bed. "I'm sorry. I didn't mean to snap at you. It's just – well – we've had another phone call."

"From whom?"

"From whoever likes ringing us up to play music without saying a single word."

"Oh no, not him again."

"It's a female."

"How do you know?" He rolled over and clutched her knee. "You don't think I've got another woman in tow, do you? It's as much as an old man like me can do to keep one woman satisfied." He expected her to say, "You're not so old." Instead she removed his hand and said as she left the room, "What makes you think you're keeping one woman satisfied?"

Ivan sat on her side of the bed, looked into the dressing-table mirror, flexed his jaws and bent his head to see his hair in the thin light. He sang, out of tune, "Darling, I am growing old/ Silver hairs among the gold/ Shine upon my brow today/ Life is fading fast away."

Two Saturdays ago they had ventured into a charity shop, he in the vain hope of finding some rare book like a Shakespeare & Co edition of Joyce's Ulysses – he usually wound up with a handful of musty pre-war Penguins – and she to look at earrings from underdeveloped countries. The old codger behind the counter, doing his good deed for the day, asked Ivan if he would like to buy some ribbons for his daughter. The man's mottled face did not alter when Sally curtly replied, "I'm his wife."

Perhaps they had done the well-meaning fool an injustice. Perhaps he thought they had a daughter at home who would like to adorn herself with rainbow ribbon stitched by the skeletal fingers of an impoverished peasant child. For further information see glossy magazines for details and stark pictures wedged between features on gourmet cooking and holidays abroad. (Why should I be bitter?) And how would the man know that Ivan's actual daughters were now far beyond the age of girlish delight. Somewhere over the rainbow/ far away/ there is a land—

"You're miles away." Sally had returned. "I'm running a bath. What were you thinking about?"

"Ribbons and bows and countries from whose bourn no travellers return."

The phone rang. Sally picked it up, held it to her ear for a few seconds, whispered to Ivan, "Again" then handed it to him.

"Now listen here, whoever you are, a joke is a joke but I'm becoming quite angry with this—" He cupped the mouthpiece with his hand. "I'm sure I heard someone laugh," he said to Sally.

"Man or woman?"

"I think it was a girl."

He replaced the phone.

"What was the music?"

"Berlioz' Symphonie Fantastique. We heard the end of the fourth movement known as The March To The Gallows. The hero dreams he has killed his beloved and is being taken to the gallows."

"I don't want to hear any more."

On the other side of London the young woman put down the receiver and looked at herself in the mirror. "Have I got my father's eyes? They didn't wait to hear Harriet's theme." As the turmoil of the witches' sabbath waxed wrathful, she took a woman-doll from an oblong box and stroked its hair.

Chapter two

Of all the dinner parties in all the towns, two in particular merit our attention. A charming couple of impeccable snobs by name of Andrew and Zena, or A-to-Z to those without a map, had sent out gilt-embossed cards to three other couples, inviting the recipients to their des res in Richmond (Surrey) for an evening of scintillating conversation, mood music and a bellyful of haute cuisine. Sally and Ivan had received an invitation.

Ivan groaned. "Not them! And on a Sunday too. Write and tell them that we've been forbidden by the authorities to mix with healthy people. Incipient bubonic plague suspected. Besides, I must stay in to watch the programme about the history of Venetian music," he added, suddenly feeling precious.

"You can tape it." She dialled a number. He began to protest, but she hushed him with an imperious flick of her hand. "Hello, Zena and Andrew." She spoke to the named couple through the intermediary of an answering device. "This is Sally speaking. Ivan and I are looking forward to seeing you both on Sunday. Good-byeee."

Ivan had a mind to re-ring A-to-Z and tell them – via the above device – that he had anthrax or at least Chinese flu; but he knew life would be unbearable for at least a week afterwards. It was not that Sally would refuse to speak to him. On the contrary, she would refuse to stop talking, explaining over and over again how important it was for a freelance journalist to maintain contacts with people like Andrew who knew someone who knew someone in the Media.

"By the way, what does Andrew do?"

"He's an accountant." (We shall meet another accountant later in the story.)

"I knew there was a good reason for disliking him. And what about Zena?"

"She's writing her Novel."

"God help us."

On the other side of London, within a horn's toot of the North Circular Road, preparations of a frantic and chaotic nature, garnished with peppery words and spicy imprecations, were being made for another bunfight. Far less formal than the A-to-Z affair, it was one of those family events to which half the family hadn't been invited. To conclude before we continue, part of the party of the first party are related – both in the abstract and the absolute – to the party of the second party.

Sally looked reluctantly in the mirror. "Jesus, imagine twee Zena saying, 'How quaint. A Laura Ashley. How brave of you.' Damn, I'll wear the red dress instead. But I've only worn this once and that was three months ago. I wonder if anybody will ask us to their wedding." She opened the bathroom door to call down to Ivan but a blast of Berlioz swept up the stairs and smacked her ears.

Ivan sat on the sofa, having swept two cats off the cushions, his stockinged feet on the cluttered coffee table and a newspaper on his knees. His left hand waved to the beat of the music and his right hand held a pencil against his cheek. "Let me see now. 10 across. (6) Old snake-hair confuses us with honied drink."

Sally bustled into the room and turned the volume down. "This noise will make you as deaf as a stone," she said in a firm voice. "I'd expect such a racket from your youngest daughter but—(Why mention the youngest?)"

Stone! Youngest daughter. Youngest of three sisters. Three Wyrde sisters. Gorgons. Of course. Medusa.

She twisted her arms behind her back and undid a row of buttons. "Let me help you," he volunteered as he swung his feet onto the floor and scattered a heap of magazines. But she had tackled the last button and was now pulling the rejected dress over her head. She stood freshly fleshed in her underwear. "I said, how could you think with the music so high?"

"It was higher when you played The Doors."

"I was never so high as when I opened the doors of perception."

Two mundane thoughts crossed his mind. 1) You can tell the age of ex-students by their record collection. 2) 11 down. 5 letters. Medics embrace love again and again. First letter D. Yes, Doors.

He expressed the first thought while writing down the second. "And how were you able to think when mighty Morrison blared from the speakers?"

She smiled and turned to look at herself in the mirror. "One doesn't think when everything appeared as it is, infinite."

He stood behind her, placed his hands on her hips and slowly brought them up over her waist and her breasts as if shaping an urn on the potter's wheel at evening class. She moved sideways and asked, "Have you shaved?" It was such an irrelevant question. "An hour ago," he replied testily. "Good, I don't want any of this last-minute panic." He advanced his cause again. "What would your children say if they could see you now?" asked Sally rhetorically.

The mention of his children, who had children of their own, was as a douche on hot determination. "They can say what they like for all I care," he replied aggressively but the fervour was dying, the moment was passing by like a pauper's funeral and the afternoon was no longer young.

Now facing him, she held the tight red dress against her body. "Do you think this is too obvious, too revealing, too flagrant, too competitive?"

"Or too late," he muttered as he slunk into the kitchen to fill the expresso machine.

Delay was inevitable while Sally neurotically daubed her eyes and he tried to record the Venetian programme. Eventually he decided to tape over an old French gangster film. "Sorry, Jean Gabin," he muttered. "It's either being or nothing since all our pleasures are existential." As he rose to his feet, he knocked a porcelain pig off the mantelpiece. It lost its trotters. "That's an omen," he called out. "It's a sign sent from the gods warning us not to go."

There was the usual toil and moil as they tried to park in A-to-Z's street. Ivan squinted facetiously at all the knicker blinds and said rather loudly, to the disgust of a BBC floor manager passing by, "Bow, bow, you lower-middle classes, living as you do, like silly asses, with mortgages and debts up to your neck, you might as well be in Tooting Bec."

Sally trotted up stone steps, clenching a wine bottle. "This is no time to act the ragged-arsed philanthropist." She rang the bell and urgently whispered to Ivan, "Leave your cloth cap in your pocket."

Andrew – known to many as Android – opened the door and looked at them through his horn-rimmed glasses as if he were not quite sure who they were. "Ah, there you are (pause) at last. You didn't have that far to come, did you?" He swept his left arm up and gave his Cartier watch a hard stare. "Better late than never, I suppose," he said rebukingly, standing to one side. "Do come in, you two, do come in."

Zena's voice was heard at the end of the hall. "Who is it, darling?" She sounded anxious.

"It's alright, darling. The final contingent has arrived."

Sally blithely doled out bogus excuses for their lateness and thrust the wine bottle into Andrew's hands. He peeled off the wrapping paper and held the bottle at arm's length. "Ah, a dry white. How nice of you. And from Sainsbury too. I do believe I read an article in – was it the Sunday Times? – that you can get some good vintages from the supermarkets."

He led them down the hall and into the rag-rolled dining room. There were two other couples seated at a burnished wooden table (distressed rainforest). Sally noted with smirking satisfaction that the women were dressed like milkmaids. "How quaint," she thought. She felt convinced that the men were casting languishing looks at her chest. Certainly it was difficult to miss. In the interests of sexual apartheid, Andrew had placed the women on the left-hand side of the table and the men on the right. Would it be unjust, we ask, to imply he was a voyeur? It is true that he would squeeze between the women's chairs and the Edwardian rosewood cabinet ("Picked it up for a song in Clapham Junction," he smugly told his guests) to pour out wine and look them straight in the tit. If there were a Keep-Britain-Polished Party, Andrew and Zena would have been president and secretary. The introductions were brisk and glossy.

"Richard, man of the moment and the Media (tight smile and slight nod from rigid Richard), his precious spouse, Prunella (plucked eyebrows perked), George, our legal eagle and judicious genius (cloud passed over moon-face), his devoted companion

Deirdre (known as 'plus one' at parties), Sally, who sallies forth on journalistic safaris and – (Android hesitated. Ivan was not on his 'Need-to-know' file.) her constant companion, EE-Van." Standing behind Sally as if about to zip her up, he passes their contribution to the feast to Zena. "Darling, look what they brought us."

Zena holds vessel as if it were a pissing baby. "How nice, darling. From Sainsbury. I read in the Observer Magazine or was it on the wine programme, you know, the woman with the big glasses—"

Andrew raised his left arm to show her the Cartier watch. "Darling, I think we should begin." He shines a smile on his guests and says, "Let me present a musical offering—"

"Oh, I do like Bach," Ivan said.

"Quite, quite." Andrew did not appreciate the interruption to his overture. Again his hand went up to conduct the final bars. "If music be the food of love, etc, etc, we shall have Wolfgang Amadeus to excess." He vanished into the kitchen to join his wife and within seconds attenuated Mozart seeped from the two loudspeakers cunningly placed – and tastefully veneered – on each side of the Edwardian cabinet.

"I do like their wallpaper," Deirdre simpered to Sally.

"Do you mean the aural or visual?"

Deirdre's husband gave a Pekinese bark of a laugh and then, turning his round face and rimless glasses to Ivan, asked, "EE-Van? Are you Russian?"

"No, I'm actually Rastafarian."

"Rastafarian? I thought they were West Indian."

Sally delivered her first kick of the evening to Ivan's shins. "Don't mind him, George. His great-great-great grandfather came from Minsk or was it Omsk but now he's—"

"Yes, he was known as EE-Van Grocer. He had a shop just off the Nevsky Prospect."

"As I was saying, Ivan is as Romford as the beer."

Prunella spoke in a prudish voice. "Romford? Changed, changed utterly. I was driving through the area only last week on my way home from seeing friends in Cambridge. Do you know

Professor Clutterbuck? Well,the noise, the dirt, the crowds and, of course, at least every second face one saw was black."

Sally fired a warning look across the bow of the table at Ivan and then shot up out of her seat. "If you'll excuse me, everybody, I must—" She stood in the kitchen doorway. "I'm sorry to bother you, Zena, but could you tell me where—"

Andrew was placing shallow bowls filled with a white gelatinous substance on a tray while Zena slipped Cellophane and tinfoil packages into the oven. The colourful discarded sleeves were crammed into the dustbin. "If they make sure to put the heat on mark 5," thought Sally, "the second course will be at least 25 minutes."

At the precise moment that Sally was manoeuvring their humble car into the mingy space left by a Granada and a Porsche – she drove and Ivan gave non-driver's advice – on the other side of London in a dilapidated street of gangrenous Georgian town houses, a 2CV squeezed itself between an overflowing skip and a battered transit van and whined to a stop. A young woman, legs first flung forward, stepped out and for a second or two stood to view, with deja vu eyes, the cracked plaster on the false pilasters, the scarred and paint-peeled front doors, the gouged leaded lights, the dumped cars and the two boys, one white and one black, burrowing in the skip.

She shook her long pale hank of hair, retrieved a tissue-wrapped bottle and an executive briefcase from the front seat and climbed up the steps of a house. Some 30 seconds after she had pressed the third button in a row of ten, a sash window on the second floor was pushed up and a frenzied perm appeared.

"Yoo-hoo. Who is it?" The voice had a quavery quality.

"Yoo-hoo-whoo," echoed the white boy. His black companion giggled.

The young woman stepped back a pace. "It's me, Amy. Angelica."

The sash window slammed shut and half a minute later a young man stood like a matador in the front doorway. What he lacked in stature he gained in pomposity as his chest pouted. "You're here at last. You hadn't far to come, had you?" He swung his left arm up and transferred his fixed glare to the face of a shock-proof, satellite-seeking, time-bleeping wrist-watch. "I suppose you'd say it's better late than never."

"May I be allowed to enter my sister's palatial domain, Alex?"

"Do what? Oh, yes, sure. Don't let me stop you."

She pushed past him, the bottle hugged to her thin bosom, the executive briefcase swinging from her left hand. He had one more authoritative task to perform. "Hey, you," he shouted at the impudent urchins, "clear off from there." They yelled back, "Angie lick my arse" as they scampered down the street.

The dingy former drawing-room of Georgian high life was now cluttered with undistinguished furniture and noisy children. Most of the latter were being hypnotised by a television set. A woman, she of the frenzied hair, sat near the table with a squirming creature on her lap. "Look who's here, your Auntie Ange (to rhyme with flange)," she gushingly said to the bubble-blowing infant.

"Am I so late?" the new arrival asked as she ruthlessly swept a bundle of magazines from a rickety cane chair and sat down.

"Late or not, it doesn't matter. Nothing's ready yet as usual." Alex entered left, crossed the room and vanished through a door right. "He's in a bit of a tizz as well. If it's not one thing it's another." The squirmer slid off her lap. "Do you want to say hello to your Auntie Ange, then? She knows you, Ange, you know." The pant-filler and snot-dribbler waddled hopefully towards Angelica. "Tweeties, tweeties," it burbled. 'Auntie Ange' coolly brushed the sticky paws aside before spraying herself with a killer blast of designer defoliant. The brat bawled and returned meekly to its mother.

Alex and a fattish female appeared. She surveyed the chaos and shouted, "Isn't anybody going to lay the effing table?" The bawl was over. The party began.

Chapter three

That which has been written was in the nature of a prologue or, as they say in the trade, a scene-setter. Before we continue with the party of the first party and the party of the second party, it is moot that we should introduce the dramatis personae in rounded characters rather than figures of a single dimension leaping from the sweating forehead of the scribe.

Whenever the party of the second party gathered in one place for family occasions like weddings, funerals and divorces, they ended up having a good gossip about Ivan and Cleo.

Cleo? Backtracking through the preceding pages will not discover a Cleo. We will come to Cleo.

A few years ago the leading question was: "Seen Dad lately?" Yes, now it can be revealed. These are the children of Ivan. Whoever replied in the affirmative would then mention Dad's newest female friend when they called in to see how he was coping with his alleged single state. But, to be cynical, anxiety about his welfare was not the main item on their agenda.

Sometimes his companion of the moment could be mistaken for a grown-up daughter. His children's various reactions were predictable. a) Disdain: "You know what they say, there's no fool like an old fool." b) Avaricious: "Throwing his money away on these young girls but you try asking him for a loan." Loan was a code word for a donation to their distress fund. c) Grudging praise: "Still, for a man of his age—".

In fact his female friends were all well past the nubile stage, and, rare avis, knew the difference between Tolstoy and Tolkien. Some could even chat about Kant and Hegel. All but one of Ivan's offspring, if asked, would hazard a guess that K and H were German delicatessens. The nearest they ever came to the pure reason of our ponderous philosophers was in heated discussions on the categorical imperatives of necessity. Or, to translate into the vernacular, 'You gotta lend me five quid till Friday 'cos I'm bloody broke.'

Ivan's women had another characteristic in common. After a month or so of his estimable company, they suddenly left for foreign shores, or at least Scotland and Wales, undoubtedly highly enriched by his erudition. Perhaps Ivan choose them for this endearing trait. Whatever, he never seemed unduly distressed by their departure and in less time than it takes to change the library books, another one was perched on his sofa, drinking his dark coffee, smoking his Gaulois and listening to his mellifluous voice and his records of Bach's cello concerti. The traffic through his third-floor flat confused his children. "Who did you say was there? Was it Ha So?" "No, she went back to Tokyo." "Is he still seeing Sheila?" "She went back to Melbourne a month ago." "What about the black-haired nutty one?" "She sent him a postcard from Rio."

At least the comings and goings provided a small topic of conversation during dull moments. The constant factor of inconstancy did not generate sufficient rejective power for the alien body injected into the family organism.

Sally was different. Sally was interesting. Sally stayed.

Here then is the generation of Cleo and Ivan. Cleo being she that was wedded and bedded by Ivan in their youthful years when Eden seemed attainable and the Land of Nod was East of their dreams.

Cleo's role in this drama is offstage. She has many names: "She-who-curdles-milk" (Sally), "That woman" (Ivan), "The old dear" (her children), "The old bag" (her children's children).

She was born within the Bermuda triangle of Balham, Clapham and the Junction, the third daughter of an itinerant harmonica-player ("My father was an artiste") and an auxiliary nurse in a mental hospital ("My mother belonged to the caring profession"). She was fancifully christened Cleopatra because her mother conceived while standing near the alleged Needle by the Thames. [Clinical note: injection and conception are not simultaneous]. Her father's surname was Mugglethorpe but in later years she excised the Muggle part – too plebeian. When she was about ten, her father left to improve his prospects in Lytham St Anne's where he took up with a chicken plucker from Liverpool and was never heard of again. Cleo was wont to claim royal connections, treated the local railway-bisected park as her rightful domain and always enjoined her children to avoid marrying "beneath themselves".

"As I unfortunately did," she would add in later years. Though she was keen to learn and wished to become a Doctor of Philosophy, she studied sociology as a last resort. She first met Ivan on a bench in Cannon Row Police Station after a rather rowdy protest rally in Trafalgar Square. When they were charged and fined the next day (under a law which sought to deter soldiers and sailors from molesting church-goers after the Napoleonic Wars), they wandered hand-in-hand to the nearest folk club, sang soulful songs about sorrowing crofters and agreed to live and lie beneath the banner of all radical hearts' desires. Ivan thought she was six years younger than he – she was actually seven years older – and, because of the two-yard scarf she wore, an LSE student. She had bought the woollen winding sheet at an ideologically sound bazaar the previous Christmas. Meanwhile her innate snobbishness detected in his talk the lisping speech impediment of an Old Etonian. In fact, he had forcefully struck a policeman's fist with his face and it was some weeks before the wound to his inner lip had healed and he was back to his normal educated Essex accent.

By then, of course, it was too late to renege on their delusions, truth was tucked under the pounded mattress and in between spatting they were begatting.

As the first shall be last and the last first, the final begat of the generation of Ivan and Cleo was Angelica. When Cleo missed a month, her heart missed a beat, she frantically checked through her secret diary (third loose floorboard to right of dressing-table) and held the diaphragm up to the bathroom light for possible minute perforations. Could she have made a mistake – another mistake? – when they settled their latest row more in the manner of a physical assault course than a bout of marital bliss? Or could it be—? This thought did not get beyond conception.

As her womb began to bloom, Cleo quailed at the fear that this partridge of her parturition would be a bird of a different breed. She groused about it in her secret diary, a squiggle here, a scribble there and as difficult to decode as a smudged DNA symbol. (Even

Ivan, who had once completed a form for MENSA, found it difficult to decipher whenever he had a surreptitious read.) A ribbon of worry wound itself around her in the last month. Three weeks before the final outcome, a party was held to give Angus MacClaggan from the Mull of Oa a good send-off on his arduous journey to the heart of Africa. He was a close friend of the family, a frequent visitor, an ardent activist in many good causes, and his sudden decision to share the benefits of his erudition and Islay accent with the barefooted Onga tribe (Approx number, 200.) wandering the sand-scoured plains came as a great surprise to everybody. Cleo said nothing and dropped her eyes when someone, with a innocent laugh, suggested that if the child was male she should call it Angus. Angus did not say anything either but his rubicund blush competed strongly with his carrotty head of hair and burning-bush beard.

When, eventually, the snuffling piglet was held in the midwife's arms for a fingers-and-toes inspection, there was no way of telling whether the bristles on the throbbing skull would turn black, blue or carmine. The Mendelian theory of dominant and suppressive genes could explain dark hair following fair hair – it is a biological gamble, after all – but no actuary would give you odds-on for a carrot after a leguminous crop of blonde peas.

Cleo's anxiety evaporated when the said bristles grew into soft jonquil threads and she drooled over the drooling podge. "My angel, my little angel," she crooned. The naming of the infant was the next question. Naturally Cleo avoided any that had Celtic provenance. "Something French," she insisted. Ivan became so annoyed with this that he suggested Ennui and would have carried it off if Cleo had not checked in the pocket French/English dictionary. "Your father was bored with you right from the beginning," she iterated to Angelica. About that time, an acquaintance brought Cleo the complete works – in paperback – of Sergeanne Golon which detailed the improbable adventures of a busty French beauty called Angelique. Cleo anglicised Angelique to Angelica. For his part, if the child had been male, Ivan wished it to be named Harry after a famous left-winger but was willing to feminise it to Harriet.

Thus in the generation of Cleo and Ivan to the fourth part,

Angelica Harriet came into being. When the child was about two and could make her own way to the potty, Cleo developed a passion for Espana and spent every Tuesday down at the local community centre, her fat ankles prancing the flamenco under the dark-eyed tutorial of Senor Enrico. Thursdays were also set aside for an occasional in-depth and exclusive study of the Iberian language, folk customs and cuisine with Senor Enrico. Cleo now addressed her child as Awn-gel-lee-kah, with particular stress on the penultimate syllable. This state of affairs (I use the word advisedly) continued until Cleo discovered that Enrico came from Scunthorpe, not Seville, and that his parents were Italian fish-and-chippers rather than rancheros. Worse, other castenet-clickers had shared his private paellas during their exclusive tutorials.

Ivan, a man of principles, used the name of Harriet, though gruffly, as in, "Eat your muesli, er, Harriet." The child, unsure of what he meant, stuffed the brown mixture into her maw with such speed that she invariably gagged. The snatch of Berlioz played during the mysterious Sunday morning phone call was the part known as the idee fixe, or Harriet's theme. Ivan saw no reason in principle to mention this to Sally.

Angelica's brother and sisters called her Angie-pangie-pudding-and-pie and in school, because she was thought to be a teacher's pet, the other children nicknamed her Angie-licka-pants. Later, her brother and sisters told their children to address her as Auntie Angie. It is not surprising that with this imprecision of names, she should precisely choose to be an accountant.

After their first meeting, Sally said to Ivan, "Your youngest is the oldest of your children. Those cold eyes give me the willies."

"It's the brains," he said in the facetious manner he adopted when trying to avoid an uncomfortable subject. Why, you may ask, should the subject of his clever daughter be uncomfortable? Perhaps it was the word "cold". Another five minutes of the ice princess's company and permafrost would form on the coffee cups. "Have I ever told you that when my snow-bound great-great-great grandmother took steps to desert the frozen steppes of outer Siberia and retrace the steps of Michael Stroganoff—"

"Was he the inventor of the famous stew?"

"No, that was Michael Mulligatawny from Ballypoteen. Yes, my three-times great-grandmother settled in Omsk and had a binary relationship with Lobachevsky, the great Russian mathematician and—"

Sally was not listening. "With that hair and those eyes, she's like Medusa."

Ivan's early extra-cultural awareness had been bred and buttered on Penguin Classics and he was not too pleased with the comparison. "You mean the biddy and her two sisters, the Gay Gorgons, who sat with their bums at zero temperature on a granite rock to the North? She whose phiz turned men into stone?"

Sally had read a different book, Boccaccio's Concerning Famous Women, which she took down from the shelf to show him the tale of Medusa, Daughter of Phorcys. Though outwardly mollified, inwardly he felt this was a devious ploy.

As we have seen, Angelica's birth was fraught with peril for Cleo. Ivan was also caught by surprise but he bore his forbearance with the same patience as Cleo bore her fortuitous burden.

When Alexander was born, Cleo had been involved with a hearty, wholesomely healthy, outwardly bounding young man whose rippling torso would have been the delight of ancient Athens, not to mention Earls Court. "He sees me more as a mother figure," she would simperingly say to her sceptical confidantes. But the matrix of the young man's emotional problems was less Platonically fixated than a tent peg. To her chagrin, he thought camping was also an indoor sport.

It was he who loaned Cleo and Ivan his favourite canvas for their fortnight's holiday just outside Salcombe. They hated it. It rained every day till eleven at night, stopped for a few hours and began again at about three in the morning. There were very few enjoyable moments in this diluvian downpour, but the consequence of one was Alexander.

The ritual choosing of a name for what could be a web-footed whelp was taken up by a committee from the Womens' Study Group which Cleo attended every Friday. The consensus was that as Alexandra Kollentai was the heroine of the month, this sturdy agitatoress should be commemorated, if not in song and story, at least in the person of the expected child. There was no question about it being a female. Cleo's ancient aunt, bribed with a bottle of port and a bag of chocolate sweets, had patted the ballooning stomach with her gnarled claws and pronounced that as the foetus lay high in the womb, it must be a girl. Ivan made no effort to disguise his pride at the eventual sight of the pink piddler, standing like a decapitated worm on the mound of squirming flesh.

Ivan wished to lay a screed of literary names on the child. James (Joyce) Flann (O'Brien) Oscar (Wilde) Leo (Tolstoy) Maxim (Gorky). Less-lettered friends suggested Alex after all. Though the great Kollentai could not be honoured, there were heaps of great Alexanders to be recalled. A. Fleming, A. Nevsky (and his prospects), A. Pushkin, A. Volta (a current favourite), A. Pope (no Dunciad he), A. Neill and, of course, A the Great himself.

Alas, in this age of instant gratification, the cash nexus and the take-away culture, instant greatness needed more than five minutes in the microwave oven to be anything other than a flash in the tinfoil pan. Alexander did not strive for greatness, nor did greatness strive to discover him. Rather, he sought instant gratification and therefore achieved a smug self-importance that did little to disguise his limitations.

In other words, he grew up to be an ordinary person, scanned tabloid newspapers, drank diluted gnat's piss, spoke computer jargon, married when young, divorced when older and, with the aid of his various plastic cards, ran into debt. Debts, as we have mentioned, gnawed the vitals of at least three of Ivan's children. Though they were well past the fledgling stage, they still squawked like importuning starlings for succulent tit-bits to be rammed down their gobs.

One day BS (Before Sally), Ivan was unwrapping a boxed set of five baroque records in his third-floor flat when Alexander called in to see if the old man was okay. It was Ivan's first real luxury purchase for a long time.

"That must have cost a bomb, Dad," Alexander said, his face registering gloomy disapproval of this outrageous extravagance.

"No, not really. It's a special bargain offer from The Observer. It works out at about half the cost per record."

Bargain or not, so far as Alexander was concerned, the money lashed out on a bunch of long-haired fiddlers could have been more usefully directed towards a worthwhile cause. And when his father was old and grey, what then? He blurted out his reversed logic.

"The way you're spending your money, Dad, I hope you don't expect us to provide for you when—" Even Alex sensed the crassness of that remark and hastily tried to make amends. "I like some of the classical stuff, you know. The Air on a G String, for instance, is one of my favourites. They play it in that cigar advertisement on television. Have you got it?"

Ivan placed the record on the turntable and flicked it with a lens cloth. "Could this unstructured philistine really be my son?" he wondered. He stood back as Alessandro Marcello's Oboe Concerto resounded through the loudspeakers. "It's very apt that you're the first to hear this."

"Do what?"

"The composer's first name, Alessandro, Italian for Alexander. Now what were you saying about me spending my money?"

"Oh, well, what I mean is, you know, the way things are, what with engineering going through a bad patch, I suppose you'd get a redundancy pay-out if the worst came to the worst, but would it be enough for you to buy luxuries like—" Coded message in this garble: Would you have enough to provide me with an interest-free loan? Alexander blundered on. "And what about insurance? Suppose you were to—"

"Drop dead?"

"Well, even that can be expensive. Who would provide—"

"Providing I had any concern with my inevitable demise. But if I knew I had a short time to strut and stride upon this mortal stage (Alex sighed. Dad was off again) I'd find a buxom doxy and between us and my money, we would provide ourselves the many pleasures of the flesh. And when I am dust, she'll inherit the ashes of my worldly goods."

Alexander was horrified. "She'd go through your money in six months."

"If I choose correctly, she'd go through it in a month."

"But what about your children?" Alexander bleated. "What would you give them?"

"I've given you life. Isn't that enough?"

Chapter four

Sally's speed in retouching her mascara was such that she had little time to inspect the bathroom decor, except to note it was all very Idyll Home and that the shelf-load of bottles and jars were variations on the theme of feminine flesh restoratives. "What does Andrew do to titivate his schoolgirl complexion?" she idly wondered. Her hurry had less to do with the social imperative to be ready for the meal's starting orders than the need to suppress, by warning frown and sharp crack to the shin, Ivan's provoking remarks.

"I can't leave him for a minute when he's in one of his moods," she grumbled to herself as she came down the stairs. Her haste was justified. "Actually, I'm Sally's live-in lover," Ivan was saying as she entered the room. When she sidled crab-wise between the seated women and the rosewood cabinet – a Mozartian Gran Partita tickling her thighs – both Richard and George looked at her with renewed interest. It was difficult to tell what thoughts, prudish, prudent or prurient, churned beneath the women's lacquered hair.

"He's not my lover," she declared. "He's my husband."

"Sally only married me for my body." Ivan received his second tap of the night.

"If we're sitting comfortably, we shall begin," said Andrew with the jolly urgency of a vicar at an old people's Christmas treat.

"Ooo, Egg Jacqueline," Deirdre cooed insincerely. "How absolutely marvellous of you, Zena. I wish I had your magic touch. Gourmet cuisine is hardly my forte."

"My gormless cousin who is now forty—" Ivan began but Sally overrode him with a loud, "This is really delicious, Zena."

"Absolutely delicious," George chimed in.

"Listen to the hymn of praises, darling," burbled Andrew, "and just like your novel, this is only the first chapter." (Does he mean she has only cooked one chapter?)

Ivan scraped off the baked top layer and made a few exploratory digs with his fork. 'First chapter, indeed. I wonder how long that's been stewing?' He skewered a sliver of almost translucent flesh on the prongs and held it close to his eyes as if studying a specimen from the deep. "Is this a trilobite I see before me?"

"Don't you like my Egg Jacqueline?" Zena inquired tremulously.

"What is this?"

"Prawn!" replied mine hostess huffily. Sally drew her foot back.

"Dublin Bay prawn?" said Ivan. Sally's foot started its curved journey. "Did you catch it yourself?" Sally's pointed shoe made contact, his mouth opened and the sliver slid down his maw.

The dinner party on the other side of London was not so polished. Amy, she of the frantic hair, cried foolishly: "What can I do to help? I'll fetch the plates and things." She plonked the snivelling squirmer on the chair and flurried into the kitchen. Alex began to organise the seating arrangements. "The kids can have theirs on their laps," said the overweight blonde with the overbearing personality and then told the quarrelsome children to shut their racket or she would turn the television off. Alex added his bit. "That goes for you too, Shel, and you, Darren. Behave yourselves or I'll never bring you here again," was a threat that sounded more like a promise to his disenchanted offspring.

While the hustle and bustle continues, we will return to the brief life of Alexander the not-so-Great. His scholastic attainments were patchy and his endeavours to master any tough subject depended on instant praise lavishly bestowed. Ivan was disappointed and said so in very harsh terms. Cleo, of course, took an opposing view. "He's a late developer. How many O Levels did Einstein have?"

After a handful of indifferent jobs, he went into computers. We apologise for this apparent solecism and offer as a feeble explanation for our impropriety the fact that current terminology, now deified by modern drudging lexicographers, uses the word 'into' instead of 'to be involved with'. Do not suppose a person 'into' alcohol has drowned in a butt of malmsey like the poor old Duke of Clarence, though sometimes drunks have been known to cut out the middle man in this drastic fashion.

No one knew what he did exactly in computers – repair man?

service engineer? – though once, when asked by Sally, he replied with a superior sniff, "I'm a national expert." He was indeed an expert in jargon and his conversations were peppered with capital letters, numbers and brand names.

In the course of time, his fancy turned to Tracy, a receptionist from Deptford. They wedded, bedded and begat Michelle (Shel for short) and Darren. After a decade of coursing time, Tracy – subsequently known as SHE – became bored with RAMs, REMs and kilobytes and left him for a video salesman from Broxbourne. "What did you expect?" Cleo said. "You married beneath yourself. As I did." In the period of our story, Alex is now contemplating marriage to the lovely Dawn, a hairdresser from Mitcham. Cleo's thoughts on this are unrecorded.

The children were restless. It being Sunday, the various TV channels were unvaried in their failure to hold the attention of questing young minds. Grasping hand grabbed remote control from grasping hand. Flick. Choral singing (an array of goldfish mouths gasping for God). Flick flick. Re-run of yesterday's sports events (And that was a near-miss from Bloggs). "Gimme it." Flick. Avant-garde version of Aida being performed in a scrapyard. "Ooo, what's that fat biddy yelling her head off for?" Flick flick. Discussion between three eminent dreary droners about destructuralism and the catastrophe theory of life.

Alex once again ordered Shel and Darren to behave themselves. Amy, the wriggling contents of whose lap had formed an escape committee, said her lot were always as good as gold at home and she didn't know what had come over them tonight. Angelica stayed silent while the busty blonde shouted, "Alright then, alright, I'll put on a video only if you promise to eat up all your dinner." The first offerings were rejected with disdain, particularly by Michelle. "Lady And The Tramp? Mum's got that. It's soppy. Snow White. Ugh. All them dirty old men. Anyway, Mum's got that. Sleeping Beauty? Boring." The woman pulled a video from its package. "Yes, I know, your Mum's got it. Has she got Chicago Cops V?" Triumphantly she slid the cassette into the slot.

The rewind button had been pressed on the pre-prandial mutiny and the start button locked. The four adults, plus squirmer, began to jab the Worcester sauce-smeared avocado halves with apostle spoons. The children were given melon slices. "Don't like it," said Michelle petulantly. "I want a Coke."

Two incidents threatened the uneasy equanimity of the meal. The first proved that the peasants were still revolting. In between the video's graphic illustrations of how to excavate somebody's chest with a sawn-off shotgun and incinerate the occupants of a speeding car, the watching children were happily and innocently flipping melon segments at each other. Darren had to go and spoil this happy game by emptying an oozing mess down Michelle's back. Alex shouted, Michelle bawled, Darren loudly denied his guilt, busty woman turns off television, other deprived children protested. A minute of turbulence passes. Alex tells his son, who is now studying the tips of his shoes, that when he, Alex, was the same age, he, Alex, would never never do such a horrible thing to his sisters and why, because Alex's father would have given him a good smacking. (Angelica opens briefcase, takes out notebook, writes, "Violent beatings for minor childhood misdemeanours common." Replaces notebook, snaps briefcase shut.)

Blustering tone of voice from Alex. "Is that what you want me to do, Darren, is that what you really want me to do, eh?" Darren's reply was just above a whisper, "Sorry, Daddy." That was not good enough. "Louder, Darren, louder. I can't hear you." Four times Darren had to repeat, "Sorry Daddy" and each time louder than the last. The boy was truly sorry.

Michelle returned from the bathroom to the clucking sympathy of her aunts and, with child-guile, thought she was in a fairly strong position to resubmit her earlier demand. "May I have a Coke, Auntie Arni?"

Aunt Arni, aka Busty Blonde, replied, "No, not in this house, I don't stock poison. You can have a glass of pure orange and that's all." Michelle grimaced and crouched down beside her brother. They put their heads together and began to whisper conspiratorially.

We can now reveal that the above Aunt Arni, hereafter known as Ariadne, is eldest sister to Amy, Alex and Angelica and first-born in the generation of Cleo and Ivan. We will say more about her later and give her a role in proportion to her size.

"I'm surprised, Alex," said Ariadne bossily, "that you encourage young madam there to rot her teeth and wither her brains with this Yankee cultural narcotic."

Alex was not quite sure what was meant by Yankee cultural narcotic when it was at home. (Of course, a fervent fan of Chicago Cops I, II, III, IV and V would immediately recognise the unique role of the Narcotics Squad. Making holes in chests and burning felons in upside-down cars.) Normally he would have countered her animus with feeble and fatuous semi-detached jokes about water drinkers drinking half the nation's piss but today he needed friendly ears.

"You know me, I only want the best for my kids, but I ask you, what control have I got over their diet? (Repetition is good for the rhetorics). None at all. SHE has them five or six days a week and God only knows what cheap muck SHE shoves down them and with my money too and SHE's asked for more money—" Gasps around the table at this outrage. "Because, SHE says, now I'm getting re-married—"

Ariadne. What's it got to do with her?

Amy. It's ages since I've been to a real wedding.You're having the full ceremony, are you?

Alex. (Preens himself) Oh yes, all the trimmings. Champagne reception after the register office, then church blessing, sherry reception, wedding breakfast—

Angelica. That will mean a lot of money. Is it cost-effective?

Alex. (Exasperated). What a ridiculous question. (Sotto voce). More effective than your in-and-out marriage to Kevin, anyway.

Angelica. Opens briefcase, takes out notebook and calculator.) Wedding dress? (Looks over to Ariadne who purses her lips and gives an estimate.) Tails etc for bridegroom. Horse and carriage. Video. Say, total cost, £8000. Invested in a building society deposit account at the present interest rate of (prods calculator buttons) blah-blah.

Alex sits tight-lipped and pales slightly at the itemised costs. Last year's tradition was that the bride's parents paid. This year's tradition is that the bridegroom defrays a proportion of the expenditure.

Now for the second disturbing incident. Amy listened to the figures, her mind torn apart by the wild horses of romantic ritual and miserly regret. If only she had half, no, a quarter, but what was the use of thinking like this. She dug a lump out of the avocado and shoved it down the squirmer's gob. The child began to choke and Angelica asked in a disinterested manner, "Amy, why is your baby turning blue?"

Panic, chaos, shrill scream from neglectful mother and conflicting instructions ensued. "Turn it upside down and hold it by the feet," Alex barked. Amy obeyed the order. "No, no, not that way," yelled Ariadne. "Turn it right way up and slap its back." For a few seconds the child was revolved like a sluggish ship's propeller until its puny engine spurted into action and avocado fragments, plus earlier tit-bits, were spewed out across the table. The table cloth and soiled cutlery were removed into the kitchen by Ariadne and the squealer was removed into the bathroom by Amy.

Alex redirected the children's understandable excitement at a near-death in the family by switching the television on and stood behind them to watch three bodies hit the sidewalk under a hail of bullets. Angelica wiped an unidentifiable yellowish blob from the matt black briefcase and continued with her calculations.

While the first two are out of the room we are free to talk about them and their positions in the generation of Cleo and Ivan.

Cleo was determined that her second-born should be called Amelia. She claimed it was a family name on the 'royal' side. Caroline Amelia, smelly wife of George IV, was a hard-done-by heroine of hers who had unfortunately married beneath herself. To Ivan's small circle of literati, the name was inspired by the eponymous heroine of Fielding's novel (Cleo had read the first chapter). She had been friendly with an Italian olive-importer who hailed from the Perugian city of Amelia but it would be unjust to imply more than an intimate interest in the language of Dante when the two sucked spaghetti in the Trattoria Paradiso. Besides, the child was blonde.

The ultimate reason, and the one she stuck to ever afterwards, came about when visitors called in from the Women's Collective to coo over the new-born and give thanks to the Great Goddess Gaia, Almighty Creatoress, for the birth of another female. "Amelia," they exclaimed. "How super!" Their joy took flight. "Amelia Earhart, the first woman to wing her feminist way across the Atlantic." They muttered darkly about dark conspiracies in the final mysterious disappearance of the lady-flier. "And don't forget our very own aviatrix, Amy Johnson," one swooped in with a touch of national pride.

Amy did develop at least one characteristic to justify the aerial appellation. When there was a need for any form of definite action, she would fly off in all directions. She was a podgy child, tended towards breathlessness and had a touch of rheumatic fever. The podginess stayed with her in her early teens, which led to cruel jokes about her being the only known grounded female dirigible. The flying connection again.

But later she shed some fat, became a comely maid and was taken into marital custody by Robert, a local constable.

She did her duty as a policeman's wife and they begat a flying squad of their own. During the year-long miners' strike, begatting was put on hold while Bob vigorously upheld the cause of law and order and earned enough overtime for them to take out a large mortgage on a detached house in Cheam, buy a Porsche and send their children to a private school. They were heartbroken when the miners went back to work. The printers' strike had possibilities, as had the Poll tax agitation, but both fizzled out in no time and the most Bob earned from either was a grazed knee during the Trafalgar Square fracas. It was back to the Panda car and slim wages.

Occasionally Amelia visited Ivan and Sally. She was in fact a conduit of mostly muddled information about them. "What does she want?" Sally would fiercely whisper to Ivan in the kitchen. "To see her dear old Dad, of course," he would reply. "And to show him his lovely grandchildren."

"That lot," Sally snorted.

"A policeman's lot is not a lovely thing."

And now the first of Ivan and Cleo's generation shall be the last. Ariadne! To know Ariadne is to know Cleo. Ivan had a severe case of amnesia when asked to give the provenance of his first born's name. "Let me think now," he would reply with massive wrinkling of brow. "Perhaps it was after your woman who was a Grecian guide to tourists entering the maze and used to entertain them by singing the flower song from Billy the Bullock. Or perhaps, in an amazing way, we took it from the byline on a series of erudite features in New Scientist." Or perhaps he was too embarrassed to recall the early days of youthful fervour when Cleo and he huddled together on the single bed in their one-room flat, a time before passion was replaced by pique and petulance.

Ariadne was carried side-saddle and then wheeled to meetings, rallies and marches. There is an old grainy picture of her waving a miniature banner with the legend, "Babies Against The Bomb". The cause of good causes stayed with her in adulthood and could be accused as the cause of her becoming an archetypal Earth Mother. Her clutter of children were the products of several allegiances and the dates of past parades could be detected in their birthdays. Yet, with all her outward show of partisan attachments, there was in her the nullity of a priest or priestess who continued to perform the rites of a religion in which they no longer had either faith or belief.

Sally and she did not take to each other on their first meeting. Ariadne's imperative was to give this newcomer (or intruder) an illustrated history of the family in the years BS and to this end photographic albums, in chronological order, were laid on the table.

Faded black and white photos filled with fading pale faces flickered before Sally's flickering eyes. 'This is Mum and me in my sun bonnet in Brighton. There's Mum holding Amy. This was our terrace house in Clapham.'

Album No 2. Pictures of age-washed colours. Holiday shots. (Remember, Dad, that awful caravan site.) School group (That's me fourth from the left. Have you still got a copy of it, Dad?)

Album No 3. Brash colours. Faces grinning inanely. School studio studied poses. Family groups. (That's Amy, Alex, Mum and me.) Events. (Cousin Elsie's wedding.) Relatives (Aunt Aggie. She's dead now) and so on and so on. Fourth and fifth album followed. Everybody a bit older. Sally's eyes glazed but, with jaws set in a rictus smile, she continued to chirp exclamations, partly to prevent herself faling into a stupor and partly to exhibit a polite interest for Ivan's sake. It was early in their relationship. "Is that really Alex?" "How awfully cute Angelica used to be." Small error halfway through the fifth album. They had moved onto the children of A and A and A. Above exclamations inappropriate. Quick correction. "My, she has his eyes, hasn't she."

(What is Ariadne's coded message to me in this display? You are invading our territory?)

There were gaps and omissions. No pictures of Alex's first wedding. No trace of Tracy. And from album to album a diminishing number of Ivan that reached zero number in the fourth and fifth albums. Had he become the invisible man?

When the collected, selected works were returned to the shelf Sally sipped the by now cold instant coffee and asked, with a contrived air of innocence, "Aren't there any more?"

Ariadne rooted in an overflowing drawer and produced several oblong packages. "These were some we took when we were in Spain last year."

"Spain! How lovely. All that marvellous sunshine, Agaric."

"Agaric?" Ivan, who had hardly spoken for the preceding half-hour, looked sharply at Sally.

"No, not Agaric. We went to Alicante."

Sally pointed to a photograph of two over-tanned mounds of scorched flesh oozing out of inadequate swimsuits. "I never knew you had a twin sister."

"That's Mum and me," Ariadne replied stiffly and she returned the snapshots to their packages.

No more coffee and biscuits were offered, the conversation died in the graveyard of long silences and after fifteen minutes Sally and Ivan said goodbye.

"What did you mean by Agaric?" Ivan asked on the way home.

"You know, those litle mushrooms with those dear little red spots."

"You mean the poison mushrooms?"

"Oh no, I was thinking more of those Mabel Lucie Attwell illustrations. Your Ariadne reminded me of the fairy princess dancing round the toadstools in the glade."

Chapter five

The passage from the first course to the plate-scraping end of the second at the Richmond party was a glissade or, rather, a glissando of tinkling laughter, merry but mild quips, baritone chortles and an occasional sombre note. Politeness in the abstract was preferred, controversy was curtailed and fame, in a minor key of G.A.B, was the theme.

The mingled Mozartian variations came to an end and Andrew did his slide-trombone act, surreptitiously glancing at the heaving bosoms as he sidled by. Within seconds he returned, exchanged a few 'darlings' with Zena and took the scenic route back to his seat. Schubert, in slippered feet, seeped from the loud speakers.

Sally was in that near-satiated state where sharp colours are blurred and sharp thoughts are suppressed. She wondered whether to ask Zena where she bought the ready-to-cook cuisine – preheated oven, mark 5/200C, 25 min – or sneak into the kitchen and rummage through the waste bin.

At the beginning of the evening she had worried about Ivan. At least once a day Sally made a point of worrying about him. Last Thursday night, very late, she realised she had not worried about him once all day. This began to bother her and her second stage of solicitude ranged from the mendacious to the macabre: that is, as she lay she lied to herself and then moved, in mind, to that last lying-in state when the flesh is lye to the soil and all worry is wanton.

His elemental mischievousness, the seemingly naive remarks, the mordant humour and the ingenious use of words all unnerved her. Happily, the prawn incident had only resulted in Zena dashing into the kitchen and smashing a plate. Happier still, for Sally, he appeared to have taken on the role of an attentive listener with a nod here, a smile there and an occasional amused glance in her direction. But she knew he was not subdued or impressed (perhaps oppressed) by the company. She was sure that like a cat watching the spider-foraging birds in the grass, he was waiting.

He did make one mental muscle-flexing move when the main course was brought in, accompanied by mouth-sennet trumpeting from Andrew. "Tar-ra,tar-ra. My lords and ladies," proclaimed their host, "We present Fillet of beef Italienne with gnocci Romana."

"Ah poor cow, I knew her well," Ivan said. Zena looked at him warily. "Butchered to make a Roman holiday."

To kick or not to kick? It could have been worse. He could have made one of his endearing remarks about eating corpses. "I beg your pardon," Andrew said stiffly.

Sally hobbled her kicking foot. "Ivan is quoting Byron."

"Ah yes, Childe Harold." George wiped his glasses, pleased with himself that he knew the origin of the quotation. The others picked up on the Roman Holiday. Deirdre was simply dying to return to the eternal city, toss pennies in the fountain and soak in the grandeur that was Rome. Prunella complained about the dust, the noise, the crowds. She did seem to have problems with crowds. Andrew sneered at the Italians' lack of discipline and Richard spoke loftily about meeting a famous Italian film director when he was at one of those international media events.

Sally nervously anticipated another explosion. When they first arrived, she had nearly shrivelled with the cold; but within an hour, what with eight bodies in the room (Ivan the engineer stated that each adult body generated one hundred watts of heat) and warmth wafting from the cooking area, she feared she was expanding beyond the elastic capacity of her red dress. She saw herself, as if in a slow-motion film, bursting out of her flimsy carapace and the fragments rocketing across the table. Would they notice? Zena hastily dashing into the kitchen to put another Mark 5/25 min tinfoil package into the oven, Deirdre asking if her underwear was Janet Reger – thank heavens she had bought a new bra in M & S yesterday – Richard, rigid smile and glinting eyes, mentioning a female presenter of some TV clothes show, George removing a shred from his gnocci and countering one quotation with another from the works of the limping lord. Had it happened? No, she was still intact, if not virginally so.

George: 'All tragedies are finished by a death,
All comedies are ended by a marriage.'
Deirdre: (Sotto voce) Oh George. Must you.
Ivan: (Feigned heartiness) No truer word, Lord George, and as the gay Gordon went on to say,
'Dreading that climax of all human ills,
The inflammations of his weekly bills.'

If Sally knew what they were talking about, if she had not allowed herself to retreat behind the palisade of her own thoughts, she could have made a foray with an apt quote, one to disarm Ivan.

Andrew, the accountant, pontificated. "People become unnecessarily hot and bothered with weekly and monthly bills when there are facilities like debit accounts." Richard made a weak joke about laying all one's charge cards on the table and then added, "Marriages repeat themselves. First as tragedy and then as farce." Prunella shot him a sour glance. "If you ask me, there's as much farce and comedy in a first marriage as a second or third, that's the tragedy."

"What is going on here?" Sally wondered. Ivan's grin did not give her a clue.

The dreaded Deirdre of the sorrows turned to her. "From what Ivan said (What did he say?) you're his second wife?"

(What did they want? A case history from the Marriage Guidance Council?)

"I'm his official second wife." Who is this stranger I take into my bed? 'He was the mildest-manner'd man'. Yes, when he sat with feet on the coffee table, listening to his big-band Bach. 'That ever scuttled ship or cut a throat'. Once he was coerced into shooting at a rabbit. He missed by a mile but the bunny died of heart failure. 'With such true breeding of a gentleman'. They did breed gentlemen in Romford. 'You never could divine his real thought.' True. True.

Ivan's thoughts at that point were too divinely silly for words. He was likening the table talk to the art of the fugue as he sat there with a foolish smile stitched to his schmig. This he explained in great length and harmony to Sally later in the week.

Example. Zena or George to Sally, "Andrew tells us you write for magazines. (Introduction of subject.) Sally, "Yes, I do. (Answer.) Zena or George. "How interesting. What do you write?" Sally, in lower key. "Features. Mainly about celebrities." (Enters theme of FAME.) Deirdre: "Oh really, anybody we know?" (Contrapuntal.) Ivan gives list of improbable names like Attila and Joe Stalin's mother. (Counter-subject.) George, light nervous laugh. "Never written for the Times, then? Old Thunderer not what it used to be, though that Jewish chappee, what's his name, can be quite acerbic." (Second counter-subject.) Deirdre to Prunella, "Sally writes for magazines." Prunella to a spot above Richard's head. "Really, that must be interesting. Tatler? Cosmo? I didn't think I recognised your name." (Subject and counter-subject.) Andrew: "Well, what a coincidence. Two writers at our table. Zena, of course, with her novel, is more of the literary kind. You must tell our guests about your novel, darling." (Various bogus cries of anticipation. This is known as the Episode.) Zena, with becoming modesty. "It's only a draft at the moment, darling, and I've yet to finish the first chapter." Andrew to Richard, "You must be used to being surrounded by writers." Richard, "Now that you mention it, it was only last Friday I was having lunch with a famous writer at Caprice/Groucho's/The Garrick—"

Sally, at end of explanation. "I don't quite understand. My musical education stopped when the Doors were closed."

Ivan, patiently. "Let me put it another way."

Sally, suppressing yawn. "Tell me tomorrow, ducky."

Two fractious bites of conversation came from the women's side of the table. Slippershod Schubert quivered.

Prunella. "And how long have you two been together?"

Deirdre. (Her hand on Sally's arm) "You really really must agree with me on this."

Ivan lilted, "We've been together now for forty years."

"Who's been together for forty years?"

"We have, me old Dutch cap." (Sally regretted asking.)

Deirdre continued with her usual intensity. "What I mean is that for any relationship to succeed, people should talk, not just write it down on paper as if that's any comfort. But nevertheless there must always be a will."

Ivan chortled. "Let's talk of graves, of worms, and epitaphs/

Make dust our paper, and with rainy eyes/ Write sorrow on the bosom of the earth/ Let's choose executors and talk of wills."

George looked up with the bright alertness of the top swot in the class. "Those are exactly my words. Choose executors and talk of wills."

Deirdre removed her hand from Sally's arm and shivered. "But let's not talk of graves. That's morbid. And I hate worms."

Richard leaned forward so he could look down the table. "That's a quote, isn't it – from – let me see now – it was only last week I was at the National with Sir – remind me, what's it from?"

"A poor benighted namesake of yours."

Richard drew back. "Of course, I should have known."

Prunella returned delicately to the attack like the most shy and retiring of sharks. "How long have you two been married then?"

Ivan feigned deafness in that direction. "It was Will who willed his most worldly goods to his will-less wife." Sally felt another quote being willed. "For God's sake, let us sit upon the ground and tell sad stories of the death of kings."

"I never willingly sit on the damp ground," said Deirdre with a touch of peevishness. Richard hid his expression behind his wine glass.

"But you must have sat on something damp, dear," said George sweetly. "I found a green stain on your coat."

"What are you?" hissed Deirdre. "My wife?"

"Am I alone in thinking," thought Sally in the manner of Disgusted of Tunbridge Wells writing to the editor, "that there is more to George's chiding than concern with a dry-cleaning bill?"

To her right, Deirdre was now cooingly asking their hostess in what 'John' did she write, (John? As in lavatory?) and to her left, Zena was twittering on about "writers' block". (Was this some municipal building in which authors, putative or otherwise, were housed?) At the other end of the table, Andrew was expressing loud astonishment that some very famous person Richard knew (who didn't he know) was in reality a very dull chap. None spoke to Prunella. What was wrong with Prue? Did she have wind problems?

For his part, Ivan in his usual jocular manner was telling George that the only good reason for marrying again was to prevent rapacious children from inheriting everything. Was he talking about their marriage? Did Laura Ashley do a line in black lace?

The lunar landscape of George's face shone as it came out from behind the fleecy clouds. "Ah, as with so many people who have not had a grounding in the legal niceties of jurisprudence, you labour under a misapprehension. To reiterate and re-emphasis your apt quotation from the Bard – choose executors and talk of wills." He licked his judicious lips and, inclining his head towards Ivan, laboured to demolish the walls of misapprehension.

Sally strained to hear what was being said, but Deirdre buzzed like a peevish bee. "Never, never ask George anything about the law. He just goes on and on and on. I wouldn't mind so much but he just hands out free advice to all comers as if it didn't cost him a penny to be trained in the first place."

That night, when Sally had locked the car in the garage and came into the kitchen, she asked, "How long do you think their marriage will last?" Her audience was a pair of cats on the window sill and since their interests did not stretch further than the food tray, their answer was a non-committal meow.

Chapter six

When Amy returned with the freshly-washed squirmer, steaming dishes heaped with depressed vegetables had been laid on the table. "Where's everybody?" she asked, ignoring in her aimless way the fact that only her sisters were missing. Alex was leaning over the back of a chair, his right hand fiddling with the lock of Angelica's briefcase. He jerked upwards, momentarily startled. "Everybody? You mean A and A. They're getting the rest of the dinner. We've had to wait for you to clean It." 'It' blew a bubble through the nose dribble.

Amy was in no mood to be intimidated; she had enough of that at home."What were you doing with Angie's briefcase?" she asked sharply.

She could have predicted his response. In this he had hardly changed since he was caught with his two-year old fist stuck in a sweet jar. First a red flush to his brow, then an air of bland innocence. "Do what?" Next a blustering denial of any wrong-doing. If that failed to convince, he would then find some plausible reason for his crime. "Well, if you really must know, Ange said the lock was stiff and I was having a look at it." Next, aggrieved tone. "I don't know why I'm always picked on when something goes wrong." Whisper who dares, "Because you were brought up in a houseful of females."

But Amy was not listening. Squirmer had tossed a fork on the floor and in bending down to pick it up, Amy had bumped the child's head against the table leaf.

Ariadne made a boisterous entrance, bawling for all to take their places and bearing at bosom level an oven dish filled with sizzling chicken legs. She was indulging herself in her favourite Earth Mother role of the goddess Gaia. The waxen Angelica thinly followed her in with a heaped plate of fish fingers.

The distribution of the comestibles was done with the maximum of shouting, scraping of chairs, shuffling of feet and clattering of plates. The division was even simpler. The adults had chicken legs, the children had fish fingers and everybody had carrots, peas, potatoes and sprouts whether they liked them or not. Angelica, who did not eat animals that were smaller or dumber than humans, simply ignored the carbonised leg of what must have been a genetic marvel: a spider-shaped hen. One taste of the sprouts and they too joined the great rejected. Michelle led a puny mutiny of short duration by nasally whining, "I don' like 'em" when midget carrots were dumped on her plate.

By a supreme effort of executive will-power, Alex did not stamp his tiny foot or threaten her with exclusion from any future event in this commodious mansion. (Second-storey flat of.) Instead he gruffly told her to eat what she was given or do without for the rest of the night. Michelle bowed her head, face puckered for a whinge. Was she repentant? (Michelle's secret thoughts. "When we get home I'll say to Mum, 'Mum, me and Darren couldn't eat those manky carrots and we're ever so hungry,' and Mum'll say, 'Course you are, my darlings. Sit down there and your real Mum will cook up some oven chips, you love that, don't you, and while you're waiting here's a bag of crisps each.' ")

The two separated groups of this extended family settled down to enjoy (or not) their meal.

And what is a family? A profound question. Give answer on one side of paper. Family is a collective noun for a collection of individuals, who, given half a chance, would not be seen with, dead or alive, these blood (or bloody) relatives. Proof. If consanguinity had not been the binding factor, would prim, accountable Angelica, with her life organised in a briefcase, have enjoyed an affinity with Alex?

Not that Alex failed to take an interest in his 'little' sister with whom he once took baths. "How's things with Screwitt and Scrimpet? (His name for her accountancy firm.) Still helping the filthy rich with their tax evasions?"

"Avoidance," she corrected. "Evasion is illegal."

Every time they met, he asked the same questions and received the same replies.

"Six of one and half a dozen of the other, that's what I say." Alex was noted for his idiomatic endeavours. "Honestly, it makes me sick to think how they can get away with it while people like myself—" And so on

Angelica prodded a potato, Amy masticated a slice of cardboard chicken into pulp and shoved the morsel into squirmer's mouth while Ariadne bawled to the children to "keep the racket down". They had turned the sound up for the 2nd re-run of the Chicago Cops V.

Alex stimulated the topics of conversation as the leading simulator of outrage or disdain. If the table had been other than round, he would have insisted on sitting at the top.

And what were these topics?

From Alex, the dawn of a new marital age for him with Dawn from Mitcham and the cost of the ceremony thereof. Then there was the diatribe against SHE (1st wife Tracy) whose name must not be confused with the H. Rider Haggard heroine and the perfidious demand SHE had made for more money. SHE even had the bloody nerve, the cheek, to ask for various household items – fridge, vacuum cleaner – from their marriage.

"Think of the cost of replacing them," he moaned.

Amy suggested he gave them back. "After all, your new wife wouldn't like to cook your meals in pots your first wife used," she soothingly said. Ariadne rather rudely intimated that the second wife would have no objection to the same cock the first wife used.

All of the above was spoken in hushed tones with frequent glances over to Shel to make sure she was not listening. Michelle had a fey and dreamy look on her face.

From Ariadne? Complaints about the travails of bringing up various children with little or no help from their various fathers, the cost thereof and the reluctance of said fathers to pay maintenance. "Believe you me, I was so strapped for cash I nearly didn't go to the Bob Dylan concert. (He was her great hero and she had a scratchy collection of adenoidal albums.) Mind you, that was a bit of a swizz, he hardly sang any of his classics and I had to sit right at the back."

From Angelica? Nothing much. Just listened. Seemed to be calculating.

From Amy? Burden of increased mortgage interest rate.

Children's school uniforms, private education and the cost thereof. None showed much sympathy for these problems. Ariadne sniffed and asked what was wrong with sending the lot to state schools instead of making them mix with a bunch of toffee-nosed wankers. Alex suggested they should join the junior branch of the police and get free uniforms just like their Dad, Sergeant Plod.

"Sergeant Plod? Are you referring to my husband Robert?" Now and then, Amy poked her head out of her mousehole and squeaked defiance. "You know very well that Robert isn't a sergeant, but it's not for the want of trying, he's sat the examination, he's gone for interviews, he's very rarely had a day off—"

"Especially during the miners' strike," Ariadne muttered.

"And the only things that stopped him from getting on are jealousy, he doesn't waste money boozing with the other policemen and he's not a member of—"

"The Women's Institute?" asked Alex hilariously.

"You know very well what I mean. The Freemasons."

And it was not for the want of trying in that direction either. Robert had spoken of his great admiration for the Brotherhood in the hearings of his superior officers, hinting that he wouldn't mind being asked to join. He was not asked.

Ariadne asked if he had fully recovered from the injury received at the Trafalgar Square anti-Poll Tax fracas.

"Oh yes, he's better now. He did have to have a week off at the time and he still has a bit of trouble with his leg."

"Come on now, Amy, who are you kidding," sneered Alex. "You're not talking to the compensation board now. He tripped over a placard and grazed his knee. Remember the big picture of him in the papers being helped by some WPC. Thugs beat up police hero, my eye. She wasn't bad-looking for a policewoman. WPC Wendy, if I remember correctly. And from his station as well. I bet he's handy in the Panda with her."

Amy leaped up, tucked squirmer under her arm and dashed out to the bathroom.

"You and your big mouth," Ariadne said to Alex.

"What have I said, I ask you, what have I said?"

Other than the family connection, what else links the above topics? Answer on back of postcard. The Cash Nexus.

Secondary topics of conversation.

No. 1. Cleo/Mum/Old dear. Their itinerant mamma had recently settled in the well-known Sussex watering-hole of Eastbourne. Though mateless and lacking the wherewithal to feather her nest, she had perched on the top-floor eyrie of a redundant hotel where she had a fair view of the Beachy Head suicides, the rolling sea and an eagle-eyed sighting of the hardy souls braving the sharp winds along the Parade. The obdurate telephone people insisted that she owed them money for their services at a previous address – or it could have been a previous-previous address – and not a bleep-bleep would sound within her four walls till they rang up the charges of her account. She was adamant that if They continued to deprive a lone woman of the means to communicate with her loved ones, she would take the case to the International Court of Human Rights. Meanwhile she had to use a public pay-box.

The above information came from a long letter Cleo had written (What else can I do, stuck up in this crow's nest?) to Ariadne. "Mum tried to ring you two but all she got was those bloody answering machines. Besides, she was going to reverse the charges."

Unfortunately for Cleo, her children's money problems nagged them even more than she could.

Her distance from them had its enchantment. Ariadne read from the screed, 'How about paying me a visit soon and having a nice day by the seaside? Next weekend or the following weekend? Until I get a bigger place, it's best not to bring any of your children.'

"That cuts me out," Alex said with barely concealed satisfaction.

"Me too," said Ariadne. "What about you, Angie? Mum hasn't seen you for ages and thinks you're neglecting her."

"She always says that." Angelica opened her briefcase, took out her digital diary, erased an entry – "I won't need this any more" – and tapped in the new address.

Later they were to arrange a visit for conspiratorial rather than filial reasons.

Secondary topic of conversation.

No 2. Ivan/Dad/Old man.

Secondary secondary topic of conversation. Sally, hereafter known as HER, as in, "Dad's a changed man since he met HER." He was, they agreed, less fatherly (and not at all grandfatherly), less generous – "When was he ever generous?" snorted Ariadne – less caring and so on since he took up with HER. Amy and Alex quoted instances when they had called in to see him and had indirectly mentioned their money problems. Did he dig his hand into his pocket? Oh no, not with HER listening to every word.

Alex recalled the occasion (BS) when Ivan said (jocularly?) that he would leave all his money to a bimbo.

"Suppose, for the sake of argument, that Dad was to suddenly drop dead tomorrow and—"

"You shouldn't say a thing like that," Amy fluttered in fright.

"I only said suppose. I mean, he's got to go sometime. It was just a thought."

"And what were you thinking?" Ariadne asked, her own thoughts quickening.

"Ask yourself, what would happen to his property and his money?"

"Everything would go to HER."

"Exactly."

"No, not exactly." Angelica bent to pick up her case and then changed her mind. "I'll show you later. His estate would be divided between his legal inheritors, which is us and HER."

"What you are saying—" Alex's brow furrowed. "Even with the depressed state of the market, his house must be worth – let's see – two hundred thousand divided by four, no, five, can't cut HER out legally – forty thousand each and that's not taking into account his savings—"

Michelle opened lustrous eyes wide. "Is grandad going to die then?"

"Jeez," swore Ariadne. "She must have radar ears." Not technically correct but her meaning was clear. "I think it's time for pudding."

Ariadne was opening a large tin of custard (10% extra) in the kitchen while Angelica doled out slippery segments from a family-size tin of fruit cocktail (10p off next purchase) into shallow bowls on the breakfast bar when Alex came to stand in the doorway.

"'Ello, 'ello, what's going on here then?" he said in a mock-baritone voice. Ariadne's reply was curt. "You've got eyes. Give us a hand for a change." He lowered his voice. "He's come to move them on." "Who? What?" "PC Plod, who else, from Railway Cuttings Police Station, East Cheam."

Robert, husband of Amy, stood by the window, a long buff raincoat covering his uniform, his hands behind his back, his legs set apart, his eyes surveying the room as if to challenge any unruly element to upset his day. He was a big man with a handsome, blank face and, as he stood there, he flexed his muscles and gave his brains a rest. Amy had Squirmer tucked under her right arm as usual while she cattle-prodded the other children into line.

Ariadne, bearing a trayful of shallow bowls, led the small procession from the kitchen. "Hello, Bob. How are you? Just come off duty, have you? Care for a cup of coffee?" She never found it easy to speak to a policeman and always suspected it would be taken down and used in evidence.

Bob slowly proceeded to answer but the sight of trim Angelica proved strangely distracting to him. It is possible that in this chaotic enviroment of crumpled clothes, her neat business suit of navy blue blazer and pleated skirt was the nearest thing to an uniform; and Bob liked uniforms. He had met Amy dressed in her Girl Guide captain's apparel at a County Fair. If he ever had the power, he fantasised, he would introduce a new Act of Uniformity. Then everybody would know exactly where they were.

Faced with the possibility of a minors' strike from his fretful kids, he cleared his throat and barked, "Hurry along there, hurry along. We haven't got all day."

As the troop trampled downstairs, Amy stood in the doorway, cradling the Squirmer and facing her siblings. "I'm ever so sorry we had to dash off like this. Bob's been on his feet all day." She lifted Squirmer's paw. "Say goodbye to Auntie Ange, Auntie Ari and Uncle Alex. It's been so nice – families should stick together – you must come to my place one Sunday – when Bob's duties allow – I wish we hadn't said that about Dad – I sometimes think." Eyes became moist. "—When I woke up this morning and saw the flood of sunshine, all this spring sunshine, I felt so moved and so happy! I felt such a longing to get back home to—"(Exit rapidly)

"What's that about?" Ariadne asked. "It's not even spring."

"She was quoting from Chekhov," Angelica replied. "I'll make the coffee." (Exit to kitchen)

"Who's Chekhov?" Alex stood by the window. "He'll never fit them all into the Porsche. Hold on, they're getting into the manky old transit van."

"They had to sell the Porsche. He does a bit of moonlighting with an ex-copper who's now a bailiff."

With the departure of Amy's crowd, the turbulence of children diminished and was further abated by Ariadne slipping Arizona Avengers III into the video slot. Michelle did whine a bit about the cherries in the fruit cocktail looking like blobs of blood – giggle from Darren – and she hated custard anyway. When Angelica remarked that surely they should be in bed by now, Alex snorted, "Tomorrow's another bloody school holiday" and then ranted on about those lucky school teachers and concluded with, "Wish I had taken up teaching."

His sisters had heard all this before and apart from a cutting, "You should have taken up learning first," as they cleared away the empty bowls, neither made any further comment.

Angelica made room for her briefcase on the table, opened it and took out a small brown plastic bottle of tablets and a crumpled manilla envelope. "What's that?" Alex asked as he took the bottle from her hand. He rattled it and tried to read the label. "Digitalis da da, can't make out this. Saw something like this in Dad's bathroom cabinet when I was last there."

"When was that?"

"Oh, it was, let me see, the week before they had a burglary. That envelope, I saw that there as well. You do know they had a burglary?" He looked at the label again. "This is from an Epsom chemist! You didn't, did you—"

Ariadne returned from the kitchen and Angelica gave her the envelope. "Old photos. That's Dad when he was young. He wasn't so fat then, was he?" She took out a booklet. "I remember this. Mum's always going on about how she put her money into this so-called literary magazine." She reached out for the plastic bottle. "Who brought this? You know I don't allow tablets of any kind in the house, not since what I saw when I was a chemist's assistant." Ariadne had worked for six months in Boots and as a consequence regarded herself a medical expert. "My God, whoever these belong to is in dead trouble. You know what they are? They're tablets for chronic heart sufferers. The person taking them could die at any moment."

Alex muttered, "Suppose, for the sake of argument, Dad was to drop dead tomorrow—"

Ariadne looked from Alex to Angelica, "Are these—?"

"From your experience and knowledge of these matters, Ariadne," Angelica asked crisply, "what would cause that final fatal heart attack?"

"Oh, anything like, say, rapid exertion—"

"Doesn't say much for his sex life," sneered Alex.

Ariadne ignored his bad-taste joke. "A fright, a sudden shock, a sharp noise, worry. For instance, if a load of bills came in all on the one morning—"

"That would make anyone collapse." Alex spoke from the heart.

"Or, as another example, if the person was to hear that his wife was carrying on behind his back—"

The three fell silent. Alex produced a packet of cigarettes. "They're not the strong ones Dad smokes, are they?" Ariadne asked as she took one and inspected an old photograph. "He has put on weight, hasn't he. That doesn't help, does it?"

"A shock? A fright?" Alex blew circular smoke signals.

"And it would be sudden?"

"Very sudden."

"And soon?"

"Very soon."

"The sooner the better."

Chapter seven

The Richmond party ended on several tinkling notes from the ornamental clock in the hall which, now that Schubert had been put to bed, could be heard during a gap in the diminishing chatter. Richard's wrist watch went 'beep beep' in response ('Just the sort of person I like sitting behind me in the theatre,' Sally thought) and all stood up to a chorus of, "We've had a splendid evening. How can we thank you for such a lovely meal? How lovely of you to come. How lovely. How lovely."

There had been small signs that host and hostess wished to see the backs of their guests.The wine had ceased to flow and the emptied bottles on the table stood like mute signposts to the exit. Sally and Ivan's contribution had not even had a walk-on part. Then there was the chill. Twenty minutes before exeunt had become the order of the evening – Do not stand upon the order of your going. Go! – Sally had trotted up to the bathroom and checked the radiator. Yes, they had turned off the central heating.

Ivan said little more than yes, no, I think so, perhaps, to Sally's speculative questions about their fellow guests and simply remarked that George was a good old stick. Praises indeed. He was usually quite voluble on the homeward journey, happy to be no longer burdened with the self-elected task of navigator. But tonight he seemed morose and tetchy.

Perhaps the final scene of the final act still irked him.

Scene: Pavement outside A-to-Z's house.

Richard: (Suavely. Touch of false gallantry) Can I drop you two anywhere?

Sally: (Pointing to humble blue car wedged between two ostentatious gas-guzzlers.) No, thank you, Richard. Our humble blue car is over there.

Pruneface: How wise of you to have such a small car. We rarely find a parking space big enough for ours.

The drill of putting car in garage (backwards) was: – 1) Sally drives vehicle fast up the lane with full headlights to dazzle neighbours' cats and visiting foxes. 2) Stops ten yards beyond garage door, skewing car to 15 degrees. 3) Ivan jumps out, puts latch on passenger door, runs to heave clattering doors across broken concrete. (Neighbours wake up and say, "They're early tonight. It's only twelve o'clock.") 4) Sally does a six-point reverse into garage and listens for yells as she drives over Ivan's feet.

Amendment to 4) since burglary. Ivan hurries down path, fumbles with keys, opens back door, dashes into house and turns on all the downstairs lights.

Sally stepped into the kitchen, blinked and asked that fateful question. "How long do you think their marriage will last?" Whose? Pick one out of three. The pair of cats on the window sill stretched, knocked a wilting fuschia into the sink and greeted the great provider with a meow-meow.

"Ivan, where are you?" Silence. Feline fur rubbed ingratiatingly against shivering legs. Call again. Louder. "Ivan, where are you?" Stealthy approach to door leading into hallway. Cats point noses in direction of feeding tray.Voice quivering. "Ivan, answer me." Quavering. "Ivan, stop fooling about."

Sally stands in the hallway, the open door leading into the see-through lounge on her right, the cat-infested kitchen on her left and the shabby stairway leading to the opaque landing in front of her. A sighing sound came from the dark above. Sally braced herself for unseen horrors in the Stygian gloom.

Film scenario:
Scene: Interior. Entrance to ancient house. Doors creak. Window shutters flap. Cobwebs trail down from ceiling. Background music of orchestra playing rum-tii-tump-dii-tump. (How did they get in?) Man and woman in raincoats stand looking up the stairs.

Woman: (Michelle Pfeiffer playing Sally) Darling, I'm frightened.

Man: (Sally's fantasy figure played by Gerard Depardieu) Shsh, darling. Did you hear anything?

Woman: It's quiet, darling.

Man: (Grimly. Stares at camera.) It's too damn quiet.

(Cats screech and run away)

Woman: (Eyes dilated. Stares at camera) What – what is it, darling?
Man: (Eyes narrow.) My Gawd, it is—
Woman: (Tremblingly) It is – it is my husband.
Man: (Twice as grimly. Takes Biretta from inside raincoat.) It WAS your husband, darling.
(Shot rings out.)
Woman: Darling. Darling.

What was that bang from the bathroom? It sounded like the lavatory seat dropping. Perhaps when Ivan was carrying out his security check of their fortress home he was ambushed by a vile intruder hiding in the airing cupboard. "Ha ha," said Ivan as he grappled with the vile intruder, "You thought to take my CD classical collection, did you?" The vile intruder's claws clutched Ivan's throat. "Bah, I've twice as many CDs as you," he sneered. They rolled on the floor. "Maybe on another occasion we could do swops but for now I want to abscond with that beautiful, intelligent woman in the red dress whom you call your wife." They tussle violently. "Never, never," cries Ivan but those were his last words. His noble heart cracked and his manly body lies stretched on the cork tiles.

What should Sally do then? Weep bitter tears. "He died calling me his sole inheritor." But what if there is more than one vile intruder? She scurried back into the kitchen for a weapon to defend her honour against a swarm of invaders, stumbled over the cats and grabbed a blunted pair of scissors. Ivan had broken the end of the blades when making a forceful entry into a tin of drinking-chocolate. An alternative possibility entered her mind as she crept up the stairs and tried to avoid the creaking steps.

An immensely rich person who employed assorted ruffians to steal priceless art works, rare books and CD collections sat on his damask-covered gold chair in a state of intense dissatisfaction. "I need a jewel for my crown," he said to his hirelings. Like many rich people, he could only articulate in cliches. "What you need, sir," said sycophant No 1, "is a beautiful and intelligent woman."

The hirelings duly enter the house (through the roof?) and after a titanic struggle, Ivan's lacerated and perforated carcass is left slumped over the edge of the bath. "I hope they haven't chipped the new ivory hand basin," Sally hoped. She stopped on the last step to catch her breath. "Why," she wondered, "do I keep bumping Ivan off? I'm getting morbid. I blame the wine."

Ivan was kneeling in front of the lavatory bowl in apparent contemplation. He turned a pale face towards her, grinned and clumped over to her on all fours to nuzzle his nose against her legs. "Woof, woof," he said.

"Christ, Ivan, have you taken up Nephritic worshipping in your dotage?"

"To be Sirius, as in dog-star, I worship a god of a different kidney." He struggled to his feet and rinsed his face in the basin.

Sally was vext. On the way home he had been grousy and hardly said anything and now, when she ached for a warm soak to finish off the night he stood foursquare in the bathroom, prating and playing juvenile pranks. "Why didn't you answer me when I called? What were you doing ? I imagined the worst. You could have been lying here—"

He stood up and went back to the lavatory bowl. "Hang on, my fair lady of the dark silk knickers." (That was another thing. The centre seam was killing her clitoris.) "Humour an old man in his dotage." (She knew he was secretively sensitive about his greying years and regretted her inept remark.) "Remind me of the delectable dishes that passed our lips tonight."

"Oh really, Ivan, must we regurgitate—"

"An apt word, regurgitate."

It was then she understood and became quite contrite. "Oh, you poor dear.Was it the Egg Jacqueline—"

He held the cistern's handle. "Fare thee well, jocund Jacqueline, may all your ovaries be small ones and a prawn be on your soul."

"It could have been the prawn. You were the only person to swallow one. I did doubt if the beef Italienne with gnocci Romana was past its used-by date."

"Vale, Papal Bull and bones of Petrarch, my love to your Laura. May your die be cast forever Tiber."

"Then there was the Bulgarian wine."

"Ah, the vulgar bulgars, buggers all." He pressed the handle and as the water whirled he intoned, "We must down to the sea again, the rolling polluted sea again, where the oil slicks sway and the detergents spray and the final fishes decay."

"Look, dear, why don't you make yourself a nice hot milk drink, I'll put on the electric blanket. Then, while I'm having a bath you can pop in between the warm sheets." She slid back the small cabinet door. "I know what'll settle your tummy. I'm sure we have a canister of arrowroot here. That's funny, they're missing."

"Don't bother with the arrowroot. I'll make myself a cheese sandwich."

"No, wait, here's the arrowroot. It's the other bottle that's missing. The one with the tablets. Remember I put them here for safety—"

But she was talking to herself. She turned on the bath taps, threw a handful of salts and half a bottle of foam into the swirling water and struggled out of her tight red dress. At least that was a qualified success. As she passed along the landing, she could hear him having a few words with the cats in the kitchen. Before switching on the bedroom lights, she stumbled over the sprawled eiderdown and drew the curtains.

A small car had stopped opposite their house. When she had pulled the covers over the bed and switched on the electric blanket, she returned to the window and opened the drapes a crack. The car was still there. Somebody visiting a neighbour? At this hour? Or someone lost?

A hand slipped around her waist and another grabbed her breasts. "Ah ha, caught you in the act," Ivan said. "A peeping Thomasina. But you're doing it the wrong way around. You should be peeping in, not out."

She removed his marauding paws. "Not now, Ivan. Let me have my bath first. Anyway, you're supposed to be below par."

"It's an ill man indeed who can't enjoy indoor sports. I thought I'd put in a bit of practice."

"It's still there.That car."

He looked out. "It's one of those French yokel cars. You're not ecologically sound unless you have one. The driver must be lost. I wonder why she doesn't turn on the inside light?"

"She?"

"Yes, if it was a man he'd get out to have a gander at the house numbers or the street signs. Shall we invite her in for a cup of tea and a chat? It'd be nice company for me while the suds tickle your fanny."

"My bath," Sally shrieked. "It'll be overflowing."

"I'll go out and see if I can help her."

She dashed in to turn off the taps. "You do that but don't ask anybody in. And be careful. It could be a mad axewoman."

Sally took off the rest of her clothes, put them in the laundry basket and then inspected her naked body in the mirror. "Am I getting fat? Perhaps a bit too much around the love handles." She twisted around and looked over her shoulder. "Perhaps a bit heavy on the haunches. I hate that gross word cow, but sometimes I feel like one."

The front door slammed. Sally called out, "Is that you, Ivan?" What would she do if it wasn't? Curt reply, "Yes, it's me." "Everything alright then?" Second curt reply. "Yes, it is."

When the temperature was to her sensuous satisfaction, not scalding like a bitter woman, not too hot like an angry man but as warm as desire before fulfillment, she stepped in and stood upright for a few seconds. The steam rose to surround the reddening blush of her skin like a Zeus-inspired mist and scattered in tattered banners as she lowered her hips into the floating islands of foam.

The sound of voices came from downstairs. Surely he had not invited the mysterious driver in for a cup of tea, as he had threatened. Or perhaps he was talking to himself? One night he soaked the bed with sweat and loudly called out, "The time has come," but when she shook him awake he opened his eyes, grinned and said, "To talk of many things."

She slid beneath the suds till the water lapped against her lips and her breasts bobbed. She moved herself into a more comfortable position and a tiny regatta of foam scudded in the whirl to be caught on the tips of her teats. "Now what was that rude rhyme from the little boys' book? One day the captain's daughter fell into the water (that doesn't scan) and delighted squeals announced that eels had found her sexual quarters. Just how do sea creatures do it? Lubricity without lewdness, no squashing you up against the bedhead. But would you get barnacles on your bottom? If it wasn't for the slimy seaweed and the nipping crustaceans, I wouldn't say no to a life beneath the ocean waves myself."

She drifted into a dream-stream. Suddenly a scream slit the curtain of mist. Sally opened her eyes and shivered. The placid water was chilly. So much for liquid sensuality. Liquidated!

Two more screams, in quick succession, and what sounded like a thumping noise, came from below. "What shall Sally do?" Sally wondered. What Sally did next was to climb out of the bath slowly and carefully.

If Ivan was strangling the mysterious driver – two more screams indicated that it was taking him a long time – he wouldn't need her help. In that case she could give herself a hearty rub down, shake oodles of talcum into and around the crevices, wrap up and then creep down.

Sally crept down the stairs and peeped around the door. Ivan was sitting on the sofa, his feet on the coffee table, a plate on his lap and the crumbs of several cheese sandwiches scattered on the floor. An old black-and-white film was on television. Several distraught people scurried through a subterranean passage, followed by a flapping cloak. One of the pursued – a girl with long flowing hair – stumbled, turned a terrified face towards the camera and screamed and screamed again. The scene was overlaid by a dripping-blood logo, 'The Return of Dracula's Daughter.'

Sally marched across the room and switched off the television. "You're supposed to be ill and in bed."

"Oh, switch it back on, Sally. It'll be soon over. It's a smashing film (How that word 'smashing' grated on her teeth.) It's about this girl from Whitby who goes to Transylvania to look up her relatives and discovers that Dracula is her Dad."

"What happened to the person in the car?"

"There are no cars in this film—oh, you mean the bell tent on wheels. Funny, that. As soon as I came down the path he or she revved up and disappeared up the road."

When the film was finished he fumbled and stumbled his way into bed in the dark. It seemed as if he had just dozed off when Sally thumped him in the small of his back and urgently muttered,

"There's somebody or something downstairs. Can you hear the tapping?"

He listened for a second. Yes, there was the sound of a tiny tattoo in the kitchen. "It's the wind." He padded downstairs. "It's them bloody cats," he grumbled as he turned on the light. The wakeful animals, expecting an early-morning bonus, followed him as he went to the far end and jerked at the blind. When it flip-flapped up and around the roller, a white shape, like a sheet of paper or a startled face, shot away from the window into the darkness. He stepped back, his heart taking a sudden lurch, a squealing cat taking the full weight of his heel on its tail.

For a full half-minute he stood facing the demons of imagination. Taking his courage in one hand and his collapsing pyjama trousers in the other, he approached the window to stare out at the ragged shapes of bushes and trees. 'Why are men always expected to be braver than women?' he wondered miserably. He sucked in his breath and pulled the blind down again.

Sally had recaptured his side of the bed. "What on earth was it?" she brooded."I thought I heard a screech."

"It must have been a white cat in the window. That mad red-eyed one from two doors down, the psychopath which keeps beating up the others. It's a witch's familiar and its mistress was burnt at the crossroads 300 years ago. That's why cars keep crashing outside this house. We're too near the corner."

"Cat. Cathy," she murmured dopily. "Poor pussy locked out. Move your feet away. They're like blocks of ice."

As the warmth gradually returned to his lower limbs, he too began to drift into sleep. "Cat, Cathy, All locked out. White face cries, 'Let me in, let me in'. Heathcliff, give me heat, heat me in the cold ice night good night white face good night, fair ladies, do go gentle into that ice cold night Daughter of Dracula."

His eyes closed. A car whined past the window and sped into a new nuclear family age.

Chapter eight

"Each system contains within itself the seeds of its own destruction." Who said that? Could it have been an Hegelian Kant from Marx – a spectre is haunting Europe – or Spencer's synthetic philosophy and the decline of the vest? One bereft of suitable reference books would be inclined to dial-a-quote. Presuming, of course, such a referral body reclines within the systematised covers of the telephone directory and is not a spectre haunting one's imagination.

Presuming, then, that one scribbles down the found number and with trembling index finger prods the required digits. What then? An epicene voice emits from the earpiece. "We are sorry there is nobody at present available to answer your enquiry but if you'd like to leave your name, number and your question after the tone we shall get back to you as soon as possible. Thank you for taking advantage of our world-wide Dial-A-Quote service. Beep. Beep."

Therein lies the seed threatening to destroy the telephone system, that is, the answering machine, and therein co-joins the above quote with one of the multitude banally uttered by the famous Oriental philosopher Thai Saih. This ancient sage is unique inasmuch as his name is always put in front of the quotation. For example, "Thai Saih: There's no smoke without fire" or "Thai Saih: Television has killed the art of conversation." And the gnomic utterance most apposite to our thesis: "Thai Saih: The telephone has killed the art of letter-writing."

Sally was sitting in front of her word-processor, staring at the screen as if mesmerised by the blinking cursor. "Blinking hell," she growled to herself, "I could have written the synopsis of War And Peace in this time." A passing thought: "Thai Saih: The typewriter and the daughter of the typewriter, the word-processor, have killed the art of calligraphy."

Ivan came into the study (euphemism for tiny room cluttered

with desks, chairs, books, papers and so on) and stood behind her, his paunch pressed against her scapula, his spatula thumbs pressed into the chair's back rest. "If he pokes me in the ribs (an endearing boyish habit of his)," Sally silently said, "I shall poke my fingers in his fly and pull his pubic hairs," but Ivan was fly to her threats on his privates and made no public assault on her person.

His breath wafted across her alert hair. (Must make an appointment for a crimp. Hope Jason is available.) "You've laid out our address and telephone number very nicely on the top right-hand corner." (Was he being ironic?) Another year or two and you'll get the hang of this contrivance."

"What are you hanging around here for?"

"You shouldn't finish a sentence with a preposition."

Sometimes he could be very irritating, particularly when he pontificated about grammar. "Could I proposition you to finish your sentence elsewhere?"

"Alright then, if that's the way you want to operate. I brought you these books (there were two tomes under his arm) to help you with your feature."

"What feature?"

"The one about mad, bad George—"

"Now you've mentioned George—"

"Gordon, also known as Byron, the limping lord. Did he or did he not write The Vampyre?" He laid the books on the desk.

"I'm sure they'll be a great help. I've written a thousand words so far but this is a thank-you letter to Android and Zena."

"Surely they should thank us for swallowing their stock of cheap vulgarious Bulgarious plonk. It would be quicker to phone them."

But Sally had. A tinkle of Telemann and then a trill of Zena. "We are very very sorry that neither Andrew or I are in residence at this moment in time to take your call but—"

The phone rang.

"See who it is, then."

"How can I see who it is? Surely you mean hear who—"

"Go. Go. Out, damn spot."

Exit Ivan reluctantly.

Sally typed: – 'Dear Andrew and Zena, My husband and I'

"This is too queenly. And shouldn't Zena be first? After all, she was the one who had to open all the tinfoil."

Type: 'Dear Zena and Andrew, Ivan and I—'

Ivan returned. "Who was it, then? Oh no, not another one of them—"

"Yes. Schubert's Death And The Maiden this time. I'm going to put on the answering machine."

"Wait a minute. Talking of George and The Vampyre reminded me—"

"Old Byron and his alleged poem?"

"Well, not exactly. I was thinking more of George the solicitor, what he said about making a proper will and that other vampire, your ex."

He was now really grumpy. "We'll discuss it later. When you've finished your later. I mean your letter and—"

"And?"

"And I'm not properly willed to be gravely laid in a designer sarcophagus."

Five minutes earlier, and not a grave-stone's throw from Highgate Cemetery, Angelica had entered her neat and sweet-smelling (thanks to pine-fresh discreet scented sachets. Banish city mustiness with odours of wild flowers and sea breezes) designer tomb-size flat. As with most women, be they mother of six from Tunbridge Wells, Miss Whiplash, lady brain-surgeon or high-flier in the City, she carried two plastic carriers as well as her executive briefcase. We are all bag ladies under the skin, sisters. When did you last see a man carry a briefcase and a plastic bag?

Her routine was simple. She stepped over the pile of letters behind the door, took three paces forward and laid plastic bag with bookshop logo on the divan, placed briefcase on plain wood table-cum-desk, turned, took four paces into kitchenette (not suitable for plump person), put plastic carrier with delicatessen logo on worktop, poured water into expresso device, poured fine coffee into perforated container, switched on device, returned to first room, slid selected CD into player, switched on same, dialled number on phone, laid receiver on table, polished collection of minature glass ornaments, returned to phone, listened, smiled and replaced receiver in cradle.

Of course, we all have our little routines. In a later chapter we shall consider the habits of Alex. When the expresso device had expressed its steam through the granules, she poured the coffee into a delicate cup: no sugar, exploits female cane-cutters. No milk, exploits dumb female animals. (Wait, I hear you cry, what about the cowled female coffee-bean gatherers, so picturesquely depicted on the package cover? Well, we must all make some compromises in this life.) Then she prepared a snack of wholemeal wafers smeared with vegetable-oil margarine and a spread of vegetarian cheese.

Back in the first room, she pulled an office chair up to the table, opened the briefcase, and then click-click, exposed the hidden tape recorder and checked the tape-length. Next, the post. Envelopes containing wordy slogans – Getting Britain On The Move and so on – from Left, Right, Centre, Greens, Revolutionary Workers and Bury The Tunnel political parties. Is there to be an election? Each had an inane smiling portrait of 'Our (male) Leader'. Into basket reserved for recycling. Followed by 'Your Chance To Win £1000' and several other similar enticing offers. 'On the Margin', a season of feminist theatre, was put to one side for future reference. Also, brochure from the CD mail-order company.

Books from plastic bag No 1 laid in neat pile on table. 'Wills And Probates.' 'The Law Of Inheritance.' 'Dictionary Of Benign And Noxious Plants.' 'Have A Heart. How To Avoid Cardiac Arrest.'

'Play' button on answering machine pressed.

No 1. From Ariadne.

"Hello, Angie, it's me, Ariadne. (Words rushed. Panting. As if running. To where? From what?) Listen, what we were talking about the other night, remember. I was thinking if we could get together, Alex, you and me, not Amy, she gabbles too much and talk things over without any little ears flapping. How about us three going down to see Mum and take her out for a meal. Mustn't say too much over the phone. Never know who's listening. We can go down in Alex's car. Makes him feel important. Give us a ring or drop a note. God bless."

Buzz. Buzz. Message No.2. Kevin.

('Kevin?' we hear you ask. We have mentioned Kevin. Briefly.

But then so was the marriage of Angelica and he. Out, out, brief candlewick, was their wedding night farewell.)

"Hello, Angie. Kev here. (Defensive deserving-artisan tone.) Got your letter yesterday. Okay, fair enough, I had two hundred off you before you walked out but a hundred's rightly mine because you took one of my paintings with you. It could be worth quite a bit in years to come and anyway—" (Angelica yawned and flipped through the poison plant book as Rotherhithe's own Rothko went on to bemoan the collapsed market in charlatan art. Would he too give a broken bottle the elbow?) "—you'd better send me a stamped addressed envelope cos I'm not going to waste my money supporting the post office."

Buzz Buzz. Message No.3. A Friend.

"Hello, Angelica. (Womb-trembling tone, probably accompanied by dilated eyes brimming with tears.) You didn't answer my last phone call or the one before that. Are you so busy or – (Pause. Sniffle) don't you want to see me again? What have I done wrong? I ask myself that a thousand times a day – (Pause. Another sniffle) and night."

Angelica rose from the table, switched on the word processor and slotted Beethoven's Pathetique Piano Sonata No. 8. into the CD player.

The Friend was still tremulously talking. "—I've videoed every episode of Prisoner Cell Block H since you left—"

Angelica grimaced fastidiously. Yes, she had watched those bloated, butch and smelly female crims in their cardboard cells just to please—"Whinger, whinger," she shouted at the answering-machine. "Why don't you leave me alone?"

The Friend's voice was cut off in mid-whinge.

Buzz. Buzz. Message No.4.

Angelica quickly pressed the 'Hold' button. She began to type.

'Kevin,

Please don't think I am harassing you for the money you owe me but, as you know, I do like to tie up all the loose ends. I admit I did take one of your paintings (to strengthen the box of books) but £100 is too much for it. Costing it at one hour's labour, £10, square of hardboard, £5 and paints, brushes etc,

£10, you therefore owe me £175. I am enclosing a S.A.E for your speedy reply.
Yours etc.'

A second letter.
'My dear friend,
Of course I'm not trying to avoid you but I'm too busy even to go to the theatre at the moment. I might have a few nights to spare next month. Could you send me the 'On the Margin' listings? Mine seem to have gone astray. I am enclosing a s.a.e, for your speedy reply.
Your dear friend.'

Angelica wrote out names and addresses on four long envelopes and then fished out a small bottle from the briefcase, squeezed the rubber bulb and smeared the sticky fold of two envelopes with a viscous substance extruded from the teat. "Let us consider it as a scientific experiment," she told the array of glass figurines.

'Play' button on answering-machine pressed. Message No.4.

(Sound of traffic. A slight cough.) "Hello, Angelica, I am just ringing to remind you that your mother is still alive, although with the way you've neglected me these years (I saw you five months ago) I might as well as be dead. And even then would you visit my grave, I wonder."

Bleep, bleep, bleep. Rattle rattle.

"I haven't much change and I can't afford to keep ringing and talking to a machine. I'd write to you but all you'd say is there's Mum moaning again and anyway why don't you send me a letter, God knows it's little to ask—"

Angelica went over to the CD player, turned up the volume and then sat down in front of the word processor. The piano rattled through the final movement of the Appassionata sonata and finished with a presto flourish.

"—are you fonder of your father than me, I ask myself, even though you know how terrible he was to me. If it wasn't for HER, you'd have gone to live with him—" Bleep, bleep, bleep. "I've no more money. Come down and—" Bzzzzzzz.

Scene from a domestic life. Time: years ago.

Cleo: (In a high-pitched voice.) For all you care, I might as well be a pillar of salt.

(Angelica, as a very young girl, enters)

Ange: (Brightly) We were told about a pillar of salt today, Daddy, in school and how Lot's wife—

Cleo: Don't interrupt me when I'm talking to your father.

Ange: What's a pillar of salt, Daddy?

Ivan: It's for cows to lick.

Cleo: That's right, go on, teach your daughter to call her mother a cow. Let me tell you, Ivàn know-all, there'll come a day, and the sooner the better, you'll be living a lonely life with nobody to keep you company and then you'll be sorry.

Ange: Where will you go to live, Daddy?

Ivan: (With benign smile) I rather fancy a cave. There's some nice big ones along the South Coast.

Ange: (Claps hands) Oh, can I come with you, Daddy? And bring Amy as well? Just like Lot and his two daughters and we'll buy wine and—"

Cleo: (Neck turning red. Pushes protesting Angelica out of room) Don't let me hear you saying such things again.

End of Scene 1.

Angelica began to type.

'Dearest Mummy,
I was so sorry not to be in to take your call. You could have reversed charges and we could have had a long chat. Of course, I'm not neglecting you but I've been so busy these past few months and, besides, I only received your new address last Sunday from Ariadne. We've been talking of driving down the Sunday after next. It will be lovely to see you in your new place. As for Dad, I haven't seen him for years now and—'

Scene from a domestic life. Time: a few years ago. Place: Ivan's flat.

Hallway. Doorbell rings.

Ivan: (Opens door.) Hello, Angelica. Didn't expect you today.

Angelica: (Enters.) Hello, Dad. I was just passing.

(They exchange pecks on cheeks.)

Ivan: Didn't I give you a key?

Angelica: You promised to have one cut. As I'm here, I'll take it, that is, if you remembered. (Walks down hallway.)

Ivan: (A little awkwardly.) Well, I did remember but—

Angelica: (Stops in doorway.) Oh, you've got company. Perhaps I'll call back tomorrow.

Ivan: (Stands behind Angelica. Hand on her shoulder.) Of course not. You'll stay and have something to eat with us. Sally, I'd like you to meet my youngest and brightest daughter, Angelica.

Sally: (Rises from armchair.) Hello, Angelica. I've heard such a lot about you from Ivan. (Holds out hand.)

Angelica: '(Takes proffered hand limply. Coldly.) I've heard nothing at all about you.

Ivan: (Forced joviality.) What do you think, Sally? She's not only inherited my good looks but my brains as well. (Puts cigarette in mouth.)

Sally: (Sharply.) Ivan, you promised! (To Angelica.) I'm trying to make your father cut down on his smoking. (Smiles sweetly.) Look, why don't I put on the coffee pot and slice some cake (To Ivan, patting his stomach) and only a small slice for you, and leave you two together. You must have a lot to talk about. (Exits.)

Angelica: Your latest, Dad? And how long do you expect her to stay?

Ivan: (In an embarrassed manner.) Well, actually, we were thinking of buying a house together and, in the near future, getting married. I expect her to be with me for a very long time.

Angelica: (Looks at wrist-watch.) I don't expect to be here for a long time.

End of scene 2.

Angelica took an oblong cardboard box from the bottom desk drawer, opened it and laid a woman-shaped doll in front of the word-processor. Then she removed a long needle from a sewing kit and stabbed the doll in the heart.

Sally clutched her breast. "Oh God, I'm getting chest pains sitting in front of this bloody machine." She switched off the word-processor, went into the lounge, rooted in the bottom bureau drawer, took out an oblong cardboard box and removed a fistful of coloured postcards. She selected one with a William Morris design (have nothing in your house that is not useful or beautiful, and that goes for the husband too) and hastily scribbled, 'Dear Zena and Andrew, Ivan and I were simply delighted to—' She then shoved the finished note into an envelope. "I should have done this right from the start." Suddenly she screamed, "Oh no!" and dashed into the study.

The startled Ivan quickly followed and found her staring at the word-processor. "What's wrong, guv?" he asked.

"Wrong! Everything's wrong. I switched it off without removing the floppy disk and now, weeks and weeks of work has been totally erased. Somebody must have put a curse on us."

Chapter nine

Like a Tarzan with a tarantula in his dhoti, Sally's mood swung from the undergrowth of despair, despondency and desperation up through the forest's shadowy umbrella where she saw the glimmer of shining hope and the little tent of blue which prisoners called the sky. Then she came crashing down again, her limbs lashed by thorny shoots and barbed vines.

"The curse has come upon me," she cried.

"It's not that time of the month, is it?" Ivan asked a little anxiously and glanced at the Renaissance Art (this month, Titian's Venus of Urbino) calendar beneath the cracked mirror. Apparently the Duke of Urbino had died the same year that his lusciously limbed wife had been so nakedly portrayed. "Your woman's seductive flesh with her hand coyly hiding her essentials would make any man's heart falter," he thought. What with this and that, he had not had much chance to check out his own cardiac resilience and now, if the moon was in the wrong quarter, his hopes would have to be deferred for another week.

Sally was chanting a litany of cursed events. "There was the burglary, those phone calls at all hours, the attempted break-in the night we came home from A-to-Z's dinner party (Ivan would have included the last-mentioned among the lesser curses), although you pretended it was a neighbour's cat, and then you threw up in the bathroom. Talking of which, one of ours sicked a half-digested bird outside the bedroom door—" She gave a theatrical groan. "And now this. Three months' work gobbled by a maniacal machine. And I thought we had it house-trained."

Ivan refrained from saying, "Why don't you make copies first?" He would only state the obvious under duress and this was somebody else's duress. Anyway, it would be of little consolation to the bereft and grieving Sally to be reminded that she had nil scores due to a double fault. He switched into an avuncular role – fatherly would be too incestuous – put his arm round her shoulder and muttered platitudes. But this was like dragging her through the mire. "You've got notes, haven't you? And surely you can remember—"

She shook her head violently. "No, no, it's no use."

"Perhaps there's some electronic way of recovering the files. I'm not a know-all in the bits and bytes of matters electronics but I know someone who says he is. Why don't we ring up Alex. He's a national expert."

"National expert!! You're joking." She tore away from his clutch and started to rummage through the drawers. "Yes, you're right, I do have notes. Yes, here's one notebook and here's another." The fury of battle was in her. "And another thing, if you tell that so-called national expert anything, anything at all about my mistake and have him sniggering at me for being a stupid woman, I'll be so angry—"

Ivan smiled. His ploy had worked.

As we said, everybody has their little routines though not all keep to them. The self-proclaimed national expert was no exception.

Alex never carried a briefcase. The Saturday shopping ritual was the only occasion when he allowed the palms of his manly hands to be creased by the weight of plastic carriers. Now and then he could be seen hurrying along Cheapside with an important frown on his forehead and an equally important looking clip-file folder clutched to his chest; but an observer would not have guessed that tucked between the brochures and technical hand-outs was a recent purchase of Bunty or Judy. He had a strange fascination for little girls' comics and vetted Michelle's reading matter every week. His choice of (tabloid) newspaper was determined by the company he kept: his real taste was for trash but when he visited Dawn's house in Mitcham he made sure that he had a middle-market rag tucked importantly under his arm. Her mother had once stood as a Conservative candidate in a local council by-election. To her intense chagrin, she trailed by 50 votes behind the successful Labour candidate. "I wouldn't mind so much," she complained, "after all this is a democracy, but he was a black man."

On this particular night, as with most other nights, Alex plucked the letters and freebies from the mat, stood for a second or two in the doorway to make sure nobody had broken in, dumped folder, newspaper and post on the settee, switched on the television and watched it for another two seconds, plugged in the electric kettle in the kitchen, poured two spoonfuls of instant coffee into a mug, removed the Cellophane from a steak and kidney pie (Made from prime British beef), switched on the small portable radio permanently tuned to a 24-hour pop station and lit a cigarette with such an apologetic amount of nicotine in it that it might as well have been made of chocolate.

When the coffee was ready, he settled down to enjoy himself heckling quiz-show competitors.

The unctuous compere, darkly dyed hair smarmed, leered at a pudding-faced woman contestant. "Now, Sharon, for ten more pounds, and you already have fifty pounds in the kitty (Scattered applause from audience. Oleaginous compere frowns at blue card), for ten more pounds, Sharon, answer me this, who were known as the Fab Four?" Sharon looked desperate.

"The Beatles, of course, you dimwit," Alex shouted. "Everybody knows that. God, how do these people get on the show?"

Thunderous applause, compere grins, Sharon simpers. She had given the correct answer. "It must have been a fix," Alex growled." One day, when I've less on my plate," he told himself, "I'll apply to go on one of those shows."

Frequent fantasy:

Compere: Now, Alex, you've done splendidly so far. You've answered questions on maths, politics, history, sport – this man is a genius. Give him a hearty round of applause – (Thunderous applause) right, Alex, for £1000, I would like you to tell me—" Scene fades to various awestruck friends and relatives saying to each other, "I didn't realise Alex was so clever."

A rap version of Adam Faith's "Wot Do You Want If You Don't Want Money?" was blaring out of the radio. He levered the steak-and-kid onto a plate and returned to the settee. Pictures of houses burning, people running. Voice-over: "As riots spread to other major cities, the army is moving in to regain control and—"

Flip to another channel. Situation comedy in which husband and dotty wife try to cope with noisy children and intrusive neighbours while preparing for their buxom daughter's wedding.

The answering machine was blinking. Press play button.

Message No.1.

"Hello, Alex, luv, it's me, (pert) Dawn. About next weekend, in case you've made any plans, it's off. Carol in work is getting married and she's invited the girls to the reception and the disco afterwards. And the following weekend, well, Mum says I ought to go down with her to Tunbridge Wells to visit Gran because she, that's Gran, is too old to come to our marriage. Mum's sent you a letter about the wedding costs. Do you think you could get your Dad to help out a bit? Bye bye for now and God bless."

How could Dad, aka Ivan, help out with the costs with HER leaning on his chequebook? But if Dad had a severe shock and suffered a cardiac arrest, that might arrest the wedding. "How can I be riotously happy when I've just attended the last rites for my dear old father? Let's put off the joyous event till his memory is cold." How long? Six months? Six weeks? Six days? Six hours? Or until probate has spread the honey of his money among his grieving children.

Message No.2.

"Angelica here. Relating to what we touched upon the other night. It's imperative we talk again in private. Ariadne has had a good idea. She suggests we, that is, you, her and I, go down to see Mummy together in the one car. Ariadne and I will be free the Sunday after next. We can finalise details on the way there. You could make some excuse to Dawn for not seeing her; you're always making excuses anyway. We thought we'd go in your car. You know the route and you're a far better driver than either of us. Let me know what you decide soon."

Alex smirked and went through his post.

Circulars offering fabulous prizes. Into waste basket. Political waffle – and we can rely on your vote. Into basket.

MENSA: "We regret to inform you that—" Into basket.

"It was a stupid test anyway and couldn't really measure real intelligence. I mean, take the question, 'Kill. Slaughter. Execute.

Assassinate. Die. Which is the odd one out?' There's five different answers to that. Didn't want to join them in the first place and spend good money so I could meet snooty know-alls like Dad or Angie."

Blue envelope, hand-written name and address, faint whiff of scent.

Dawn's Mother. (Typewritten)

'Dear Alexander,

As you can see, I am exercising my old skill on Janice's electric portable which we bought for her 21st but now she is married and gone to live in Basildon with her husband (Yes, yes, we've heard about Janice, youngest of three daughters and her rising young executive husband. Skip this bit.)

'I have mentioned to you that before I was married I was personal and private secretary to the senior partner of Skrimpet and Skrimpet in the City (Yes, every time we met. More than likely she was the tea lady. Skip this. Turn over page.)

'—and I have enclosed two clippings, one from Bride Magazine and one from Wedding Magazine, which I think you will find useful as a guide. Of course, we do know that it was traditional for the bride's side to pay for everything but traditions do change (Yes, since the last showing of Dynasty and Dallas.)

'—and we also thought we could leave the hiring of the ushers' morning suits in your very capable hands (In other words, pay for those as well)

'—everybody is very excited – relatives coming down from Scotland, Wales, Hampshire (For a free meal) – sending out invitations now (We'll end up hiring the Albert Hall. Who'll pay for that?)

'—and now for a delicate matter. Are you inviting your father AND his young wife? And if so, will he want to sit at the top table? I don't want to upset your mother, she is such a lovely woman and has had such a wretched time, what with your father leaving her for a younger woman and then losing most of her money in the Crash and having to sell her Spanish villa (What fancy story is this?) '—perhaps your father might be willing to make a contribution to your costs. You did say he was quite well-off. (Why not present him with the estimate? That should bring on the required heart attack.)

'—do send me a list of your guests. (On a postcard?)
Kindest regards,
Felicity.'

Cutting A. On light blue paper (Touch and retreat to a safe distance) "Who pays for what." The groom is responsible for: (For what? Creating a black hole that swallows every spare penny?)

Cutting B. Cream paper. Headings in red. (That is where I am heading.) "WHO PAYS. The Groom: Rings, Fees, Flowers, Transport, Presents." (Presents? Will all those present please stand and put their hands into their pockets or purses. Donations welcome.)

Alex groaned as if his steak-and-kidney pie were in visceral turmoil and then tossed the haranguing letter plus cuttings across the room. Yet fluttery Felicity had a point about asking Dad for a contribution to the expenses. What if he sent Ivan one of those "Release the capital tied up in your house" leaflets.

Scenario One.
Scene: Ivan's see-through lounge.Time. Very near future.
(Alex has just finished explaining to his father the economic advantages of releasing his tied-down capital.) So, Dad, with all that cash-flow available, you'll have money to spare to advance me sufficient for the wedding costs.

Ivan: You certainly have a brain for these financial matters, Alex. I'll certainly take your advice; and to fulfill my parental duty (Takes out cheque book) let me help you out with your immediate expenses. Will a thousand do for now?

Door crashes open. Sally storms in. Ivan cowers.

Sally: (Strident) Don't you dare, Ivan!

Alex lapsed into sullen contemplation and the scene darkened. This will not do at all.

Surely the best possible scenario will be as an aftermath to the successful PLOT, scheme of which has yet to be executed.

Scenario Two.

Scene as above. Time likewise.

Sally: (Cowering on sofa. Weepy.) And when I came in – oh my God – there he was lying on the floor. Alex, I know we didn't see eye to eye in the past but you're the man of the family now. Tell me, what am I to do?

Alex: (Standing, facing Sally. Very stern.) Do, woman, do? What you will do is vacate this house immediately. My father's property is to be divided between you and his children and we need this house empty for the sale. That's legal and that's final.

Sally: (Holds hands together as if in prayer.) But Alex, surely it'll be legal if I gave you some of your inheritance now?

Alex: I'll consider it.

Sally: (Takes chequebook from handbag.) Is ten thousand worth your consideration?

Alex: I'm only taking it out of pity for you.

Sally: (Grabs Alex's hand before he can pull away and kisses it.) Oh, Alex, you're wonderful.

Scenario two faded but Alex's attempt to re-wind for a repeat of Sally's highly improbable humiliation was shattered by the ringing of the phone.

Tracy: Alex! Is that you, Alex?

Alex: Yup. What do you want? Children okay?

Tracy: They are now, no thanks to you. Not that you care all that much in spite of what you say to everybody else.

Alex: What's wrong with them, eh?

Tracy: You'd know if you'd read my letter. That's all I'm saying. Read my letter. (Phone slammed down)

Read my letter litter. Here it is. Second-class stamp. Typewritten. Is typing the latest trend? Are ancient Remingtons being taken down from hundreds of lofts? Could they become collectors' items and be worth heaps of money?

'Alex. My solliciter says we got to comunicate by letter and copies kept so I borrowed this machine from the woman next door. First thing is that Shel and Dar were sick the day after you had them and I know you took them to yr sisters cos Shel told me. When you take my kids out for the day, it must be to a clean place. So you cant have them for the next two weeks. Besides their going to a party for my brother Tone on Sunday next whos just won the area boxing championship cup.Second thing is them things I want . Theres more and theres a list with this letter. Third thing is, seeing as how yr getting married again my solliciter says we must settle the extra maintnance for the children cos the cost of living just keeps going up and up. Answer this soon before I have to go to court. Trace."

Was there no end to these torments? Wherever he turned, there was somebody trying to drain cash from his veins. What could he do? Be a masterful man and take executive decisions. Ignore Tracy's and Felicity's letters, write out the list of ways to kill your father by shock and claim a big portion of his money. Do this after the murder mystery on TV but – but firstly make the first executive decision.

Stab phone buttons in a decisive manner. Beeep, beeep. Beeep, beeep. Doeful music. (Shit, she has her machine on. Pretending not to be in. Trust Angie to have her dreadful dirge on the answering-machine.) "Hello. I am not available at this precise moment but if you care to – thank you for calling."

"Er, hello, Angie, it's me, er, Alex, returning your,er, call – cough cough – anyway, I've told Trace it's about time she had the kids for a weekend or two so it'll be okay for us to go down to see Mum. Let me, er, know, er, where we'd meet. Of course, I'll do the driving if you and Ariadne will chip in with the petrol money."

The TV murder mystery was a complete let-down. Anybody with half a brain could see that the man with the black moustache was the murderer but then they had to go and spoil it by drowning him before the first commercial break. Alex was disgusted and would have switched to another channel if there had been a decent quiz programme showing. As it was, he continued watching just to see the mess they made of the plot.

Two hours later, in the kitchen, he filled the kettle for another fortifying cup of ersatz coffee and turned the radio up so he could fully hear the music in the adjoining room. Then, from a cupboard in which he kept drawing books for the children, he took out sheets of A4 plain white paper, a plastic straight edge and several HB pencils. Spreading the sheets on the table he drew with the straight edge a transverse line on each near the top and then two equally spaced vertical lines underneath. He wrote above the left-hand column 'Ways', above the middle 'For' and above the right-hand one 'Against'.He was going to write above them all, 'In Alphabetic Order: Shocking ways to kill a person with heart trouble and claim your inheritance' but decided against it. What if Michelle should find it?

Having made yet another executive decision, this time not to do something, he sat down to compile the list.

He had reached 'E' for 'electrocution' when his head fell on the table in a deep sleep and he dreamed of a wild wedding party being showered with banknotes instead of confetti while dancing around a sarcophagus.

Chapter ten

And now for an intermission. Theatre-goers are familar with the lacuna known as the interval when the safety curtain comes down, the actors hurry off for a gin and tonic and the audience rub their sore bums as they shuffle to the bar for a snorter of over-priced drink. Do they excitedly ask each other, "What happens next?" or are they too busy craning their necks to see if there are famous persons among them? As for the latter, any famous person worthy of a photo-opportunity has already been to the first night on a complimentary ticket.

But what has happened between the first act and the second? The play's programme says: Act Two. Ten Years Later. When the curtain rises, a clutch of decaying family retainers relate the apposite parts of the past decade's history in their local yokel patois. 'Arr, Rebecca's a right sharp one she is and her in Americay these years and not knowing the master's been taken to his bed with the dry rot and the mistress is keeping herself to herself in the East Wing and the young master he's had a limp since Black Betsy, the gypsy mare, rolled over him in the wet meadow last summer.' Pregnant pause for audience to finish their choc ices. 'Arr, and they do say as how Rebecca married a rich soya-bean farmer and as how he fell into a volcano on their honeymoon, leaving her with a fine strapping boy and all his money.'

The intermission/interval gap, then, is a useful device for the author to shovel in all the odds and bobs that are relevant to the plot but, if written and acted, would cause the paying customers severe rectum-rigidity.

By coincidence, our intermission also has – in the words of the reader of tea-leaves – a space of ten; in this case, ten days.

Sally had been commissioned by the androgynous editor/ess (Talk about having the best of both worlds) of a certain female-interest magazine to write a feature on the Pride and Passion of Slavic Women; to be sub-titled, 'Are Ice Maidens Nice Maidens?

Niet or Da Da?' As an aid to traversing the tundra of the subject, she had obtained two tickets (free) for a West End production of Chekhov's Three Sisters. This was the fifth version of the sororal shilly-shallying to be presented this year in the London area alone and, according to the drama critic of the Guardian – "a statement of spiritual affinity" – and The Mail – "an ecstasy of energy" – it promised to be an iconostasis of the Russian soul. "Ah, an array of talking pictures," Ivan muttered when he read the last statement and made a note to send a cutting to Private Eye's Pseud's Corner. He did this at least once a week but never actually posted off an extract; arguing, perhaps justly, that the mailbag for this particular column must be the largest in the country.

Sally had already seen two of the previous productions. Of the French company's mime version, mentioned en passant in chapter one, she had not a word to say and her gesticulation was unprintable. In the second critically acclaimed (sub-text: audience-bereft) presentation, the roles of the tiresome trio were performed by real-life sisters from a famed Irish acting dynasty and the scene was set on the bleak, gale-swept bogs of gaunt Galway. Even the names were changed (Oona for Olga) to protect the guileless and the characters moaned on and on about returning to Dublin. 'Why not Kilburn?' Sally had scribbled in her notebook.

She had foregone the pleasure of seeing the other two productions. One was a codpiece version performed at a converted morgue in Hampstead, retitled The Three Brothers. The second, a rave at the Edinburgh Festival, was spoken in the vulgar vernacular of outer Troon and was performed in darkest Croydon.

Sally and Ivan ploughed through the crowd in the miniscule foyer and were ushered to their end-of-row seats in the stalls five minutes before the beginning. A notoriously dopey actress, the inconstant companion of an infamous film director, pushed archly past them without apology and tried to hypnotise Sally with Coke-dilated eyes. "Are we supposed to be mind-readers?" hissed Ivan. The audience gabble subsided and all eyes were fixed on the grand-daughter clock standing downstage. Three actresses in long off-white nightdresses appeared backstage from behind the clutter of Edwardian furniture and silently advanced on the time-piece.

At that precise moment, another pair of latecomers materialised beside Sally and Ivan.

The male of the two growled, "If you don't mind" and the female simpered, "Thenk kew, thenk kew." They left in her trail one hacked shin belonging to Ivan and a low-flying cloud of Savage Moron aftershave.

"Wasn't that Richard and—?" Ivan whispered. He was interrupted by a fit of schoolgirlish hysterics from a 60-year old actress, whose tempest-tossed gestures were hidden by the grand-daughter clock. Those in the middle of the stalls were forced to lean sideways as if seasick to see the performers, all members of the Ruddigore dynasty. There was much squealing, weeping, javelin-throwing, tumbling, hugging, kissing, face-slapping and falling down in heaps of flounces. A hockey match organised by Angela Brazil could hardly have done better. Such avant-garde intensity left the audience in a state of nervous exhaustion.

When the curtain came down, Ivan stood up, his two hands pressed against the small of his back, and declared rather loudly, "For this relief much thanks." He avoided going to West End productions of Chekhov because of his great love of Russian literature. In fact, he had mastered the Cyrillic alphabet and spent hours with language tapes in the hope of some day reading the Great Works in the original; but he floundered with the arcane grammar and the verbs of motion almost paralysed him.

He fumbled in his pockets for small change and ambled towards the ice-cream usherette, beaten to first place in the queue by two old ladies and second place by a pair of portly American tourists. A whole minute passed while the old dears, having first proffered a £10 note, searched in their purses for the right amount and the Yanks overcame their problems with the currency.

"You know chocolate gives me spots," said Sally ungraciously. She took a chance on a faceful of monstrous carbuncles and dug into the rock-hard sweet while trying to peer over the heads of crowd at the bar entrance. She liked to mingle, no matter how thick (in both senses) the throng, whereas he regarded a half-full restaurant as a dreadful example of population explosion.

"You were right," she said to him. "Richard is here."

"With old Pruneface in tow?"

"No, not Prunella. Deirdre."

"George's fluffy—"

"Quiet. They might hear you. And guess what? They pretended not to see me." He knew that nobody could pretend not to see her a second time. They drifted back to their row. "Perhaps they're too shy to meet us and have gone home, his place or hers," Ivan suggested. Sally clutched Ivan's arm and pointed across the auditorium. "Isn't that your daughter over there?"

"Who? Which?"

"Medusa."

"You mean—"

"Angelica." The audience noise died down and two people quickly brushed by Ivan and Sally. "Hello, Richard. Hello Deirdre. Are you enjoying the play?" said Ivan with malicious glee, as if addressing Mrs Lincoln.

Suffice it to say that the reputation of Chekhov was ritually slaughtered on stage during the second half. After one curtain call, Ivan was ready to flee but Sally placed a restraining paw on his arm. "Let's wait a minute, just to say hello and goodbye. Perhaps we'll meet your elusive daughter as well." Ivan protested that he was starving but she was incandescent with curiosity. The last of the audience had trudged out and the attendants were closing the doors when Richard and Deirdre appeared. They tried avoidance tactics but Sally was in the mood to be horribly hearty. "Well, well, I was sure it was you," she cried chirpily. "Didn't I say so, Ivan, but you said it was too much of a coincidence."

"What was?" Rigid Richard was as stiff-faced as ever.

"Why, meeting you two here and also, I'm sure I saw Ivan's daughter in the audience."

"Oh really. How interesting. Well, it was very nice meeting you again but I'm afraid—"

"Look, look, there she is, Ivan," Sally cried excitedly and pointed towards a group standing by the traffic lights.

Several things happened at that moment. The junk-fed Americans and the old ladies, the very last to leave the theatre, came down the steps together. A squad of middle-aged rubber-neckers with loud voices and beery breath surged up the path from the left, a mixed troop of gawping Swedish youths trundled down from the right, the traffic lights changed and a truculent young man in simulated leather gear made a swipe at a posh car.

In the consequent melee, our quartet was split asunder like a molecule struck by a particularly vicious neutron. When the spin of confusion had abated, they had reformed into a pair of binaries. Binary one, Ivan and Deirdre, had been shunted three feet to the left and their face-to-face confrontation was so close he had a full view of her crooked front tooth and the nervous twitching on the right-hand corner of her mouth. "Perhaps," he self-consciously thought, "She can see the blue vein on my nose and thinks I'm an alcoholic." Her lips seemed to be opening and closing at an inordinately rapid rate.

"—and of course one could not turn down the chance to see the Ruddigores in the flesh, so to speak, there's more of a je ne sais quoi in the theatre, and to see them in Chekhov, I simply adore Chekhov, don't you, did you see the Irish version, not the same ambience, and George couldn't come, not that there was a ticket to spare but he was going to his legal aid thingy, all those feckless people with their problems, why he does it I don't know, there's no money in it, and what thanks will he ever get from those people, mind you, there's no point in taking George to the theatre or even the cinema, he always gets up before – I mean, he never finishes anything, he never reads the last chapter of a book and Prunella was feeling ghastly, so Richard said, he knows I love the theatre, he said—"

The second binary, Richard and Sally, had been swept towards the traffic lights. Now that the flow had changed to an ebb, they returned towards the first binary, chatting away like two old friends. Ivan was not sure he liked this transformation and noticed that Deirdre too seemed less than enchanted.

"Richard, you did book a table at Caprice, didn't you?"

"Oh yes, but it's alright. We've five minutes to get there." To Sally and Ivan. "It was so nice to meet you again. Must keep in contact."

A quick wave of the hands, a 'goodbyee' from Deirdre and they vanished into the swarm of non-Londoners going towards the Eros statue.

It was not until Sally's car was stolidly negotiating St George's

Circus that mention was made of their brief encounter. "Do you think there's anything going on there?" Sally asked. Ivan, who was thinking he could murder a bag of chips right now, stared out of the window. "I can't see anything going on."

"Stop prevaricating. I'm talking about Richard and Deirdre of the Sorrows."

"I dunno," said Ivan laconically. "You and Ricky-Ticky became quite matey. She wasn't very happy about that."

"Oh, he's alright once you penetrate his carapace." She did not add that the turtle beneath the hard shell had invited her to lunch at the Harpo Club. This was a new literary watering-hole for Groucho Club dissidents who felt that that place had become the haunt of secretaries on the make, tabloid gossip columnists and publicity junkies. Ivan contemplated Deirdre's remark about George never finishing a book. Didn't want to reach the climax? Was that the coded message?

"And I'm convinced that was your daughter I saw in the theatre and crossing over the road by the traffic lights. She was carrying that bloody briefcase as usual. When I pointed her out to Richard, he said she looked like someone who worked in Andrew's office, Andrew is Richard's accountant. And that reminds me, I must get in contact with George about making our wills. Should I invite your children to your funeral?"

A combination of hunger and ennui was making Ivan grumpy. "If you'd bothered to read that book on the Catastrophic Theory and the Improbability Factor in the Analytical Approach to Social Stratification – " (But she had tried, just to please him and had read chapter one in the bathroom. Yawn. Yawn.) " – you would have seen that the chance of meeting someone you know who knows someone else related to yòu one night in a 300-seat theatre from a population of seven million—"

"Talking of catastrophes, remind me when your birthday is."

"Don't remind me. It puts ages on me."

"Oh, any excuse for a party."

"I hate parties. You never see any of them till election time."

"As an alternative, I'll take you to an alternative theatre to see a Pinter play."

"Give that man another Pinter."

Two escaped characters from an altered Pinter play called on Angelica.

Scene: Angelica's flat. Time: between 6 and 7 pm. She is sitting at the desk. Writes in notebook, 'S in animated conversation with (?), a man, near theatre.' Opens grubby envelope from distraught Kevin (can a Kevin ever be distraught?) and reads out aloud, 'Can't answer your letter because Jackson Pollock (his multi-crossed lurcher) ate it. You won't believe this but he got sick later on and died. You must have written a poison-pen letter. You never did like my dog because you're a hard little bitch.' Angelica laughs, crumples letter and throws it into wastepaper basket. Picks up oblong envelope, sniffs it and puts it to one side. Selects Rutter's Requiem on CD, slides it into slot, presses 'Play' button. Imperative knock, knock on door. She frowns, rises, fits chain in groove, opens door a crack.

Voice (Man's):	Evening, Miss.
2nd Voice (Man's):	Nice evening, Miss.
Angelica:	I don't want anything this evening, thank you.
1st Voice:	No need to thank us, Miss.
2nd Voice:	What is it you don't want this nice evening, love?
Angelica:	Towels, dusters, biro pens, note paper, vacuum cleaners, lavatory brushes, plastic bowls, bleeding hearts.
1st Voice:	How about encyclopedias, Miss? All human knowledge is there.
2nd Voice:	How about life insurance, home insurance, endowment insurance? All human assurance is there.
Angelica:	(Closes door) No thanks.(Imperative knock knock. Re-opens door as before.)
1st Voice:	Evening, Miss.
2nd Voice:	Nice evening, Miss.
Angelica:	You two again!
1st Voice:	Again, Miss? We haven't gone away.

2nd Voice: Anybody been here, love, pretending to be us?

Angelica: I don't want to buy anything. I don't want to join a political party. I don't want to discuss religion. Are you bailiffs? I haven't defaulted on my mortgage. Right?

1st Voice: Quite right, love. You don't have to do anything you don't want to.

2nd Voice: You stand on your principles, Miss. Right?

Angelica: I am not Miss Right. Right? Now, if you don't mind—

1st Voice: No, Miss, we don't mind in the least as long as you—

2nd Voice: As long as you answer our questions.

Angelica: Why?

1st Voice: If you don't mind, we do the questions. Show her your identification, Stan.

2nd Voice: And you do the answering, Miss. You show her your identification, Olly.

Angelica: The police! (Closes door, releases chain. Opens door fully.) Why didn't you say so in the beginning?

(Two men in large raincoats stand in the doorway. Owner of 1st Voice is jocularly known as Olly to the squad cars. About 45 years of age. Plumptious. 2nd Voice is sometimes known as Stan. About 35 years of age. Skinny, snappy dresser.)

Olly: Didn't we say we're the (lowers voice) police, Miss?

Stan: Couldn't you guess, Miss?

Angelica: No.

Olly: We'd like to have a word. And we'd rather proceed with our enquiries behind closed doors.

Stan: You know what they say, Miss, corridor walls have ears.

Angelica: (As the two enter her flat) Thai Saih? Isn't that the Chinese philosopher? (Closes door)

Olly, who has some wit, elaborately ignores the sarcasm and favours her with the searchlight stare.

Stan: (As he affably peeps into the kitchenette and then

inspects the CD player) Nice piece of music you've got on there, Miss. Nice bit of equipment too. Got something like that myself. I like classical music.

Olly: Not to my taste, all this classical music. Jazz, that's my choice any day. Kid Ory, King Oliver, Miles Davis, you know what I mean. The blacks could certainly play and none of them could read a note of music. Unfortunately we're not here to enjoy ourselves. I take it you've proof of your identity, Miss. Passport, driving licence, bank card, works badge, library ticket, membership card or cards, you know, club, that sort of thing?

Angelica clicks open the briefcase. Stan and Olly lean over to look into it. She takes out driving licence, works security lapel badge and a charge card, hands them to Stan, he gives them to Olly who stares at them and then returns them to her. Both men lean over again to look into her briefcase and then quickly straighten up when she clicks it shut. She then goes over to the desk, followed closely by Stan, takes a key from a chain round her neck and opens a drawer. She hands Stan the passport, membership cards for the National Trust, British Film Institute and a female-only theatre club. He gives them to Olly, who stares at them in turn.

Olly: Olly: Well, you are who you are, there's no question about that. (Returns them to Stan who blithely passes them back to Angelica. She puts them into the drawer and closes it.). We've reason to believe you're acquainted with one mumble mumble and you've corresponded with her on various matters, including a theatre club called – (Looks at notebook) yes, On The Margin. Are we correct?

Angelica: (A little distracted as Stan looks closely at her glass figurines.) Who? Oh yes, I know that person. Why do you want to know?

Olly: As I said, we'll do the asking. And have you had any recent correspondence from her? And can you tell us when you last saw this young woman? And when you last spoke to her or corresponded with this young lady, was your relationship friendly, quite friendly, less than friendly, unfriendly or what? And, one more—

Angelica: (Sharply to Stan who starts to touch one of the figurines.) Don't touch them. (Less sharp.) I'd rather you didn't handle them. They are very fragile.

Stan: (Grins wolfishly.) Know what you mean. Gotcha. My wife is the same with her collection, only hers is birds. She won't let nobody else touch them and every night she cleans them with a special cream one by one.

Olly: (Chattily.) Mine goes in for photo albums. She's got dozens and as soon as I get home, out they come and she sits there arranging and rearranging them and making lists. Drives me spare. Well, Miss, to proceed with our enquiry. As I was asking you—

Angelica: Yes, of course, yes, we did exchange letters now and then and—

Stan: (By desk. Points to oblong envelope.) This looks like the sort of envelope she used. You haven't opened it.

Angelica: Oh that. It's not from her. I know what's in it, it's a theatre listing, that's why I didn't open it.

Stan: Fond of the theatre, are you? Took the kids to a panto at the Palladium last year. Waste of money if you ask me.

Olly: It's those anti-police plays on TV that really get on my wick. Now, Miss, as you were saying—

Angelica: Well, yes, she was kind enough to put me up while I was buying this flat but I've only seen her once or twice since then.

Olly: At the theatre?

Angelica: Yes, but that was about six months ago. (Hesitates.) But why are—(Stops.)

Stan: (Reads title of book.) 'Dictionary Of Benign And Noxious Plants.' Can't be too careful these days with some of the foreign muck they bring into the country.

Olly: And in your opinion, Miss, is there any reason why she should—(Pause.)

Angelica: She should—

Stan: (Forcefully.) Take her own life?

Olly: A tragedy, that's what it was. And she so young.
Stan: A waste.Her whole life in front of her and she had so much to look forward to.
Olly: It's her parents I pity.
Stan: There's always someone left to suffer—
Olly: The pain and—
Stan: The sorrow.
Olly: As the poet said, the brave man does it with a sword.
Stan: And the coward with a kiss.
Olly: But who does it with poison, I ask you?
Stan: They say that's the woman's way.

A few minutes later the pair concluded their enquiry, thanked Angelica for her cooperation and promised to keep in contact (Why?) Exeunt.

As if released from a spell, she rapidly walked around in the confined area of her flat, touching ornaments, table and desk, all the while muttering, "I'm sorry, I'm sorry, I didn't mean it that way, it was just an experiment, I'm sorry." She picked up the oblong envelope, dropped it into the basket, retrieved it, put it on the table and then threw it into the basket again. But where was the crumpled letter from Kevin? Gone! THEY had taken it. How dare those men invade her space and molest her with their questions.

In a fury of loathing and disgust, she ran into the bathroom, returned with a slim glass cylinder of lavender (environmentally friendly) spray, pressed the nozzle and squirted left, right and centre. As she stripped off in the bathroom and stood beneath the scalding water from the shower, the scented miasma laid a damp patina on every flat surface.

Scene from another time. "Angelica darling, say hello to a very dear friend of mine. Charles (or Harry or Stephen or Fred or Bill), this is my youngest daughter." Overlong clasp of clammy hand, leering smile, smells of tobacco, drink, Old Goat aftershave, fumbling attempt to kiss, kiss. Wash. Wash. Wash.

Chapter eleven

What were the other characters in our story doing during the ten days' intermission, you may ask? They had, so to speak metaphorically, gone to the bar for a jar. To satisfy raging curiosity, here, in brief, are their brief lives in alphabetic order.

Alex moodily brooded over his unhatched clutch of vipers' eggs, stowed the begging letters in the dark recess of a cluttered drawer and stopped at 'E for electrocution' in his patricide list. This, he felt, was sufficiently shocking to be the current favourite. He tried to calculate the probability of winning the football pools or unearthing a Meissen vase.

Amy's obscure location, limited mobility allowance (relying on Bob's van) and lachrymose tendency made her eminently forgettable.

Ariadne clucked at her untidy nestlings and, when within the tossed sheets of her midnight bed, indulged in the recurring fantasy – and sometimes disturbing dreams of unsettling sensuality – that one day, with money in her fist, she would erect a shrine to he whose 'songs are carved from the bones of ghosts and have myths and vision.' The last was a direct quote from an overwrought article in The Guardian. If Alex had gone to a certain car-boot sale that Saturday to find the precious Meissen vase heavily disguised as a table lamp, he would have met his eldest sister frantically rooting in grubby cardboard boxes for additions or replacements to her Bob Dylan collection.

Ariadne was a great one for badly organising good causes; and at a meeting of the Peoples' Charter committee (Consisting of a retired schoolmaster, a disillusioned Marxist and herself. The delegate from the 'Cyclists-against-the-M25' group was in hospital with multiple injuries), she heard of the legalistic device known as the Anton Piller Order. More of that later.

Sally did ring up George the solicitor to invite him and – a mite mischievously – Deirdre to dinner; but he politely declined and offered as a reason his madly busy schedule. He disingenuously added that his dear wife was reluctant to stay up too late more than one night in the week. "She's fanatical about her eight-hours sleep." Sally then made an appointment to see George in his office the following week. She did not immediately tell Ivan of her arrangements.

Note on the programme. Act Two. Scene one.
Within the environs of and within Ariadne's apartment.
Sunday morning, ten days later.

10.25. Angelica's 2CV swung into the vacant space and came to its usual whining stop five yards from a large mattress and a late Victorian wardrobe (mass-produced and stuck together with fish glue), both leaning despairingly against the overflowing skip. "Another broken marriage," she said sotto voce to herself. She had arranged that Alex and Ariadne meet her here at 10.30 and set off on their Eastbourne Ho! journey no later than 11.00. Her brother and sister always needed the cattle-prod of a deadline.

She stayed quite still until Alkan's Requiem For A Dead Parrot had finished, switched off the radio, opened her briefcase, clicked on the tape recorder and listened to the final part of Stan and Olly's enquiry into the death of a young girl by an unknown but noxious substance.

Olly: And the funny thing was—
Stan: Not funny REALLY.
Olly: No, I suppose not, under the circumstances.
Stan: Peculiar! That's a better word.
Olly: How about funny-peculiar?
Stan: Okay then. The funny-peculiar thing was—
Olly: There were no bottles, phials, jars, pill-boxes—
Stan: Nothing with suspicious substances
Olly: The same with cups, mugs, drinking glasses, spoons.
Stan: Not a trace of anything.
Olly: So we asked ourselves . . .
Stan: How could she self-administer poison and not leave a teeny-weeny bit behind?

10.29. Angelica switched off the tape, shut the briefcase, stepped out of the car and clip-clopped up the steps. There was not a single buzz from the surrounding hives of humanity (to coin a cliche) and the only other living creatures to be seen were a scavenging cat in the skip, coo-cooing sex-mad pigeons and a pair of rotund West Indian ladies wearing dark clothes, large hats and clutching black bibles to their ample breasts as they stolidly strode past on their way to a jolly gospel sing-song.

She had her finger poised above the button when the door opened and a pink face with a gap-toothed smile confronted her. "Ah der ye are Angeleena me darling girl and how are ye dis fine bracing Sunday morning?" If he had said 'bedad' and 'begorrah' she would not have been surprised."And yer off den, yourself, herself and d'udder feller to see yer oul mudder by the say so. Be all d'accounts she's a darling woman, a darling woman though I never clapped eyes on her myself."

A ten-year old girl brushed past them, ran down the steps and turned to stand and stamp her foot on the pavement. "Come on, dad, come on. You promised me a burger and I'm starving."

"Aren't you going to say hello to your auntie?"

"'Ello, Auntie Ange. Come on, Dad, you promised."

"A promise is a promise and that's my word on it." He seemed for the moment to have forgotten to play the stage Irishman. He grasped Angelica's hand – she in her turn forgot to stiffen with rejection at the male touch – and she became aware of the brightness of his blue eyes. "Not a word, on your honour, Angeleena darling, to your ladyship about me taking young Bridgie for a burger now. It's a rare treat for the child, God help her."

"No, Shamus, not a word. I promise."

"You're a fine strapping girl, you are. Do you ever fancy coming out for a jar? There's the Biddy Mulligan in Kilburn and they have lovely entertainment there. Have you ever heard the song, Red Roses For Me? It's a darling song."

"Come on, Dad."

He ran down the steps, waved his rolled newspaper (The Observer) as a farewell salute and, with a laugh, called out, "As the poet said, 'We must down to the sea again." '

Angelica resented the subtle way he had scratched her glazed insularity. "Damn that fraudulent Irishman. He's not the bog-trotter he lets on to be, not if he can actually quote Masefield correctly."

10.32. "I'm afraid I'm a trifle late," she said when she entered Ariadne's flat.

Her sister had the phone to her ear. "Well, maybe it's not what you think. I mean – no, of course not but – circumstances can change." She put her hand over the mouth-piece. "It's Amy. She's in a bit of a state. It was Bob's day off but he volunteered for the Sunday shift, he'd do anything for money, and he's now out in the patrol car – with WPC Wendy. Make yourself a coffee. You're early." The ornamental clock on the mantelpiece was 15 minutes slow though the ghastly sun-burst one by the kitchen was 20 minutes fast. Ariadne uncovered the mouthpiece. "Yes, Amy, yes. I was listening. Angie has just come in. Do you want to speak to her? Alright then. No, we weren't keeping our trip from you, I know, yes, I know you'd like to see Mum, but we thought Bob would be at home and besides we're not taking any of the kids, you know what Mum is like if there's a lot of kids racketting – okay then, I'll say goodbye then, Amy. Goodbyeee." She put down the receiver and sighed gustily. "God preserve me from weepers. Did you meet Shamus on the way up? He's a right cod, he is. He takes Bridgit to a burger bar every time and he thinks I don't know." She shouted at the twins. "Don't move one inch, either of you. You know what your father's like if he sees a speck of dirt on your clothes. Bad enough as it is with him ringing up to say he'll be late." She turned back to Angelica. "It's his wife that's the bother, her and her bloody prim house in Hendon. They hate her."

She admonished a mutinous group in the corner who were muttering "We want to go to the sea" and went across to the window. "Hello, Alex's car just passed down the road. Ah ha, I know what's he's up to. The garage at the junction used to sell cheap petrol but he'll be disappointed. It was robbed three times in one week and the company closed it down. Let's go into the kitchen, make some coffee and have a private chat. It'll be at least ten minutes before Alex comes."

"About Shamus?" Angelica placed her briefcase on the breakfast bar.

Ariadne was dismissive of the blarney-endowed Irishman. "He's a fly-by-night and a chancer. Comes and goes whenever the humour takes him and one day he's all hot for the Cause and the next he's sneering at the green flag-wavers of the Kilburn Republic. But as long as he pays for Bridgit, I couldn't care less if he's IRA, KGB or the Special Branch."

She poured the hot water into two cracked mugs, spooned in dollops of instant coffee, apologised for the state of the place – "Had a small party for the BD (Bob Dylan) Appreciation Group last night. Only five came. All women. Drinking lager and lighting candles" – and grumbled about the late payments from the various fathers of her brood. The mug of brown swill she handed Angelica was decorated with the nursery rhyme about the old woman who lived in a shoe. Ariadne was about to light a cigarette when a small disturbance in the adjoining room distracted her. She heaved herself from the draining board, where she had been resting her buttock, and exited with a roar.

Angelica sensed an uneasy aura of indecision emanating from her sister and it remained hovering among the suspended molecules of grease in the fetid air of the kitchen. She poured the coffee down the sink and fiddled with the briefcase.

"Well, that's settled. Two off my hands for the day." Ariadne returned to her buttock-rest by the draining board, gulped down a mouthful of coffee and lit one of her favourite cancer-sticks. "He wouldn't come up. I think the Hendon hausfrau was in the car. Now what were we saying? Yes, before Alex arrives." A pause as she sucked in a lungful of nicotine-flavoured smoke. The grey ash tip fell to the floor. "I was having second thoughts about – you know – and I was wondering—". The uneasy aura was becoming visible. "You know how I'm involved with, well, basic humanistic causes, that's the burden I've taken on myself and I'm not one to make value judgements on others but, I was thinking, what we talked about may not be moral—"

"Moral!" Angelica was not prepared for her Cause to be corroded by the acid of a latter-day Savonarola. "That's a strange and wonderful word for you to use, Ariadne. But let's not argue any more about it." She picked up her briefcase. "If you're content to let our father treat his children with total indifference and injustice—"

"No, wait, Angie. What I mean to say—"

"While you, Alex and Amy are threatened with penury, he and Her lash out money on all sorts of luxuries—"

"Perhaps we can talk about it a bit calmer in the car."

"I'm not going."

"But why? Mum will be very disappointed and you're her favourite."

"And perhaps when you're wrèstling with your moral dilemma, you'll consider how Mum could do with extra money."

Angelica stood with the briefcase dangling from her hand, her thoughts trembling with the fear of defection, while Ariadne vigorously puffed at her fag, her mind a swirling cloud of colliding moral particles.

"It's just this, Angie. (Did she say justice or just this?) We know that he has a heart condition and we agree that it only needs a sudden shock to make him – make him – but why should it be down to us to do it?"

"Why, he that cuts off twenty years of life cuts off so many years of fearing death."

Ariadne did not understand the quotation. "You mean we'd have to wait—"

"Precisely. If it is to be done let it be well done and soon. Think of it this way, we'll only be expediting what is inevitable."

Angelica places the briefcase on the breakfast bar again and, unseen by Ariadne, switches on the tape-recorder.

Conversation as recorded.

Ariadne: (Slightly sullen tone) I suppose you're right, Angie. (Brightly) But why not concentrate our efforts on getting rid of HER? A car accident, for instance. And the effects of that could achieve what we intend in the first place.

(Thoughts which the surveillance equipment is unable to pick up.

Angelica: "And rob me of my revenge?")

Angelica: (Crisply) Too complicated.

Ariadne: And let's say we succeed—

Angelica: Succeed?

Ariadne: Yes, let's say we succeed in frightening – shocking him to (voice reduced to sub-aural level) death (voice back to normal), with all the legal complications, it would take ages for us to lay our hands on his money.

Tape recorder switched off.

Is there any truth in the theory that siblings have a telepathic empathy? Recall Alex's fantasy scenario two in chapter nine in which he masterfully confronts a bereaved Sally and, in consideration for her distressed state, nobly accepts a fat cheque as a first instalment on his inheritance. Compare it with Angelica's proposal. "There should be no delay. We'll make a full inventory of the estate, demand, legally, an inspection of his bank account, deposit accounts, etc, and then put it to HER that it would be simpler and cleaner for HER to give us our share in cash immediately."

Ariadne was loud in her praises for her young sister's ingenuity and the chalice of morality was put aside undrunk.

10.45. Alex arrives. He had wasted nearly a gallon of petrol in his futile search for a cheap supply and was most upset.

11.00. What remained of Ariadne's tribe, a mutinous crew, was dispatched to enjoy themselves at the local community centre where World Children's Day was being grimly celebrated. Earlier they had thought to stage a Stay-At-Home protest if their demand to go to the seaside with their mother was not met; but they retreated from that position when they discovered that the day's outing was a visit to their granny. Ethnic songs and dances and plates of fried rice suddenly seemed a much better alternative.

11.15. Angelica sits at the table, reading the Business section of the Sunday Times. Ariadne bustles in and out of the bathroom, fixing her makeup and adjusting her clothes. Alex fretfully paces up and down, still griping about having to buy the dearer petrol and, nearly as bad, having the fuel measured in litres. "I mean, what was wrong with the gallon, I ask you. If those foreigners want us to join them, they should take on some of our centuries-old traditions." He glared at his satellite-seeking watch and morosely announced,

"11.16." Angelica finds the section with the crossword puzzle and fills in the first clue. Alex continues, "I rushed out this morning without having a proper breakfast so we'd have an early start and—" Ariadne stops in her tracks. "You haven't had a proper breakfast?" Hurries into kitchen. "I'll only be a moment. I'll make you a sandwich."

11.25. Angelica has an attack of ennui. Bored with the crossword, bored with the 90-year old grammar-school compilers, bored with this waiting, waiting. All life wasted in waiting. Ariadne had made a sandwich for Alex, then made another for herself, then made more dreadful brown sludge, aka instant Muckwell House coffee, then with a "It's bad for you to gulp down your food" sat down to share banalities and cigarettes with Alex. "Sixty minutes ago to the minute I entered this house of involuntary confinement," Angelica said in a low unrecorded voice as she strolled over to the window. There was the seismic sound of a big bass backbeat in the street. "What revels are in hand? Is there no play, to ease the anguish of a torturing hour?" Loud youths football-bound, drunks cranking themselves up to start the day, list-clutching couples setting off for their Sunday service at the DIY store and those who found the road to God too rough and unready, ready to clamber aboard their cars for worship from the back seat. A familar small face peered around the corner of a house opposite. It looked like one of Ariadne's fledglings prematurely ejected from the nest.

11.30. "Are we going?" (What is this reluctance, for Christ's sake? Didn't these clowns want to play their parts? Which was Bottom and which was Wall?)

11.31. "Okay, let's make a start. Who's got a map? I don't need a map. I mean one of Eastbourne. What are we taking? What do you mean? For Mum, you know, box of chocolates, flowers. Gawd, I forgot. We'll get something on the way. Jesus, what with bribing the kids, the petrol cost and now flowers for the old dear, I'm nearly bankrupt. I could do with some of Dad's money right now. Okay, are we off?"

11.35. Alex, of course, is in the driver's seat, Ariadne, with a 20-year old AA Book of the Road, in the passenger seat. Angelica, after brushing down the simulated leather with a cloth, sits in the rear.

As the car lurches masterfully round the corner, she glances back through the rear window and catches a glimpse of Ariadne's issue as they creep in single file back to the house. It would appear that they had invested their mother's hand-out in cigarettes and a four-pack of lager. She did not think it necessary to mention this to Ariadne.

11.37. The journey had begun, conspiracies are set in motion, plans are afoot and plots are on the boil.

Chapter twelve

They who know Eastbourne intimately do not need us to expound on its hidden charms; they who have not visited the spume-sprayed and wind-raked Sussex town shall be spared the painful details.

The Sunday jaunt (cue for pun) of our half-baked conspiratorial trio shall be summarised, quite appositely, into three parts: The journey there, the visit, the journey home.

To heighten the pitch of our tale, to give a classical gloss to the schemers, to raise their motive above the venal (If it were venial they could be forgiven), we should apportion to each an historical or legendary counterpart. Alas, our search through the tomes and our walk by the tombs, even unto the Valley of the Kings, brought us none that could match our plotters. There was, of course, the story of Cronus who conspired with his mother Gaia to slice off with a stone sickle his father Uranus's vital equipment. Cronus went on to marry his sister and then took to swallowing his own children as a once-a-year treat to himself. A rather unsavoury lot, those early Titans. That yarn has no bearing whatsoever on our trio. Has it?

You can see our problem. Angelica certainly had that lean and hungry look but where is the female equivalent of Cassius? And where, from Rye House to Rome, was there a plotter so portly as Ariadne? Could Alex be "put-money-in-thy-purse" Iago? We wonder.

Part one. The journey there. Not one of them spoke of their fell purpose. Ariadne hoped that her children were enjoying themselves and not getting into mischief, "Robert will make sure of that," she said firmly. (He was her eldest, inevitably named after Dylan. It was he whom Angelica saw carrying the lager.) Occasionally she gave unsolicited advice to Alex about the best route while he shared his thoughts about other drivers. "Gawd's sake, look at the way he's dawdling along. It's a well-known fact that most accidents are caused by slow drivers. Typical, it's a woman. Did you see how that one cut in at the roundabout? Asian. A nation of shopkeepers. I've nothing against coloured people as such, mind you." Angelica said nothing.

He was tight-lipped with impotent rage when Ariadne told him he had shot past the A22 turn-off. Neither of them said another word till they were entering Tunbridge Wells.

"You'll have to stop here."

"Why? What for? We're late as it is."

"Well, whose fault is that? Not mine.

"Nor mine. I think we should press on."

"If you don't mind having a wet patch on your car seat,then do drive on. It also means that we've no prezzies for Mum."

Tunbridge Wells, spiritual home of disgusted letter-writers, has many endearing qualities. Tourist-infested Pantiles, souvenir-shops, vile-tasting water passed off as a health drink, real and fabricated history and a vast army of very old people. Some have dubbed it England's wealthiest white elephant's graveyard. It is also very difficult to park your car.

Bladders emptied, prezzies for mumsie bought (gift-wrapped chocolates, flowers –"oh, the cost," moans Ariadne – bottle of wine tastefully wrapped in tissue), ersatz coffee drunk, cream cakes eaten and within thirty minutes they were on the road again.

Part two. The visit. It can be sectionalised thus:—

The greeting. Effusive: Hugs, kisses, more hugs, tears well to eyes. "It's so wonderful, so absolutely wonderful, to see you all."

Wry twist to above: "It's been such a long time since anybody came to see me."

View of a room with a view:.Small, sparsely furnished, a few knick-knacks, framed photos, relics of old decency, tiny radio in tiny kitchen, second-hand television opposite single bed. "I know it's a bit of a climb-up but it's worth it just for the view." View of grey clouds and lots of sea water.

Giving of gifts and gushing like an overwrought jacuzzi. Flowers. "Oh, how lovely. And they're still fresh." Chocolates. "My favourite. And they're Belgian. A present from Tunbridge Wells. You went out of your way to buy these for me." Wine.

"How sweet. Chardonnay. In my Spanish villa – but let's not talk of the past."

Return gift: "And look what I've made for your coming." A large, brown and extremely heavy cake, unevenly topped with icing and similar in design to a neolithic mound, is plonked on table.

First refusal: "Oh no thanks, Mummy, we've just eaten." "Couldn't touch another thing, Mum." "I'm trying to keep my weight down, Mumsie."

Response to refusal: Big sigh. Expression of devastated disbelief. Face puckers. Pipes overflow. Details given of day traipsing round shops for essential ingredients and hours spent mixing, making and cooking.

Consequence of above:Visitors succumb to emotional blackmail. All sit around table while Mum/Mummy/Mumsie chops cake into chunks, pours pale tea into china cups and repeatedly tells her offspring how happy, really really happy, it makes her to see them once again sitting at her table.

Pious platitudes about grandchildren, their welfare and their prospects. Amy and her delicate state also mentioned.

Topics avoided at this point: Ivan and Sally. Alex's ex, Tracy. Angelica's ex, Kevin. Angelica's sexual predilections. Cleo's last man. Ariadne's men.

Second refusal: To listen to any unasked-for advice on how to conduct their lives.

Spats. Sharp words. Cassandra-like warning of impending doom for anyone deaf in the presence of their mother. "You wouldn't take any notice of me when I told you you were marrying beneath yourselves and I should know because I did, something I regret to this very day. I mean, apart from my children, what have I got to show for my wasted years of married devotion? No home to call my own, no money (prelude to later requests) while—" Rises from table, grabs teapot, dashes into kitchen-sink drama.

Time lapse: Two more hours. Themes repeated, reiterated, re-irritated, regurgitated.

First proposal: "It's a bit stuffy in here. Okay if I open the window?" Window obdurate because of two six-inch screws. "I tell you what, let's all go for a walk along the front. It'll clear the air in more ways than one."

The walk: 25 minutes later. Eastbourne's famous Parade is three miles long, flanked on one side by the sea and on the other by the beautifully maintained gardens known as the Meads. So much for the travelogue. On a clear day you can see the suicides leaping off Beachy Head.

They walked in pairs. Alex and his mother led the way, their shoulders hunched and every word whipped from their mouths by the wind. The sisters followed, snatching silence from the spray; Ariadne's bursting handbag hanging weightily from her shoulder, Angelica's briefcase held rigid by her side.

Excitement: Alex's satellite-finder watch went bleep-bleep-bleep. He pointed up to the bleak sky. Mother and sisters gather by him and stare upwards. One black-headed gull said to another black-headed gull, "Squawk, squawk, awk-awk-awk." Roughly translated: "Let's drop something naughty in their gobs." But second gull has seen an old-age pensioner at the far end of the parade fumble at his sandwich pack with shivering fingers and speeds off to harass and loot.

There were, in fact, two utterly forgotten football-sized satellites just then orbiting over Sussex, one Russian and one American. They were vainly trying to make contact with their mission control or some human person. Though neither could communicate in the other's coded language, they had decided to travel together.

Re-pairing. After that frisson, Alex and Ariadne tried to light their cigarettes and Angelica walked on with Mummy.

The request oblique: "I'm lost without the phone but those stupid jobsworths in the telephone company won't connect me unless I pay the last bill.I would have asked Alex to help me out since he's a rising young executive and a national expert, but then he has the wedding costs to meet. You don't think he's marrying beneath himself again, do you? No point in asking Ariadne."

The request direct: "I hate to do this and the last thing I want to do is to break into your savings but—

The question direct: "How much?"

Reaction to answer: Low whistle of disbelief. "Let me have their letters and I'll sent the amount off."

Devious reply: "They're back in my place but to save you all that bother why don't you write the cheque out to me. No, wait, I'm a bit overdrawn. Make it out to the housing agent, he's a very nice man, and when he's deducted the rent – could you make it a round figure—"

Diversion: Alex, "Me and Ari, we're freezing.What are you two whispering about?" Ariadne, "Yes, and I want to do a wee. Is there a Ladies in this God-forsaken place?"

Suggestion: "Let's go into a restaurant, you can use their toilet and we can have a meal before we set off home."

Counter-suggestion: "We'll go back to my place and I'll make you something warm. You haven't finished the cake and I thought that you can take whatever is left over home to your children."

Third refusal: "Oh no, Mum, we don't want to put you to any trouble."

Suggestions: "We'll eat out. There's a steak house over there." "I can't stand the greasy chips and mushy peas. I'd rather have an Italian or an Indian." "What about that restaurant across the road?"

Objections: "That's a snooty place if ever I saw one." "It looks a bit pricey to me."

Objections overruled: "It would round the day off nicely for Mummy." "Oh, what a wonderful idea, Angelica. At least some-one knows what I like."

Reception desk and angular maitre d'. Addresses only male among arrivals. Supercilious tone. "May I help you, sir?" Curt reply, "Table for four." Maitre d' studies ledger. "Name, sir?" Alex stumped. Angelica answers. "We haven't booked." Maitre d' re-studies ledger. "Ah, in that case." Looks towards the rows of vacant tables. "Yes, sir, we can just about fit your party in." Clicks fingers. Middle-aged waitress appears. "Table sixteen."

Table sixteen: At extreme end. Near toilets. Away from windows.

Initial behaviour: Stiff and tense while reading menu.

Attitudes after reading menu and prices: Ariadne declares that because of her weight problem she will stick to a salad. Alex asserts that there is nothing there he really fancies but to keep the others company he will have a soup.

Reasons for these attitudes: Ariadne has only a five-pound note left, she is nearly out of cigarettes and there is her expected share of the petrol cost. Alex is mean.

Alteration in attitudes: Angelica declares that the meal is a special non-birthday present (A winsome Winnie-the-Pooh reference) from her to Mummy. "You mean you want to pay?" blurts Alex. "Oh, what a divine surprise," exclaims Mummy. Menu reread with heightened interest. Alex peruses wine list with puckered frown of national expert then, with smug smile, passes list to Mum as this is her special treat. A quarter of tables now occupied.Alex goggles as minor TV personality in pink suit enters with small entourage. TV personality makes loud remarks and looks around to see his reflection in other people's eyes. Alex looks down at napkin and comments that said pink person is a big head.

Behaviour during meal and the ten to fifteen minutes between courses at table sixteen: Conversation begins in hesitant spurts and subdued tones. Topics varied but non-controversial. Voices gradually rise.

Mum's increases in pitch and changes to fluted speech. Such phrases as "Last year in Vienna—" or, "I would have simply love to have gone to Salzburg for the Mozart celebration, but, my dears, it was so commercial—" or, "Glyndebourne is full of gays, on and off the stage—" shivered the chandeliers. The last infelicity brought a short sharp halt to the merry chatter at the pink TV person's table. "The old biddy is half-cut," sneered one.

Latter part of meal: As Alex did not understand the French for burnt rice pudding, he had a mixed fruit salad with ice cream. Ariadne had chocolate-covered balls (wishful thinking), Angelica wafer biscuits with cheese and Mum, as it was her special treat and her youngest daughter was paying, had a double helping of Black Forest Gateau with cream topping.

Alex expanded and expounded on the idiocy of those whom God or Satan had seen fit to put in a higher office than he and the many occasions he was forced to amend, annul or erase some ghastly error made by the self-same mouths almighty. Ariadne shovelled chocolate balls into her gob. In defence of her increasingly dirigible shape, she raucously roared at least three times,

"You know what they say, (Yes, it's that Chinese philosopher again), thin is tasty but fat is fantastic."

The Bill: Nothing whatsoever to do with the police. Alex raised one finger, waitress nodded and with a speed that outshone her service, she returned with the Bill. This she gave to Alex and after a second or two spent dully staring at the itemised list – "Only checking to make sure we're not overcharged" – he passed it over to Angelica.

To touch or even to see a slip of paper detailing monies owed tended to stimulate Ariadne's allergy, a rash in her private parts. Rather than end the evening in an uncomfortable state, she rose from the table. "'Scuse me, folks. Must go to the little girl's room," she simpered and waddled off to the Ladies. Alex also visited the comfort-station to cudgel his wits. When, at the end of their journey, he asks his sisters for their share of the petrol costs, would Angelica reply that she had paid for the meal? He rehearsed a counter-argument. "It was you who insisted on eating in that snooty place, we didn't agree to that in the first place. Isn't that right, Ari? But we did agree to go one-third each for the fuel." Happy with the stunning logic of this, he gave a final wag to his willy to make sure no suspended dribbles were left to dampen his pants and then spent an extra minute or so washing his hands. By then the others should be ready to go and there would be no question of him contributing to the waitress's tip.

Meanwhile back at table sixteen.

Request reiterated: "While you have your chequebook out, Angelica dear, I wonder if—."

"How much did you say?"

A figure is mentioned but—"If you could round it up to—" A larger figure is suggested. "And make it out to Arthur Gunboil, he's the housing agent and he's ever so nice. He's a widower and—"

Cheque handed over as Ariadne returns.

Ariadne blunders back. Notes with satisfaction Angelica's bank card on saucer. No danger of her allergy occurring. In a jolly manner, "Well, that was a splendid blow-out. What a pity we didn't think of ordering Mum a cocktail as a night-cap."

"A cocktail? How marvellous. I'd adore a Singapore Sling."

Beckons to waitress. Mild protest from Ariadne that perhaps another occasion, when they were not in such a hurry. Waitress takes order, hurries to bar where barman opens small bottle marked Genuine Singapore Sling, empties same into tall glass, adds crushed ice and bent straw. Waitress returns with glass and bill and hands the latter to Ariadne. Fumbles in purse and produces the five-pound note. "I'm afraid I've only this—" Waitress takes crumpled note and leaves 50-pee piece on table. Skin under elastic of Ariadne's knickers begins to itch.

Alex's bad timing: Appears at table, smiles and asks loudly, "Are we ready for the off then?" But no. Mum is sipping her Singapore Sling and says that nobody but nobody can mix it like Raffles Hotel. Alex sits down, glances at his satellite-seeking watch and stares glumly at the saucer. Nobody but nobody has left a tip. Mum, generous to the last of everybody else's cash, says, "We really should leave something." Morose Ariadne says that the 50 pee is her last, Angelica has no coins and Mum hasn't brought her purse with her. Alex produces a fistful of loose change and, to his distress, the others pluck out all the pound coins.

The parting: Effusive. Hugs, kisses, more hugs. Tears well to eyes and overflow. "It was so wonderful, so absolutely wonderful, to see you all."

Wry twist to above: "Even if it was just for one day, one day only."

Counter to above: "We'll come again soon. When I am not so busy/ when I can get the children off my hands/ when I have a long weekend."

Incautious proposal: From Alex. "Why don't you come up to London for a day?"

Unexpected response: "I'll do better than that. I get so lonely down here in this lifeless place, with no one to talk to, I've been seriously thinking of moving up to London to be near you all. I'm sure you'll be able to put me up till I find a place."

Students of King Lear will have some idea of the thoughts that passed through the minds of her children.

Part Three. The return journey.

And now will there be plots and plans? Will the conspirators conspire? Will they remember the prime motive? The answer is yes, though for the first half-hour they were curiously shy about it. Ariadne's expanded form needed the roomy space of the rear seat where she fitfully dozed and fitfully worried about her depleted purse. Alex was quite disgruntled with the cost of the day's outing. Angelica anxiously fiddled with her briefcase and wondered if the rattling car would drown any conversation she hoped to record.

And then there was the threat of their mother appearing on their doorstep with laden suitcases, demanding full board for an indefinite period. To Angelica it represented the destruction of her private world.

Ariadne broke the silence with a sledgehammer. "Anton Piller!" she exclaimed.

"Isn't it typical of Ari," sneered Alex. "Stuffs her gullet all evening and then all she can think about is a Spanish hotch-potch."

"Listen, smart-arse, if we're really going to go through with what we talked about, we'd better start coming up with ideas. And my idea is the Anton Piller Order. Jeeze, why didn't I mention to Mum the magazine Dad brought out with her money." She quickly explained that the said Anton Piller Order was a legal device which empowered a partner in a defunct business to send the bailiffs to raid the premises of the ex-partner for vital material. She proposed recruiting Amy's Action-Man husband for the task.

"Oh come on, Ari. What good will that do?"

"What good?" She nearly exploded at his obtuseness. "How would you feel if a bunch of bully boys come banging at your back door at five in the morning, hey?"

"I think I'd die of fright."

"Precisely. Now what's your bright idea?"

Alex was more of a dim bulb than a bright spark. He muttered something about an electric shock.

"Well, you know the technology, after all, you're a national expert. What about you, Angie?"

Angelica was evasive. "I was thinking of Mummy and how few things she has in her place."

"There's not much we can do about that. Not right now."

"But we can. At least I can. There is a certain house in which a certain man lives with a certain woman and that house contains a lot of luxuries which—"

"You mean – but you couldn't—"

"I have and I will."

"Okay, put a name on how this will help us."

"The name is harassment. And, of course, there is the corrosive effect of poison letters."

"Poison letters?"

Angelica had not intended to mention her schema ultima until the taped conversations committed them. She casually remarked that she had seen Sally talking to a man outside a theatre. If 'a friend' wrote to Ivan, informing him that his young wife, emphasise 'young wife'—

"Ah, I get you. Giving time and place whenever possible. It'll make him fret. Distrust. There'll be rows, you know what a temper he has when roused. Then one day! It'll be the proverbial last straw."

They smiled and chortled, joy radiating from each beaming face, the tedium of the journey forgotten.

Alex dropped his sisters outside Ariadne's place and blithely drove off, humming something simple by Simply Red. Not until he opened his door did he realise they had failed to pay him for the petrol.

When Angelica drove off, Ariadne went upstairs singing Dylan's Blowing in the Wind. "How did it go today, kids?" she called out as she entered her flat. Like cockroaches suddenly disturbed by light, they scattered in all directions. Angelica listened to Schubert's Death And The Maiden.

Chapter thirteen

The doorbell went DING. It was an unusual start to the day. Ever since the burglary, the active chime had been DONG. Sally and Ivan had grown almost fond of the single lonely note, the bereft iambic tone. Now the DING had returned. And the DONG? Had it gone, luminous nose and all, to a far, far greater campanile where it would be lovingly greeted by a reborn Quasimodo with a radiant cherubic face?

Ivan kept his eyes closed in a vain attempt to hang onto the tatters of sleep and succeeded only in pulling thin rags of oblivion over his mind. He could barely recall – and was he bare at that time? – a spectral face peering, leering through his waking dream and a crouching shape settling on his chest with a growl like the devil's familiar.

DING. It was neither as sonorous nor as imperative as the departed DONG and they would miss the latter sadly. In this first stage of awaking awareness, confusion of time and place still troubled him and for now he preferred to keep his shutters down. An uneasy weight of displeasure pressing on his breast and, as each flea had another flea upon its back, so lurked darkly nagging foreboding on the shoulders of his disquiet.

But there was a real, in the physical sense, weight pressing on his sore rib cage. "Doctor, I get this peculiar pressure on my chest in the morning and—" Clinically clean hand signals silence. "Say no more. The diagnosis is simple. Take my advice and don't waste your money buying any more long-playing records." "But I only buy CDs now." "Ah, and they're more expensive too. You wouldn't want to miss the end of The Four Seasons, would you, particularly as you've now reached Winter." "I thought this was my Autumn." "With the weather we're having, it's difficult to tell one season from another. Put on Schubert's Unfinished instead. Goodbye now, it was so nice to have known you."

DING. "Gerroff. Gerroff." Sally sat up, her shift slipping off a body so Fragonardesque that it was almost fat as she flung the impertinent feline off the bed. "Ivan, Ivan, did you let her into the room? Come on, I know you're awake. You must have left the door open when you went to the loo. Don't deny it. I heard you padding about less than five minutes ago. Gawd, is it only that time?" She snuggled down among the rumpled sheets. "Now you're awake, you might as well make some coffee. Kick the cat out and see who's at the front door."

Ivan hauled a protesting domestic quadruped out of the wardrobe, tugged at his tatty dressing-gown – it had snagged on the wire coathanger – and then decided to go gently naked into this cold morning.

"What day is it?" he asked the head in the pillow.

"Day? Day? What day do you think it is?"

He went into the small lavatory and leant over the cistern at an angle of 30 degrees to the vertical so that his morning-proud pistol would shoot straight into the bowl without spattering the surround. Then he padded downstairs. The hairy cat, the only known feline drop-out left over from the 'sixties, was speculatively sniffing at the pile of newspapers and letters on the mat. "Don't you dare piss or shit on my Guardian, you bloody Tory, you," Ivan shouted. (A dreadful insult to any self-respecting hippy.) A pair of startled blue eyes stared at him and then the bundle of manky fur flew into the kitchen. "If you think I'm going to feed you, you've got another think coming."

His keys were not in his jacket or his overcoat nor were they dangling from a hook in the kitchen among the suspended scissors and tin-openers. A cool breeze tickled his bum. There were his wandering keys lying by the opened back door. When he undid the front door's three locks he opened it a crack and cautiously peeped out. Phil the Postman, leaning on his bike, and Fred from around the corner were chatting at the end of the path. They looked over, grinned, and Phil pointed to the doorstep. Crouching like a primitive primate – click-click went his blessed knees – and stretching out his left arm, Ivan managed to retrieve parcel, papers and letters without exposing himself to their rheumy eyes. "You're not exactly dressed for the weather, are you, Ivan," Fred shouted.

They both laughed. "I see your window-cleaner comes early in the day," Fred continued. "Lucky for some."

The parcel contained the double CD of JS Bach's 4 Suites. Should he play them now, just in case his autumn/winter should be unseasonably terminated? But that was a bad dream. What was this bad dream he was waking up to? And what was that old bladderer talking about? Window-cleaner, indeed.

He bundled up the papers and letters, trotted upstairs and dumped them on the bed. "Thanks," droned the thing beneath the sheets in a sub-human way. "Just leave it on the mat and I'll drink it in a minute."

"I haven't made it yet. I'm bloody freezing, galumphing around in my birthday suit."

"You haven't forgotten the birthday party then?"

"Birthday Party! How could I forget the Birthday Party, at least the part I hadn't slept through."

But there was The Birthday Party and—nag-nag, foreboding—the birthday party. George the solicitor had said with a shy smile, when they had finished the formalities of the wills, "Deirdre is having a surprise party for my birthday this coming Sunday" – coy laugh—"I won't see 25 again." (Beware of wives who throw surprise parties, it could end in tears. Sing a song, 'I'm the injured party and I'll cry if I want to.') "You'll both come, of course."

Irrelevant thought: If George knew about the proposed rave-up (Rave-up!!), how could it be a surprise? Never mind, as the man said, if God closes one of the doors of perception—Relevant thought plus sudden shock of perception and total awareness: Who opened the back door?

His streaking return to the kitchen was so rapid that the assembled cats were but a whisker away from being hit by a flying foot. They bemusedly watched him as he lolloped down the garden path, the stringy lavender bush lashing his naked flanks. He only halted when a protruding thorn from the vagrant rose tree nearly effected a belated circumcision. As he slunk back, he noticed the extending aluminium ladder against the wall under the small window and the nosy old biddy next door flickering her lace curtains. "Well, at least she saw something rare to her sight even if it was somewhat shrivelled."

"What fine madness has afflicted your mind, Ivan?" Sally was standing by the fridge, warmly clad in a padded dressing- gown, her feet snug in slippers, a yogurt carton in her hand.

Think, Ivan, think. Let us not cause panic on the home front. "A fox. There was a fox after our cats."

She bent over to stroke the assembled furry heads. "Oh diddums, was the naughty foxy-woxy chasing our pussy-wussies?" They mewed and squeaked. Surely the giant mother cat would see to their needs. They went into ecstasies of head-bumping and chin-nudging when she began to open a tin.

Five minutes later Ivan, now dressed in ancient house-decorating trousers and yesterday's shirt, brought up the coffee to the bedroom. He had locked the back door, made a mental note to put away the ladders when Sally was having a bath, buy a padlock for them and screw down the small window. He still did not know what day it was.

"You shouldn't really scamper around starkers, Ivan. You never know what you'll catch. Remember what George said."

The solicitous solicitor had said, "These wills are not legally binding till they're signed and witnessed. I'll have them typed up, let you have copies for any amendments or corrections you wish to make and then you both can return to do the necessary. That'll take a week or two." Dry laugh. "Try and not die before then, either of you. It would make matters ever so complicated."

"There's a letter for you." She sniffed the white envelope. "It's from a woman! What bit of fancy have you got tucked away, you dirty old man? And talking of dirty old men, are your feet clean? Give them a wash before you come back to bed."

"What day is it?"

"Saturday, of course. That reminds me. We'll have to buy a bottle of wine for the party and a card and present for George when we go shopping. Any ideas?"

He heaved one foot into the hand-basin and scrubbed the sole. Leaving Man Friday footprints on the cork tiles, he sat down on the lavatory seat to read his letter.

The letter: (Left-leaning sloping script as if the writer were attempting to disguise his?/her? usual calligraphy. Bundled-grammar style also a possible pretence)

'Dear Ivan,

Your young wife is carrying on with another man. I saw them at the theatre together the other night and they were very close. It may be difficult for a man of your age to keep a young woman satisfied, but it's not right she should be seeing another man. You should keep a watch on her.

Yours sincerely,
A friend.'

Offending letter stuffed into trouser-pocket for shredding and disposal at a convenient moment. Would it not be convenient to flush it down the lavatory bowl? No, that wouldn't wash.

"Who's it from?"

"What?"

"Your letter."

Be evasive, vague, generalise. "Just some woman asking about the road campaign. Don't know where she got my name."

"What road campaign?"

"Didn't I tell you? The latest motorway mania. Proposals to cut through all London parks."

To quote: 'O what a tangled web we weave when first we practise to deceive.'

She gave him a deceitful smile. "And here was I thinking my fox had another vixen in a different covert. It wasn't a fox, was it?"

He was too preoccupied with possible intruder/s, ballistic missives, and the knowledge that it was Saturday to be fleet-footed enough to dance to another tune. He did a two-step to the other side of the bed and flopped down.

"It could have been one of Corgi-and-Beth's yappers with the hanging undercarriage from down the road," she continued. "My Gawd, what if it had turned and snapped at your woggle under the impression it was a raw sausage." She giggled. "And that reminds me, there'll be a barbecue." He groaned. An animal auto-da-fe. What other horrors awaited him? She suddenly sat up. "Someone has been here," she exclaimed. "I know, I know. I can smell him, her, yes, it was a her." Within seconds, the balustrade vibrated with her call, "Ivan! Ivan! Come here."

She was standing by the bureau. "Look. Those drawers have been opened and somebody's rooted through the papers. And those magazines have been moved." Sally whirled around the room in a neurotic frenzy.

"If it makes you happy we'll check if anything is missing."

Nothing had apparently disappeared.

Apparently.

Till they arrived home from shopping in the afternoon – Ivan armed with chains, locks and very large screws (Mental note jotted on brain pad, 'Must get around to fixing the garage doors.') and she considering what to wear for the birthday party. "Can't wear that red dress again. (Why not?) Of course, they haven't seen me in the black dress – you don't think it's too revealing? My shoulders will be bare. But wait a minute, I know what I'll put on – " She ran upstairs. The minute was patiently waited and then— "Ivan, have you seen my—"

On the other side of London a letter was being typed.

'Dear Mummy,

'This is just a brief letter to say thanks for having us. We won't leave such a big gap between visits again. The sea air has certainly done you a lot of good (subtext – if the way you wolfed down the food was anything to go by) and it would be a shame to leave such a healthy enviroment to come and live in London. Anyway, you said you loved walking along the Parade and I thought you might like something warm to wrap around your shoulders when the evenings are chilly. Hope you like this Pavlova scarf. It's quite fashionable in London now. Put it on when you go promenading.

'With all my love. Kissy-poo.'

Mourning for a dark shawl did not become Sally and by the time they were driving towards the party the next day, her distress had diminished to a sigh of regret. "It was getting a bit tatty, anyway." Ivan refrained from reminding her that it was a gift from him, took up his usual position on the Cross and banged the nails in himself.

Sally sensed a morose miasma. "You're very silent." Silence. "Oh, the party will be alright," she said bracingly. " It's not that we don't know anybody. There'll be George, Deirdre, must ask her how she enjoyed the play, possibly A-to-Z (a small cloud gathered), perhaps Richard and Pruneface will be there. (Cloud enlarges.) And we're bound to meet interesting people, but if not we'll make our excuses and leave early. Look at it this way, what else would you be doing on a Sunday afternoon? Lolling in the garden with the Sunday papers, pretending to do horticultural activities, drinking coffee and then wandering in to listen to your CDs. Is that the life for a gregarious man like you?" She glanced sharply at his legs. "Ivan, you're wearing yesterday's trousers." He glanced appreciatively at her thighs. "And you're wearing black French knickers at the top of those tights." She smiled. That was more like it.

The reluctant Ivan followed Sally up the gravel path towards George and Deirdre's detached house in Outer Chippings. She clutched the corners of the white woollen shawl (bought from a roadside vendor on a trip up the Nile for the equivalent of £5 and now on sale for trendy Wendies down the Kings Road for £50) and hoped she did not look like a weekend bimbo as she wobbled on high heels.

At this point, readers of slavering sex-and-shopping sagas will bate their breaths in expectation of an expose of suburban salaciousness. Will lust be let loose behind the laburnum? Ravishing beneath the rose trees? Limb-hugging Lycra stroked by marauding hands? Will talk of spread-sheets stray beyond computer terminals?

Anthropologists, other than those obsessed with the sex-life of Samoa, will study such social gatherings with a more detached mind. Their first amendment: Delete the word 'social'.

Sally rang the bell, tapped the simulated-Victorian (grinning face of a fox) knocker on the mockingly Tudor door. It was open. Ivan narrowly avoided being felled by a coach-house lantern and they both entered (Estate agent's jargon) the deceptively specious lounge. Deirdre was standing by a long food-laden table, talking to a small group of people – "And, of course, as I always say, why sacrifice your children's education—" Notices new arrivals. Blank look. ("Has she forgotten our names?" wonders Sally.) Then tempered gush. "How nice of you to come. Have you met—

(Introductory list of names trotted by.) And these are old friends of George." Yes, she has forgotten our names.

Deirdre calls out, "Dolores." Mutters. "Is she deaf? I've a good mind to send her back to Manila." Clicks fingers. Diminutive oriental girl/woman appears, carrying a tray of long-stemmed glasses. To new guests, "Do help yourself." Sally and Ivan take glasses of white wine, sip and suppress grimaces. To maid, "Now see to our other guests and be quick about it." Oriental female nods and suppresses grimace.

Sally:	(To Deirdre) Did you enjoy the play the other night?
Deirdre:	The play?
Sally:	Yes, The Three Sisters with the Ruddigores—
Deirdre:	Oh, that play. I do go to so many. Were you there?
Ivan:	We spoke to you and Richard outside and then you both rushed off to Caprice.
Old Codger:	Didn't know you were interested in the theatre, Day-dree.
Old Codger's wife:	Is The Three Sisters a musical or am I thinking of Seven Brides For Seven Brothers?
Deirdre:	(Distracted) Please excuse me. (Flies in a flutter towards two more guests. Excessive gush.) Fiona, Harry, how lovely to see you both. (Kiss, kiss.) Do let me find you a drink and then I must show you our new pergola. George built it but it's not quite finished yet. Of course, he never does finish anything.

Awkward silence falls on group by the table. Old codger's wife, with feigned enthusiasm, declares she must try a vol au vent and the old codger insists that everybody must try the kitsch lorraine.

"Shall we go now?" Ivan, in his specially loud stage whisper, asked Sally.

"Shh, they'll hear you."

"No, they won't. They're deaf as well as daft."

Old codger and wife, as they stuff crumbling pastry into gobs, "You must really try these. They're delicious."

The maid reappears with the tray of glasses. "Completement gaga," she said in impeccable French with a nod towards the scoffers and then swishes off smoothly to the garden.

"We can't leave yet. Not until we give George his present."

The present was an illustrated copy of the Rubaiyat bought for £25 in a remaindered bookshop. Ivan had suggested an illustrated copy of the Kama Sutra but Sally had firmly placed an interdiction on the purchase. "You don't need it and George would only strain his back just looking at it."

Like orphans in the storm, Ivan and Sally wandered into the adjoining room. The anodyne music of Simply Vague crept across the motionless air.

A quartet came in from the garden. "Hi there, you two," said Android and looked purposefully at his Cartier watch. "Just arrived, have you?" Zena, Prune and Richard gave Sally's little black dress a sweep with their laser-beam eyes while Android treated everyone to an action replay of the wrist-watch display. 1) Fascist salute with right arm. 2) Bend arm like a body-popper. 3) Squint at back of hand as if looking for signs of leprosy. 4) Loudly say something about the time. "It's exactly 15 minutes and 25 seconds past the hour. We shall have to put our foot down on the gas. (God, only salesmen with undescended testicles use such ghastly Americanisms.) Pity you two have just arrived at the exact moment we're pushing off."

Fluttering Deirdre appears. "Do you really, really have to go now? The fun is only just beginning."

The maid stood behind Ivan. "Tres stupide," she said.

Assuring their hostess that they really really had to go, that they really really regretted having to tear themselves away and that they really really had had a marvellous time, the quartet moved towards the exit.

A whiff of acrid smoke and a tang of burning flesh drifted into the room. "Are we near a crematorium?" Ivan asked the old codger as he passed by.The man's face turned grey, he emitted a mirthless laugh, his false teeth clicked and he shambled back to his wife.

Final farewells were being made by the quartet. Kiss kiss on cheeks, exeunt three. Richard strides back across the room. "Sally, may I have a word? Would you excuse me, Ivan old chap."

Ivan stood alone on the patio like the stag at bay. A laager of chairs was arranged on the lawn. Bored infants threw plastic plates to each other while a few haughty cultural couples paced the greensward and inspected the herbaceous borders with intense interest. Conifers of the Thuja variety cutely flanked paths and rails. Deirdre emerged on this sylvan scene, looking nervous. "Where's George?" Ivan asked her curiously.

She darted a vext glance to where Sally and Richard were still talking. "He said they were in a hurry but he's found time to talk to HER and I couldn't get a word in private all day. George, did you say?" She waved to her left. "He's there. He would insist on having his smelly bar-bee-cue. But then it is his birthday. Where has that vile maid got to? I do so hate supercilious servants."

Chapter fourteen

The riot of primary colours constricted within the fluorescent frame of oblong glass flowed into each other and resolved themselves into a human face. The visage became larger, grew a twirled moustache and spoke. "Why does a ripe apple fall?" the deep male voice asked. "Is it because of gravity? Or the stalk is withered? Perhaps the sun has dried it, perhaps it is too heavy, perhaps the wind shakes it or perhaps it falls because the boy beneath the tree desires it."

The metaphysics of the last intrigued Ivan. Perhaps in the never-never land of Nirvana, in the No-place of Tommy More, in the no-time of the future, the ruminants grazing on the plush soil East of Eden will ruminate upon their place in the universe of things and for the great love they bear their greater lords they will willingly lay down their lives. As man and woman in their clothed nakedness pass by, the kine will raise their ponderous heads and cry, "Take us to your slaughter houses, o kind masters, so that you may eat of our flesh and drink of our blood."

Strident bugles blew, iron thunder galloped across seared fields and fettlesome horses whinnied, "We did not evolve into beautiful creatures for this." The moustachioed face dissolved, the unanswered question was shredded by grapeshot and columns of men dressed in toy-town uniforms marched stolidly through pillars of disrupted earth. A large apple with its stalk angrily spitting sparks landed at the feet of a boy. "Am I to die then?" he asked as he stared at the fruit of desolation. The stripped trees began to blaze.

Following Deirdre's curt directions and guided by the sharp smell of carbonised flesh, Ivan went seeking George and found him around the corner, standing in what appeared to be an unroofed coalshed. His smudged face was bent over a cauldron of bright embers and he prodded slabs of blood-oozing meat and chicken limbs with a long wire fork. The Oriental maid stood on his left with the tray of glasses and intently watched the sizzling fat. On his right, her bottom resting on an incomplete wall, sat a woman of immense proportions, a Centurion tank in drag.

"And what I mean to say, George, well yes, everybody knows Sir Griddlepus is dense, obtuse, obstructive and only those upstairs know how he ever became Chairman of the Tribunal—" The big woman's rapid delivery tumbled from her mouth.

George looked up from his task. "Hello, Ivan. Is Sally with you? Have you met Shirley?"

Shirley was not to be stopped by a puny male. "Mr Chairman, I said, Mr Chairman, I mean I'm not going to bow and scrape because he's a Sir, I leave that to the toadies sitting with him on the platform, anyway, I said I object to this evidence being set aside. According to paragraph 12, sub-section 2a, but he cut me short with 'According to my reading of the said paragraph, your objections are overruled. That's my judgement on the matter.' "

"Le jugement d'un cretin," said the maid.

Sally came around the corner. "So this is where you're hiding. I went over to that mystic corn circle on the lawn to ask if they'd seen you. They're a bunch of mutant weirdoes from Basingstoke. Sorry, George, I didn't mean to disparage your friends—"

"I don't know any of them. They're from Deirdre's Health, Energy and Liquid Leisure Club."

"That's alright, then. They were talking about arranging weddings for, guess what, their pets. Apparently it's the latest craze sweeping Outer Suburbia."

"Tres tres stupide," said the maid.

"I quite agree," replied Sally. "Ivan, have you given George his present?" Ivan gave the birthday boy the gift-wrapped parcel.

"Do you mind if I open it later? My hands are greasy. What is it?"

Ivan grinned inanely. "A sex manual."

The response to his joke was five seconds of deadly silence.

"Don't mind him, George. He only says these things because he knows it teases. We brought you an illustrated copy of the Rubaiyat."

"How nice. It'll fit in with my other editions of the book."

"As I was saying when you came." Shirley was bent on exploiting this enlarged audience. "I had a run-in with that old buffer,

Sir Griddlepus, at the hearing on the proposed new roadways. You've heard about it, I suppose?"

"Well, yes, I have read about the hearing but – Ivan, didn't you receive a letter from a woman yesterday who's interested in it?"

The letter was in his pocket but it was a dead end not a roadway. "Er, yes, it's at home."

Shirley slid off the wall. "You must, must give me her name and address. We must start a proper campaign. Involve people. Send out letters to MPs, everybody. No time must be lost."

"George, George, do excuse me, George." Deirdre stood there, her paws held up like a supplicant mouse. "Is it possible to move your, your bar-bee-cue back a teeny weeny bit, please. The fumes are wafting over the lawn and my friends from HELL are not used to smoke."

"What the hell," said Shirley.

"The castors are jammed and it's too hot to move by hand."

"Oh, George, don't be obtuse."

"No problem, no problem, we'll lift it." Shirley looked around the small space. "All we need is, ah, this and this will do." She poked two poles under the cauldron and asked (ordered) Ivan to grab the other ends.

"Be careful, Shirley. I've just painted them with creosote."

The warning was too late for Ivan as his unprotected palms stuck to the rough wood. When they had moved the barbecue the requisite teeny weeny bit, he surreptitiously tried to clean off the brown sticky stain with the letter and only succeeded in driving dozens of splinters into his skin.

Shirley continued to rant on. "Say what you like, George, and we know you're in the legal business, but when it come to the protection of the environment, what is the law?"

"Hee haw, hee haw." They all stared at the maid. "La loi est un ane."

"Will you please take those drinks to my guests," Deirdre snapped.

Moscow was burning on the screen, Beirut was burning off-screen, Baghdad was burning in the headlines, rainforests were burning without headlines, there were little fires in Belfast and smouldering embers within the city centre of Ivan's breast. When the ashes are packed in penitent sackcloths and the charred wood sold for suburban barbeques, we can build a six-lane motorway through the devastation.

"I'm vext with you, Ivan. God knows how we'll get those marks off your trousers." Sally drove a Juggernaut through his thoughts. She interpreted his pathetic look as a sign of muted annoyance. "You don't mind me talking through this. After all it's the third time you've seen War And Peace and anyway, the sub-titles are in English."

But he had heard the man ask his Newtonian question about the falling apple. Should he treat the conundrum with more gravitas? Apple wagons were loaded with pathetic belongings, tears of bathos were dried by basting flames and babushkas mourned the fallen heroes.

When they arrived home from the party, the answering machine was flashing. Sally went upstairs to change out of her little black dress – "I'll just have to get it cleaned. It reeks of smoke." There was no voice on the machine, only piano music. Ivan re-ran the tape. Beethoven, yes, but – it was sonata No.12, 3rd movement, 'Marcia funebre sulla morte d'un Eroe'.

"Who was it?" She did not quite believe him when he said it was a wrong number. "You mean she (She?) listened to our message before realising that?"

He elaborated on the lie. "Some old biddy asking about her long-lost son. His father had been killed in a brawl and she wanted her son to return and answer the riddle of the Sphinx."

"Either you're joking or she's Jocasta. I'm beginning to wonder about you, Ivan the terrible liar. First there's that scented letter which you've not shown me and now a mysterious phone call." Said in a jocose manner. "By the way, where's that letter?" (Incinerated on the burning coals and now scattered unblessed wafers in communion with the stratosphere.)

She squinted at the mirror above the mantelpiece as she daubed her eyes. "You don't mind, do you, me going out tonight? (Why the concern?) I know Richard isn't high on your list of warm and wonderful people but – (Yes, yes, we know. He is the Media Man of the Moment and he knows people who know people who could throw a life-line to a drowning freelance writer.) I do hope the food at the Harpo Club isn't as stale as the literary outpourings of its alleged members." (We will briefly introduce the Harpo Club later.) Sally's eyes flicked to the left-hand side of the mirror. "What are you doing, Ivan?"

With his left hand under his right armpit and his right hand under the left armpit, he had the appearance of one measuring himself for a straitjacket. He was comparing the convex cavity on the right to the concave cavity on the left. What he pretended to be doing was catching a cat-flea.

Hastily removing his hands from the warm snuggeries, he held his right aloft and pressed the index finger and thumb together. "Mark but this flea, and mark, in this, how little that which thou deny'st me is; me it sucked first." He flicked his fingers as if throwing the red leaper at Sally. "And now sucks thee, And in this flea our two bloods mingled be."

Sally shuddered with repulsion. "Bloody hell, Ivan.Remind me to put cat powder on the shopping list. And talking of HELL as in Health, Energy and Liquid Leisure, not forgetting the mutant weirdoes from Basingstoke," she laughed, "isn't it laughable the way Deirdre has become like Prune, as if she were in training to be Ricky's next consort, companion and constant rebuke. You heard the way she talked to the maid."

Having done three unguided tours of home and garden, they had decided not to linger any longer. A waving and shouting farewell to George and Shirley standing by the eternal flame. "It was a pleasure to see you both," from George. "The pleasure was all ours, George," said with all the apparent sincerity convention required. "I'll keep in touch about the campaign," promised (threatened) Shirley. A flicker of a wave (ignored) towards the lawn laager, niceties exchanged with the buffet munchers. "Nice to have met you." "Very nice to have met you." "Must say good-bye to our hostess." "What a nice couple."

Seeking the hostess was easy. March towards the sounds of the guns. Deirdre, firing rapidly from the hip, was standing face to passive face with the maid in the kitchen. "And the agency promised, really really promised, and I should remind you that I am a personal friend of the manageress, she is a member of my health club, they promised to send me an experienced and reliable person, and for the money they charge I'd expect no less." Pause for breath. "You do understand English, don't you?"

"Deirdre, Deirdre, sorry to interrupt, but we're off now. Thanks for having us."

She reverts to urbane, though slightly distraught, urban hostess. "Oh, really. Must you go now. The fun is only beginning."

Oriental maid passes between the valedictory couple with an inscrutable smile. "Excrement du taureau," she said.

At the exact moment Sally swept out to keep her appointment, leaving at home a silent subdued husband watching the winter-frozen Great Retreat and a whiff of ennui-ennui scenting the farewell air, a different bullish part was being mentioned on the other side of London.

"Suppose, just suppose, for argument's sake, he has the heart of an ox. What then?" Ariadne glared at her listeners.

"Suppose, suppose, a rose is a rose," Angelica murmured.

"And what's that suppose to mean, clever puss?"

Angelica hopped from Stein to Shakespeare with the agility of a plague-flea. "A rose by any other name would smell as sweet."

Ariadne suspected devious mockery. Angelica smelled decaying enthusiasm.

The older sister rose. "You with your smart ideas and flip talk, you're the one who started this whole thing but it'll be pricked like a balloon on a thorn if—"

"If what you told us about those tablets was wrong," Alex said.

"Yes, no, I mean, no, I wasn't wrong about that but—"

But the time had passed for the reiteration of moral arguments, repetition of doubts, evasions and counter-reasoning.

"We're presuming, aren't we," Ariadne continued, "on the basis of a bottle of tablets – and I am not going to ask how they were obtained – that Dad is the one with the dicky heart. But—" a long pause. "But what if they were HERS? Ah ha, that's got you thinking."

Alex's thinking. A scenario. Dutiful son, fighting back the cheers, visits bereaved father, firmly grasps hand and offers words of consolation. "I must admit, Dad, that Sally and I didn't quite see eye to eye (Sub-text: Because of her size and attitude problem, arrogant biddy looked down on me) but now she's gone I regret our many differences. A massive heart attack, was it?" Sad Dad sighs. "I do appreciate your comforting words, Alex. Yes, it was a coronary, she was on the Pill, brought to its arresting finale by loose electric wires in the garage." Five more minutes of such exchanges pass, then, "Out of respect, Dad, I'm considering postponing the wedding." Response: Gratitude for such filial consideration but stern refusal to countenance this noble sacrifice. "Anyway, Dad, the delay would give me a chance to put some money by. I've had a lot of expenses recently and—" Deeply moved pater moves towards bureau and chequebook.

"But wait," you might cry, "is not this scenario similar to a previous one?" Yes, is the answer. It is well known to those versed in the recondite scrublands of literature that there are 21 fundamental story-lines. Anyone who has read a new novel by A and recalls reading a similar novel by B ten years before will be acutely aware of this fact. It is not given to everybody to be aware of the 21. Some, like Alex and the above mentioned writer A, are only capable of retreading a single scenario.

Conclusion to Alex's thinking as he holds A4-sized brown envelope to pouting chest. It's all san fairy ann to me who has the dicky heart. My scheme, devised as it is by a national expert, will do the trick one way or the other.

Angelica's thinking. The wrath of an avenging angel has no substance if the object of revenge is insubstantial in life but lives in memory.

Ariadne's thinking. This is getting too too complicated and the way things are going, or not going, it will be ages before I've more than a rattle of pennies in my purse.I wish in my heart of heart I hadn't mentioned the possibility of HER having the faulty ticker. If I had the money, I could buy a CD player and listen to the pure tones of Bob's (Dylan) heavenly voice.I wish to Christ I could screw more maintenance for the kids.

The forgettable Amy, not having been invited to this conspiratorial conclave, naturally had no thoughts on the matter. Had she been asked, her ideas would resound like shelled peas dropping into an enamel basin. Yet the other three's peccant hearts beat a piquant morality on her behalf. Would she not, in her innocence or ignorance, ultimately benefit from the success of their striving?

Alex took control of the debate and brushed aside as irrelevant any anxiety as to whose aorta would clog the conspiracy. He took several sheets of paper from the brown envelope and placed them on the table. His sisters bent over to look at the various schematic diagrams. "Of course, I don't expect you to understand the technical jargon and I'll try to explain them to you in simple layman's language," said the modern Mr Pooter in a state of huff and puff.

Step A) Breaking into the garage would present no problem. The door has been hanging off its hinges for years. "You know what Dad's like. A big job like repairing the doors and he keeps putting it back for ages." Step B) An insulated wire is threaded through the enamel ladders under the roof. Step C) One end is left hanging at the far end and stripped. Step D) The other end is connected to a plug which is then shoved into a socket.

Modus operandi or words to that effect. Step E) Subject X (Sally) drives car slowly forward. Bonnet and wire connect. (Question: Wouldn't the driver get a shock? Answer: No. Car insulated from ground by tyres.) Step F) Subject Y (Ivan) will do one of the following: a] Lean down by offside with hand on car to say goodbye to subject X. b] Go around to near side to open passenger door. c] Affectionately pat departing car's boot as if rump of subject X. He's always smacking her bottom. Makes you sick.

Expected result. Subject Y gets electric shock to aggravate heart condition.

Deviser smiles smugly. Expected response from exposition of diabolical cleverness: gasps of astonishment, followed by plaudits for brilliance. Actual response. Stunned silence.

"Well, what do you think?"

Unspoken thoughts of Ariadne. 'It's got as many holes in it as my last pair of tights after that hooley we had in the Community Centre. (Actually a fund-raising social for the new anti-motorway group.) Why do men have to go in for wearing chunky signet rings?'

Spoken words. "Well, Alex, your education wasn't wasted, was it?"

Unspoken thoughts of Angelica. 'Should I leave the tape running? Yes, I will.'

Spoken words: "I presume you're quite confident that this will work?"

Confident? What a typical female question. "Of course it will. I've done a feasibility study on it."

There was no more to be said. Ariadne advanced her scheme about the Anton Piller Order. "Let's put it this way. It will drive an extra nail into—" She hesitated. Surely it would be crass to use the word 'coffin'?

There was some uneasiness expressed at the recruitment of Amy's husband, PC Bob Plod. "As far as he's concerned, we're asking for his help to claw back money Dad owes Mum. The sweetener for him is a handful of notes in his wallet. The beauty of it is, none of us will be seen to be directly involved."

An extra bottle of wine was opened to toast future successes.

"We shouldn't be too premature with our celebrations," said Angelica. ("She would put a dampener on things," thought the others.) "These are just possibilities and we should be prepared for the probability that they are not immediately efficacious." (Quick glance between eldest sister and brother contained the unspoken, "Gawd, doesn't our little sister love to use big words.")

"I don't quite understand—" It was the last big word Ariadne did not understand.

"In other words, what you're saying, Angie," said Alex, "is we should have a few other schemes, just in case, up our sleeves. That's right, isn't it?" Angelica nodded. The tape was still running. "Well, I'm not a one-idea man, you know." (True, he had two ideas on his incomplete alphabetic list. The second began with B)

"So, what's your second big idea then?" Ariadne asked.

"It's not fully worked out yet but – I was thinking of Bridgit's father, Shamus."

"That Irish fly-by-night. What about him?"

"We know you met him at one of those Troops-Out meetings, Arry, and everybody knows it's an IRA front."

"It certainly is not," Ariadne retorted.

"That's what you think but I've read differently."

"Yes, in those fascist rags, The Sun and The Star."

"I'm not going to argue politics with you. But Shamus does

come and go and I'm sure he can lay his hands on some – er – stuff. Know what I mean."

"Stuff? Surely you're not thinking of—"

"It would be put down as another terrorist outrage."

"You mean putting a device in their car? It could kill or injure innocent passers-by."

"While it's still in the garage."

"No, no, I'm right against the very idea."

"Why?"

"Why! Because that would be murder, that's why," replied the outraged Ariadne.

Angelica switched off the briefcase's hidden tape recorder.

Chapter fifteen

Purely as a diversion while our conspirators garnish their devilish broth with adder's fork and blind-worm's sting,we shall, as promised give a brief history of the Harpo Club. We did plan a 300-word thesis, a mini-monograph, you could say, as a preamble to the above, on the recurrence in later years of the pathological need to counter childhood insecurities by joining or creating an exclusive club. For example, The Silent Three. HQ, behind the coalshed. Membership: Chalky White, Ginger Brown, yourself. Honorary member: Three-year old sister, because mam said you had to look after the whinger. But we felt that a more propitious occasion could arise, or if you want to be rude, eructate, for us to exhibit our erudition. Perhaps a dense book – dense people are too thick to read – entitled: Clubs From Primitive Cages To The Carlton. A Brief History. Until then we shall just pop-Popper along, singing as we go, 'We are not Jung any more.'

Suffice to say that London, though not uniquely so, proliferates with exclusive and excluding semi-secret clubs for people with a pathological need to counter adult insecurities. If or when, for instance, you join a Flying Saucers Observer Group (FSOG), you are ushered into a cosy comforting world of people who have a firm faith in the improbable and a strong belief in the possibility that everybody else is mad. If such arcane subjects are not your cup of tea, with or without a flying Chaucer, and your aspirations are more aesthetic, erudite, artistic, cinematic or theatrical, then search no further than the environs of Central London for the club/s to your taste. Of course, you will have to apply for entry but if you have not written anything nasty about a committee member in a newspaper or magazine or said the same on TV, then you should have no problem in being accepted.

Advantages: a) Impresses country cousins/Aunt Matilda/your grocer when you mention that you dined with a semi-famous person the night before. b) If said semi-famous person – sitting two tables from you – becomes overwrought in an emotional exchange with his blond/e escort, you immediately ring up your contact on a tabloid newspaper with the gossip and four weeks later a cheque – not particularly fat – arrives on your mat. At least it pays for your supper.

Disadvantages: a) The annual subscription is equal in cost to ten good meals in any nearby restaurant. b) Really famous people would not be seen dead in the club there. c) Dead famous people grin inanely at you from blown-up photographs on all the walls. c) You are surrounded by demi-demi-famous people (used to appear on game shows), want-to-be famous people, want-to-be-seen-with-famous-people people, gawpers and tea-boys.

Here then is the brief history of the Harpo Club. A querulous group of crusty literati, once regarded as angry young men in a hurry but now seen as bilious codgers in a state of middle-aged decrepitude, peeved at gawpers and doubly peeved at no gawpers, decided to create their own exclusive-exclusive club. They hired the dingy basement of a bankrupt Soho strip joint and thoroughly disinfected the premises on opening night by every person present smoking Havana cigars. The choice of name was opportune. The original strip joint's logo was a cavorting group of bulbous-bosomed blondes circling the legend HARPY. The pulchritudinous maidens were exchanged for a month's supply of taramasalata with a Greek restaurateur and to avoid violent misunderstanding with any passing militant feminists the Y was converted to O. Of course, there were unkind persons who asserted that the chosen name was a juvenile nose-thumbing at another club (see above for description) with a cognate name. This was a minor annoyance and only equalled by the callers who thought they were stockists of a certain powdered lavatory cleaner.

Is that all? We did say it would be a brief history.

Sally parked her car beneath the Neo-Brutality edifice at Bankside and to avoid the crush of music-lovers stumbling over the pan-handlers on Hungerford Bridge, decided to take a taxi. "You an American?" the driver asked. He lapsed into a sullen silence when she said no and did not speak again until they were tearing around Trafalgar Square. "I can always tell, you know, experience, you know. As soon as I saw you I said to myself, she's not

American. Not many of them about nowadays, you know. I blame it on the acid rain. It's the same with the Japanese."

The arrangement with Richard was to meet at the cognate club for a drink and then go on to Harpo's but the young woman at the reception desk looked blankly at Sally when she gave his name and pertly asked, "Are you sure he's a member?" There was a slight distraction when a plump, pink-clad minor TV 'personality', known to be on the B list of celebrities invited to the opening of a jar of caviar but soon to be demoted to the tin of sardines section, the C list, noisily entered the foyer with his entourage of giggling young men. Embossed invitation cards to a book launch – Soho People I Knew, by a defunct journalist – were flashed and the party were ushered into the interior.

Sally was in a dither. Had she come to the wrong place, the wrong night? Had she misheard Richard's hurried invitation? Had he forgotten? And should she cut her losses and return to immobile Ivan with a lame excuse prepared for his ears? "If he's not here, he's not here," she banally and wryly said to the uninterested receptionist as she turned to push through the swing doors. A very pale youth touched her elbow and asked, "Are you Sally? Your party is here. Do come with me, please."

There was an immense crowd inside. Names were bounced from wall to wall and guffaws and trilling laughter accompanied every alleged bon mot. There seemed to be an inordinate number of flaxen-haired maidens of all sexes. 'Should we take our money out of the building society,' Sally wondered, 'and invest in bleach?' She had not noticed that someone was scrutinising her.

A tiny Oriental waitress with a trayful of long-stemmed glasses stood before her. Could this be the same woman who attended Deirdre's party? "S'il vous plait," said the waitress and nodded towards the glasses. Sally took one.

The waitress vanished into the body of the crowd but Sally's attempt to follow her was foiled by the plump, pink-clad one stepping sideways into her path. She inadvertently nudged his elbow and some of the wine – his third glassful – spilt.

"Oh, I'm extremely sorry. I hope I didn't—"

"Don't mind me at all, dearie, not at all. Everybody thinks I'm a pushover, dearie, but I'm not a pushover at all. I would say I am more of a lean-over than a pushover and I'm never one to say no to a good prod. Ha ha ha. But I jest. And who are you? Wait, I do know you from somewhere. Don't tell me, dearie, yes, were you not in—no, no, it's gone. Do tell me, are you an actress?"

"No, I'm a writer."

"Oh, really, a writer.(Waning interest.) And what do you write?"

"Er, magazine features on, er (sudden inspiration) on famous TV personalities."

(Revived interest) "I knew I saw your face somewhere. Where was it now? Vogue, Cosmo? And you are one of those naughty naughty journalists who write naughty things about me, aren't you. But I'm not one to hold a grudge and to prove it I will make myself available—ha ha, make myself available – for an exclusive interview at any time." He scribbled on the back of the invitation card. "Just ring this number, dearie, and—"

"Sally!" Richard appeared through the mob. "We'll have a quick drink and then – ah, I see you have one. Well, in that case—"

"Ricky, dearie!" The pink one landed a slobbery kiss on Richard's sweating cheek. "You've been neglecting me, bad boy."

"I'll speak to you another time, Adrian." Richard's manner was abrupt, almost rude. He grabbed Sally's arm.

"Never mind that gut rot. It's only cheap crap they buy in for launches. The duckies can't tell the difference."

He took the glass from her hand and plonked it on the tray. The Oriental waitress smiled enigmatically and said, "Bon appetit."

They stopped near the exit and Richard called out, "Julian" to the young man palely loitering by the door.After a few words together, Richard returned to Sally. "Sorry about all this. It's usually quite quiet this time of the week. If I had known there was to be another book launch – they might as well launch them straight into the remaindered bookshops and save themselves a lot of bother. And then there had to be Android's, I mean Andrew's, special occasion for members of his staff. I don't want to be here when he comes and blood is spilt on the carpet."

"What do you mean?"

"Don't let this get any further but his firm handled the accounts of a certain TV company and some Gawd-awful clangers have been dropped, money missing, you know the sort of thing. This special event is in the nature of a Last Supper but none of them are aware there's going to be mass crucifixions. And I only dropped in here to have a few words with my research assistant."

"Which one is she?"

"The young blonde woman."

Sally looked around. Thirty heads of blonde tresses quivered with merriment and the thirty-first quickly bent over a bowl of Bombay mix. Julian returned, nodded to Richard who then gripped Sally's arm as they went out to the foyer. The excitement of the night was not yet over.

At the sight of a bouffant blonde paying off a taxi, Richard muttered embrocations and vanished. The new arrival surged like a minesweeper through the swing doors towards the interior. "Excuse me, madam," the bored receptionist called out, "Excuse me, madam." (Sally asks herself, 'Why should the inexcusable be excused?')

A face of stiffened fury glared at the caller. "Yes, what do you want?" The question rang with the haughty tone of a bell summoning a servant; an art carefully learned from Joan Collins soaps by countless suburban hausfraus.

"If you're here for the launching, I must see your invitation card."

"Launching? Launching? Is this a shipyard?" inquired the new arrival with exquisite wit.

"Deirdre," Sally called out.

Deirdre gave her a wolfish smile.

"Yes, I was correct in what I heard. You're here but where is HE? Is HE in there? It's no use hiding anything from me. I repeat, is HE in there?"

"Who? George? I didn't think he'd be a member. Not his scene. But Andrew and Zena should be here soon."

"Please, Sharon or Sally or whatever your name is, please don't pretend to be obtuse. I am talking about Richard. Is Richard in there?"

"Why don't you go in and see for yourself?" said Sally austerely.

"Have you got an invitation?" the receptionist reiterated.

Sally gave the pink-clad person's card to Deirdre who, without a word of thanks or even a fond farewell, lobbed the embossed cardboard across the desk and flounced into the interior.

Houdini would have envied Richard's disappearing and reappearing act. He grabbed Sally's arm again and pushed through the swing doors into the street.

"What a pity, Richard, you've just missed Deirdre," said Sally, stirring the pot with insatiable curiosity.

They skirted five bulging plastic bags, brushed past the outstretched paw of a beggar, ignored the siren call of a sex-show barker and turned left down an alley. "I think you'll enjoy our supper at the Harpo Club. They do a wonderful line in taramasalata."

Chapter sixteen

True confessions time? No, rather a true confession, to put it in the singular or, to rephrase it, a confession of a singular lump, though the only element of mea culpa in it was the tardy telling.

Sally: Why are you sitting with your hands under your arms, Ivan? Are you auditioning for a part in Marat Sade?

Ivan: (Touch of wry humour) Ah, the mad, sad, bad lad has been had in the pit of insanity but my pit, my charm-pit, has, as our dear prince would say, a carbuncle on the pith and there's the pity.

Sally (Huffily) I don't know what on earth you're talking about. And please don't ask me, not at this hour, to pit my wits against your palaver.(It was the day after her Harpo dinner and the aftermath of the meal still lay heavily in the pit of her stomach.)

She knew he was referring to his as yet unwritten but much mentioned concise version of the drama, provisionally titled Hamlet Without Tears,

Example:
King to Queen: Madam, your lad is quite mad, mad, mad. The bad cad talks to his dead dad. And he has a fad about being clad like his cousin Vlad.
Queen: How sad, sad, sad.
(Listener: I've had, had, had enough.)
Returning to our true and singular confession.

Sally: Have we any Alka-Seltzer? I'm sure we had some in the medicine cabinet. Don't tell me it's disappeared with those tablets.Gawd, I dread to think where the Harpo people dredged up the bottled Gauleiter piss we drank. In a cess-pit under the fallen wall, I suspect. (She had left the wine selection to Richard and he had chosen a slightly sweet

German white. The memory of it flavoured her choice of words.) Favour me with plain talk, Ivan. Shit or get off the pot.

Ivan: I take it you didn't really enjoy your candlelit supper with rigid Richard. (The Harpo management had spared no expense with guttering candles but, mindful of the energy crisis – particularly among their fading members – had kept the electric lights as dim as a dull day in Parliament.) In plain words and to pot it in one, I have a growth under my right arm.

There are several other items on the agenda.

1) A singular reluctance on Sally's part to give a detailed report on her jolly night out. Why? All will be revealed in dribs and drabs.

2) Arising from the above revelation, expressions of concern, anxiety, fear, followed by:

3) a clinical visitation plus a sealed letter in a brown envelope.

4) Under correspondence: various documents of a campaigning and/or junk nature plus two sealed letters: one in a white, scented envelope, the other in a blue ditto. The aromas were different but the smells were similar.

5) Under any other business: Death before noon.

"You must go to the quack."

"Only sick people go to the doctor. I've just got a lump."

"Well, lump it or like it, you should have it seen to."

Exit Sally to kitchen. Sound of short conversation off stage. Thirty seconds later. Re-enter Sally door right. "I've made an appointment for you with Doctor Cucumber. 9.30 tomorrow morning. (Pleadingly) Do it for my sake, Ivan. You're normally so fit for a man of your age and I'd hate to think of anything horrible happening to you. (Pause) And talking of which, George hasn't contacted us yet about finalising the wills, has he?"

There were not many people in the waiting room. A bulgingly pregnant woman, her young face aged with doltish immobility, her husband who whined about having "to hang around this dump", their three restless children who were variously snapped at by either parent with, "Sherrup, Wayne"/ "Kylie,I'll give you a right smacking, I will''/''Jason, I said sit, sit'', a bent stick of an old man who coughed like an asthmatic Pekinese, a sullen-featured teenage girl with green hair. And Ivan.

A silver-haired (freshly permed) head appeared at the reception hatch and called Ivan's name. ''Doctor Cucumber will see you now.'' The whining man whined, '''Ere, we're before him,'' and then throws a lustful glance at the teenage girl's tattoed thighs.

''Well, what did the doctor say?''

''Nothing much, really. Gave me this —'' Shows sealed brown envelope '' – to take to Saint Jankers Hospital a week from now. He thinks it's glandular trouble.''

Doctor Cucumber was a small, neatly formed man who dressed like an old-fashioned bank clerk. Being a foreigner, he spoke impeccable English. He was, as they say in the trade, a gland-man, and had dedicated that part of his life which was not involved in ministering to back-aches, varicose veins, piles or playing golf, to a deep study of the role of the glands in the evolution and history of humanity. Over the last ten years he had been writing a massive tome on this very subject, provisionally entitled: 'The Acorns Of Wisdom.' (Latin glans, an acorn.) He had just finished chapter 40, sub-titled, 'The French Prostate Too Much', in which he conclusively proved that a) the Battle of Waterloo was influenced by Napoleon's diseased prostate and b) that country's riots in the 1960s stemmed from De Gaulle's fear of emasculation after an operation on the prostate.

His eyes lit up when Ivan told him about the lump. ''Ah ha, could it be a farcy nodule,'' he said softly and chuckled. He then asked Ivan what books he read, did he go to the theatre, who was his favourite composer. ''Bach? J.S. Bach? A man both prolific in music and children.'' He made a mental note to include a section on The Great Composers in his opus – Bach's ultimate blindness, Mozart's final body-swelling, Beethoven's deafness, Tchaikovsky's homosexuality. (But no, had he not covered homosexuality in the pituitary gland part?) He made an actual note with his Parker fountain pen for Ivan to take to Saint Jankers.

''Saint Jankers? But that's miles away,'' Sally protested.

''The local hospitals have been shut down.''

They then discussed the sick way the nation's health was being treated by vile-tasting doses of economy; but since both agreed on the politics of the matter, there was no need to sugar the pill.

The brown sealed letter was placed against the serpentine-stone clock on the mantelpiece. 'What on earth has he written about you,' Sally wondered.

On the other side of London, adrenalin was pumping from sluggish flow to rapid torrents, pituitaries were twitching and thyroid glands were starting to over-act.

Angelica had a few letters to write, a few thoughts to be sorted out, a few plans to be scrapped or re-worked and the account of the cognate club's special meal (sponsored by Screwitt and Scrimpett, Financial Advisers and Wizards – Just see how your money vanishes) to be erased from the files.

It was detritus time on the scattered plates at the Last Supper and most of the disciples were in a giggling state of inebriation when Judas, officially the executive manager, also know as Android, pompous-arse and smoothy-chops, began an uneasy oration. "May I have your attention, ladies and gentlemen." (Voice from the crowd, "Er, we're no gentlemen, we're accountants." Effect of revelation on surrounding tables: sudden hush and glances of disdain.)

Andrew gave the heckler a condescending smile. A less adept executioner would have sniggered. His upper teeth set into a white portcullis beneath the dark arch of his moustache and the audible words marched out in stiff well-drilled ranks.

"Splendid team work in the preceding years – dedicated efforts – trust and confidence – management and employees – through no fault of – need to slim down – thin and lean times – thinner and keener – dead wood – surplus capacity – when present unfortunate problems are – loyalty will not be forgotten—"

Merriment drained from the surrounding faces, lower jaws sagged and fuddled brains tried to stand in dignified poses before the firing squad.

"Andy Wandy!" A woman with a dismembered blonde beehive lurched against the chair-backs. Her plump, pink-clad epicene companion giggled. "Have you met my dear friend, Hadrian Wall, star of stags and screams. We've just been to a boot lunch, show my dear friend Andy Wandy your loot, Hadrian."

The pink-clad one and his cortege, all grinning inanely, opened their jackets to reveal shining copies of Soho People I Knew.

"Are you alright, Deirdre?" A patina of sweat glistened on Andrew's embarrassed face.

"Course I'm alright, Andy Wandy, who wouldn't be with such gallant knights of the night to guard one's rear (More giggles from the pink one and his troupe) as we march towards hoboes and the phalanx of photographers, singing our rallying song The London Derriere. Goodbyee." As the group surged towards the exit, she could be heard enquiring skittishly: "By the way, who's paying?"

Andrew's audience was now depleted. Two young women had gone to the lavatory to be sick, two others had followed to hold the first pair's heads and a section of the young men, led by the heckler, had decided to get away from these wankers and have a good piss-up. Their defection had put their names firmly on top of the list. When all around you lose their heads, they also lose their jobs. Andrew smiled winsomely at his diminished party and said "Cheer up." He was worried. Who will execute the executioner?

Angelica switched on her word-processor and slipped Berlioz's Symphonie Fantastique into the player. She stayed quite quiet until the 4th movement, The March To The Gallows, sonorously shook the speakers.

'Dearest Mummy,

Thank you very much for the postcard of Eastbourne. It looks lovely in summer and I'm sure you'll enjoy promenading along the parade when the warm weather arrives. (Hidden message: Stay there and don't invade my space.) Have you settled things with the telephone people? (Or have you spent my money on your pretensions?) Let me have your new number soon and then we'll be able to have very long conversations and—'

Letter a worried daughter should be able to write to an understanding mother.

'Dearest Mummy,

As you are always the one person I can turn to when—'

Letter Angelica wished she could have written.

'Dad,

'Can I come to see you and ask your advice. As you must have read in the newspapers, the firm I work for has been involved in the recent financial tangle of a certain TV company and—'

Would it be a dead letter? Press Exit button.

In another part of the other side of London, Ariadne was in a frantic state of siege as cardboard box after cardboard box was brought into her flat by her troop of unwilling helpers. She directed operations while at the same time holding a loud conversation on the phone.

"Okay, Shirley, I can get my sprogs to stuff the envelopes, about time they did something useful. I'll make sure their grubby paws are clean but listen, Shirley, what about distributions? Oh good, smashing, you'll collect the boxes and get other supporters to address the envelopes and send them off—"

Bob, husband of Amy, entered and, with hands behind his back, viewed the traffic with a suspicious frown. He nearly came out with his favourite joke: "Hello, hello, what's going on here, then?"

"Right then, Shirley, see you." Puts down phone. "Hi, Bob, nice of you to come. How's Amy and the children? I'll make a cup of coffee in a sec. This? This is the anti-motorway campaign. Nothing illegal about it."

"You wanted to speak to me about something?" (Anything you say will be taken down and may be used as evidence that I'm a bloody good copper.)

"Well, yes, Bob. Wait till I clear the decks. Would you like anything to eat?"

"I am in a bit of a hurry," explained Bob stiffly.

"Amy expecting you home soon? Give her a tinkle on the phone and tell her you'll be a bit late. She'll understand."

"I have a passenger in the van."

"Ask him up then."

"It's WPC Wendy."

"Oh." Slight nonplussed pause. "In that case, Bob, first things first. Have you heard of the so-called Anton Piller legal device?"

"I don't recall reading about it in the latest edition of Moriarty's Police Law," said Bob with deep sarcasm.

More on this later. Meanwhile, Alex completed the sixth version of his schematic drawings, checked the tools in a holdall and then hunched over a large map. "Tomorrow, tomorrow," he muttered. It was the sixth night he had muttered "Tomorrow, tomorrow."

In the words of a very famous specious statesman (Is that not an oxymoron?), a new order had begun. In the Ivan/Sally household, it was manifest in the rite of the morning coffee. For umpteen years Ivan, woken by bladder urging and/or naked coldness, clambered out of bed at daylight, leaving a sprawled Sally to spread herself across his last remaining hot spot, and padded downstairs to make the coffee.

But now it was the newly solicitous Sally, conscious of her husband's apparently dire condition, who would lay a restraining arm across Ivan's tubby tum and sweetly say, "You just lay there and I'll make the coffee, feed the cats and bring up the papers and post." She would have extended the list of labours to Herculean proportions by adding such things as pulling up the obdurate blinds, the parting of the drape curtains, the nail-breaking struggle when the fabric snagged on a hook and so on, but such a litany would be too too tedious to both hear and speak at this dry hour of the morning. He would look at her with a pained expression in his eyes; to her, a message of concern for her great sacrifice, to him, a deep wish she would remove her arm and thus take off some of the pressure on his dangerously extended bladder.

It was only Sally who was conscious of any dire condition. As the Biblical myths have taught us, Eve and all her daughters, lusting for the fruits of the tree of life and the tree of knowledge, will stop at nothing to discover what kernel lies within the womb. So it was with Sally and the brown sealed envelope on the mantelpiece.

On the second morning that she volunteered to make the coffee, an extra item was added to the list of tasks. She steamed open the brown envelope. The note from Doctor Cucumber to the specialists at Saint Janker's Hospital was terse, to the point and completely flummoxing. 'I am confident that this man has Hodgkin's disease.'

Reference books, home medical tomes – how to put a splint on a fractured pinkie – rather tattered and very out-of-date Penguin Science dictionaries and several impulse-bought thick paperbacks (American), each one titled Encylopedia, were consulted on the provenance, primacy and personality of Mr Hodgkins and his attending disease. None supplied the required information. Sally resolved to junk the lot as a gift to the next Boy Scout jumble sale and then rang a fellow freelance writer who specialised in medical features. What she was told made her go pale and trembly and hastened the need to contact George about finalising the wills.

On the seventh morning of the New Order, Sally had made the coffee, emptied a slobbering tin of Pussywillow (nutritional beefy lumps for lively felines) on the cats' dish and was browsing through the newspapers' lead stories (Princess Di breaks fingernail. Thousands feared drowned in new floods, see page 34 for full story) when several letters came plop-plop through the slot. Three were Cellopane packages which offered immense and valuable prizes if replied to within 14 days, a bill from the gas company and an oblong white envelope with the legend Campaign Against Rash Motorways Antinatural Developments (CARMAD). The sixth and seventh were a small, white, scented (Pine and Lavendar) envelope and a small, blue, scented (Anais Anais) envelope. The last three were addressed to Ivan.

"Any post?" Ivan called down plaintively.

"Usual magnificent prize offers for the delight of doddering old dears, one gas bill for the delight of none and a long envelope about motorways addressed to you." ("Why," you may ask, "did she not mention the last two letters?" We shall see.)

"That must be from shrill Shirley. I'll look at it later."

Sally's initial thoughts while looking at the unmentioned letters: This one (The white envelope) is similar in size and scent to the one he lost. Is it possible that there's a distressed woman out there, frantic to be put in contact with CARMAD, thinking that our Ivan is the proper conduit?

Sally's second line of thought: Would I be a naughty girl if I opened the envelope and sent the name and address off to Shrilly?

We are not privy to her third or fourth lines of thoughts but we can safely presume that they too had an element of self-deceit.

She laid the two envelopes on the kitchen worktop, tucked the papers under her arm and carefully carried the cups of coffee in her hands. Upstairs she gave Ivan his drink, the newspapers and his letter and, in honeyed tones, urged him to stay in bed for another hour or so. "Oh my Gawd, I forgot to feed the cats," she uttered melodramatically.

Quick boiling of water in steam-spitting kettle. Envelope No.1 held against spout.

Letter No 1. (Left-leaning sloping script.)

'Dear Ivan,

'As I said to you in my first letter to you, I have only your best interest at heart. This is why I am taking time to warn you once more that your wife is carrying on with another man. She is becoming more flagrant. (Flagrant? Is there a double-meaning here?) Last week she met this man in a sleazy Soho night club and they left arm in arm. What time did she get home that night? You should keep an eye on your young wife.

A friend.'

Sally crunched the letter, smoothed it out, re-read it, crunched it again, smoothed it out again, re-re-read it and shoved it into her dressing-gown pocket. Would letter No.2 be of the same tenor?

Letter No 2. (Familar address printed in point 8 Baskerville at top right-hand corner. Paper blue. Script long in serifs, short in care.)

'Dear Ivan,

'You may be surprised to have a letter from me but not so surprised as I was when I went to meet a certain person at an exclusive West End club, only to find that your wife and he had waltzed off together into the night. Fortunately I made friends with a famous TV personality. And don't be surprised if your wife suddenly says she has to go to a conference in Eastbourne. He has a flat along the parade. Did you enjoy our barbecue party?

Yours sincerely

Deirdre.'

Letter No 2 was spared the same crunching violence as letter No

1 though crunching words of implied violence were promised by the reader to the writer. "I'll totter that superannuated bimbo off her stilted speech and stilted shoes if I ever have the pleasure of meeting her face-to-harpy-face in the future." What maniacal fury spurs these latter-day maenads to their frenzies? For yes, the author of No 1 letter was as much a woman as the scribbler of No 2.

Short scene during meal in the opaque Harpo Club.

Richard: Have some more wine, Sally. Don't you find the taste quite piquant? I discovered it when I went last year to the Berlin Freedom Film Festival in a restaurant not too far from the Cafe des Westens, gone now, of course, where Rupert Brooke wrote that Grantchester poem. I was invited to the Old Vicarage last month. (Pause for Sally to exclaim, "Oh, really, do you know—?" She did not.) Pity we hadn't met up by then and you could have come with me. To Berlin, I mean. It was very hot and I remembered Brooke's line about the Temperamentvoll German Jews. Let me fill your glass.

Sally: (Smothering yawn.) No, thank you, Richard. I'm driving.

Richard: (Master of the segue.) Talking of driving, Sally, have you ever though of driving down to Eastbourne? Let me explain, one of my propositions, or, if you like, projects, is to have one person nationally known as a conference presenter and, of course,the Eastbourne region is a mecca for conferences. That's why I keep a small flat down there which I could make available to the presenter. Perhaps one weekend when—

Sally: (Thinks: Perhaps I will try the creme brulee.) I know somebody living in Eastbourne. Well, living in the sense in which Dracula lived in Whitby.

Richard: (Feigned interest.) Oh, really. Who?

Sally: My husband's first wife.

Secret letters are as difficult to hide in a house as an unwanted dead body; but, unlike the decaying corpse, remembered or dismembered, they can be hidden on one's own person and there is no better secret place on a chaste woman, or at least one who has kept ahead of the chase, than inside her knickers. When Sally had emerged from the shower, smothered her relevant parts with a cloud of talcum, pulled up her tights (God, they're tight) and then her silk French knickers, she tucked the two missives beneath the elastic. When she dashed into the bedroom in search of her bra, she reminded Ivan of robust Toulouse-Lautrec harpies and he made colourful suggestions. She smiled, teased him for not producing his paint brush earlier and remarked that surely one lump was sufficient for him to consider at the moment. Besides all that, she was in a hurry.

The cause of her hurry was an appointment with a magazine's commissioning editor. This in itself was a cause of some chagrin because the said editor – 23 years of age – had been a tea-girl two years ago.

"Now you take it easy for the rest of the day, and don't do anything strenuous," she said as they went into the garage. "Did we leave the doors open last night?"

"Must have been the wind." It had been a calm night. "I'll have to change the hinges."

"It's been like that for the last six months and another week won't make any difference." She revved up the engine. "Oh, Ivan, what's that wire hanging over the bonnet? Could you move it? I don't want it to scratch my car." He reached over with a wooden batten and held the wire up as she drove out. The wheels bumped over a screwdriver.

Back in the house, Ivan was restless and discontented. Their latest arrival from the book club – The History Of Conspiracy Theories – lay on the table without a single thumb-mark greasing its pages. "I know, I'll make a start by securing the small window."

He returned to the garage to slide the lower half of the aluminium ladder from the roof rack, but the wire – which he had not noticed was laced through the rungs – tightened against the steps.

He pulled, he tugged, he heaved. "Oh shit," he shouted and then slipped on cat-shit recently deposited by the hairy tramp. As he stumbled back, still clutching the ladder, he felt a tingle on the palms of his hands and then heard an anguished yowl followed by a splash.

A bit shaken, he went back into the house, replaced the blown fuse and made a cup of coffee. "I wish I hadn't given up cigarettes," he said. There were a few things to be worked out.

One. How did that wire get to be tangled in the ladder? Two. How did it become plugged into the mains? Three: Where did that screwdriver come from? Four: Who did it? Five: Why?

An unworthy thought entered his mind. 'Surely Sally wouldn't – No, of course not. She doesn't know the first thing about electricity.'

And then there was the problem of the electrocuted hairy cat and goldfish. Should the deceased moggie be buried with all due ceremony beneath the madly spreading cotoneasters and the fish interred in the herbaceous borders, or should they all be recycled in the compost heap?

Whatever, a libation to the great Felix in the sky and the golden piscines of the deep would not be out of order and Ivan saluted the departed with a full glass of catnip-flavoured brandy.

Chapter seventeen

Ariadne feared that she had bitten off more than she could chew and, to chomp that well-worn cliche still further, felt that her capacious form was being eaten by the hungry demands of her many and various campaigns, projects and plots. "I just don't know which way to turn," she said to herself as she turned from left to right to look at the piles of CARMAD cardboard boxes, the languidly leaning collection of Bob Dylan records – O hard rain beating on my heart, too much of nothing is blowing on the idiot wind – her rabble of children romping by the television set, the table laden with weighty, worthy and wordy documents (a manifesto for this, proposals for that, a charter for the other) and, snuggled beneath the last heap, her own scribbled plot to execute the so-called Anton Piller legal device.

Hauling herself from the chair, she slid a record out of its sleeve, placed it flip-side up on the turntable and selected the second track for starters. At the sounds of a twangy guitar and whining fiddles, her aghast brood gawped gape-mouthed at their mother. When a creaky, scratchy voice croaked through the loudspeakers, "Our conversation was short and sweet", they raised a protesting chorus of "Aww Mam." They were fathered by Philistines.

"Shut yer gobs," she shouted back but then, in deference to the inalienable right of every individual to pursue perdition or pleasure according to their own will, she plugged in the earphones and sat with a wistful smile on her face; only breaking her silence to intone the moaning refrain, "You're a big girl now."

Long ago and not so far away, when she would incontinently bawl because of a hurt knee, a bruised ego or a perceived injustice, Cleo, burdened with Amy or Alex or Angelica, would snap, "Shut your yelling, you snivelling ball of lard, and make yourself useful." But Dad was different. "Dry your tears, child. You're a big girl now."

Ariadne could not afford an excess of nostalgia and, at the most, doled herself a runcible spoonful in any one day by spending half-an-hour with Bob Dylan or re-reading The Hobbit. She considered that remembrance of times past was a suitable subject for a work of semi-fiction, but in the real world of grown-ups the pains of yesterday, when they stimulated conflicts of interest and conscience, could become the aches of tomorrow. Far better then to recall, even for a few snatched minutes or with a single song, those pleasant pastures, those torrents of spring as if they were on fast-fading sepia photographs. Recapture, say, the heat, the hustle, the hordes, the festival halycon days when more than a quarter of a million crammed onto an island to hear HIM. And this did then remind her, God how the years fly by like a swooping kingfisher, that it would soon be her eldest's 21st. Robert Allen! What a dignified name. And to think they nearly called him Tarquin after an English hash-dealer who lived on a houseboat in Amsterdam.

"You're a big girl now." Yes, in more ways than one and in the space between songs people change, grow apart, live differently, die differently. "Each man's death diminishes me." Ah, but you were wrong, Preacher Donne, if you but knew it, for in these days it is expected that each man leaves a little for his inheritors, while some leave a lot and others leave a mess to be sorted out by expensive lawyers.

As for the last, the cost, the chaos, the pot of trouble, can be forestalled, pre-empted, emptied, cooled off, by such clever quickie-trickies as the infamous Anton Piller legal procedure.

We will pause here for breath and a proper explanation. The name Anton Piller has been tossed into the story as if it were a golden crumb flung into the pond to make ripples or to feed a mandarin duck that would lay a golden egg. Now, at this point in the tale, it is our duty to add a middle or belly note.

In the 1970s, record companies, jean manufacturers, perfume importers, whisky-makers – nothing tweeny-weeny here, you will note – were quite quite perturbed by the vast quantity of bootleg and pirated imitations on the market; but because of the elephantine nature of the judiciary, ere our legal eagles could swoop on the coop, the assorted birds had flown to lay a few more genuine plastic Faberge eggs. Then a bright laddie, a London QC, persuaded some judges to allow him to descend on the malefactors before they had time to clean their teeth or pull on their trousers, gain entry to the bad chaps' and chappesses' premises and seize whatever was relevant to the case. Thus was born the Anton Piller procedure.

In 1975 the procedure was given the name loved by many in the case of Anton Piller K G versus Manufacturing Processes Ltd. Mr Justice Brightman refused the request for an order because he feared he might become an instrument of oppression; but hardly had the ink dried on his quill or a flea leapt from his wig than Lord Denning overturned the first ruling and formalised the condition for obtaining the order.

It all seemed so easy when Ariadne first heard of this draconian right of entry from someone who had been Pilleraged at dawn; and the coincidence of rediscovering Dad's one-off literary magazine (financed, it was said, by Mum raiding her piggy-bank) turned her mind into a whirligig. There were niggling doubts. For example, when, in the name of history, had Mum ever accumulated sufficient cash to spend on worthy causes? Give her a thousand on Monday and she would be stony broke by Tuesday.

The authorised version of her life story, however, ran thus: Cleo had a passionate period of parsimony, coins and currency notes were put into a screw-top jar and at the end of this long lenten time of monetary fasting, she spilled the golden cascade from her frugal horn and said unto Ivan, "Go forth in the literary ways of the world and multiply."

And whether or not the above is false, Ivan did go forth and multiply to the measure of 2000 copies of South-East London's latest literary magazine, containing the rolling words of Romford poets, Dagenham dithyrambs and Ilford ithyphallics and bearing on its garish cover of twining nubile forms the unique title, OUTFLAGE. OUTFLAGE??

Within the inner recesses of local pubs – before they were extirpated for by-pass surgery – dark mutterings (Title of a later rival magazine, only one issue, which was utterly spoiled by the title being misprinted, Drak Mutherings) discussed the opaque reasoning for the title 'Outflage'. In the opinions of those whose material had not been accepted for the first (and only) issue, Ivan was being too clever for his own good by squashing the words outre and flagrant. "They'd never stand for that on the Mile End Road," his detractors chuntered sententiously.

Alack, Ivan had commissioned an artistically aspiring plumber's apprentice to do the cover, innocently believing that the youth's handling of copper tubes and soil pipes would be manifested in a Neo-Cubist design upon which the magazine's logo, OUTRAGE, would be soldered. Alas, the lad was no Leger, lagging was more in his everyday line, and his only artistic influence was a picture postcard of Renoir's 'Grandes Baigneuses': the four fulsome maidens which he droolingly re-drew in the privacy of his bedroom. On the evening that he settled down to create the cover, he had mislaid some flanges. To steady his nerves and to stimulate his imagination, he had smoked several joints.

All that was long ago and as a Great Man was supposed to have said, "We've passed a lot of water since then." Most of the contributors to Ivan's magazine had gone on to well-deserved obscurity by taking up teaching or social work. One of the others had achieved five seconds of fame with a speech at a Conservative Party conference, another had become a baggy-eyed early-morning arts presenter on TV and a third was completing an Open University course in structuralism at Her Majesty's Pleasure for a multiple-mortgage scam.

Nevertheless Ivan's defunct magazine of umpteen years ago had become a collector's item. Show anybody a shelf of Meissen porcelain bottles, an 18th-century mahogany commode, a pile of shellac records, earthenware hot-water jars or brass toilet-paper holders and their eyes will glaze over. Then say "These are collector's items" and the selfsame orbs will start from their sockets.

How did Ariadne know that Outflage was such a very desirable collector's item? She didn't even know the fathers of some of her children.

The fourth meeting of the Peoples' Charter committee had been long, wrangling and tedious. The contentious point was that everybody was jumping on the Charter bandwagon. Eventually, at 10.29, they agreed by 3 to 1 to rename themselves the 21st Century Committee.

When Ariadne returned from the kitchen with the coffee, the

disillusioned Marxist and the Cyclist-against-the-M25 – his right arm was still in splints – were discussing the slump in house prices and the retired schoolmaster was reading the magazine.

"Thank you, my dear," the old boy said and looked around anxiously for the biscuits. "I do hope you don't think me rude and intrusive by perusing this most interesting, er, which I discovered on the table. I do recognise one or two names." Due to certain bladder problems, he was one of the few who actually saw the early-morning arts programme; but he confused the name of the presenter with the building-society swindler. "I do have quite a library of similar booklets, pamphlets and small magazines myself (under his bed in a battered suitcase), Gertrude Stein's 'A rose is a rose is a rose' opus, for example, most rare and, I should add, collector's items." What he refrained from adding was that he hoped to augment his pension by flogging them.

Ariadne took the magazine from his palsied hands. "And is this a collector's item?"

"Oh, definitely, yes."

She hurried into the kitchen, still grasping the magazine, and just as quickly returned with the biscuits. The question fluttering on her lips – "How much is it worth?" – was already being debated by the trio at the table. The old man was evasive. "It does depend on the rarity value. If this is the only extant copy – well – it is difficult to put a price on it and there are several considerations—"

The Cyclist mentioned a comrade cyclist, now sadly pedalling on the great cinder track in the sky, who had left his grieving widow a garage full of 19th-century bicycles. "Must pay her a visit," he said.The disillusioned Marxist pondered whether there would be a demand for his mint condition – and unread – complete works of Stalin.

Ariadne also pondered but silently. This revelation changed the complexion of her plot from pale endeavour to blushing possibility. If – no, no – when the Piller raid was put into operation, documents relevant to the case would be seized and that could mean remaining copies of the precious Outflage. Even the misprint gave it a quirky value of its own. Should Alex and Angelica be told of this new development? 'Why should they be?' she asked herself. 'Fat lot of help they've given me and, anyway, if the magazine is worth a penny or two (Sub-text, oodles of money) it'll be my bonus.'

She was annoyed with her fellow conspirators. After leaving two unanswered messages on Alex's answering-machine, she managed to catch him between a quiz show and a fifth repeat of a James Bond film.

"Hello, Alex, it's me, Ariadne. (Of course it is you. Who else spoke like that?) How did it go then?"

"How did what go?"

"You know. What you said you'd do. With the electric—"

"Shut up. You never know who might be listening."

"Who'd be listening to us?"

"You never can tell. I mean, with you mixed up with all sort of—"

"Oh paranoia balls. Just say if you did it or not."

"Yes."

"And?"

"And what was the result?"

"How would I know?"

"Well, if you don't know and I don't know, I'd better go ahead with my idea. Are you interested?"

"Of course I'm interested but I can't help you at this moment in time. Anyway, it's your scheme."

She had just as much luck with Angelica. Five phone calls before she had a living reply. "I can't see what I could do to help, Ariadne, but then you're such a brilliant organiser. You see, I've had some rotten news, a friend of mine has died. I'm so upset that I'd only be in your way. Incidentally, have you heard from Mumsie?"

"Excellent organiser indeed," Ariadne snorted when she put the phone down. Of course, Angelica was partly correct. Her sister was like the queen bee, good at rallying busy bodies around her as long as there was a buzzing hive available. Some said that one of her reasons for having a swarm of children was so that she could have a permanent committee of her own.

She did discover the results of Alex's efforts when she rang PC Bob to discuss the logistics of her plan and got Amy instead.

Amy, quivering voice and confused delivery as usual, droned

on about Bob having to do extra patrol duty in the Panda – (pause) – with WPC Wendy and she wasn't sure if his van was available at present because of trouble with the big end and the children were so looking forward to a day in Brighton but anyway the weather wasn't that good and the youngest had a cough and of course she had to go to the doctor with her own complaint and—

Ariadne yawned. Yes, yes, she had heard all this before again and again in one form or another and any moment the trembling voice would become a whimper. She opened her cigarette packet. There were only two left yet she could have sworn there were five. Which one of her brats had filched—?

"And he said, he said," Amy continued, "as long as I don't over-exert myself (I can just imagine her sex life), but with a husband and children to look after – are you still there, Ariadne?"

"Yes, yes, I'm still here."

"You went so quiet. And that reminds me, have you heard about Dad? I'm afraid it's bad news." Was it heart-stopping news? Amy, as we have mentioned, was the only one who kept up a tentative contact with Ivan. "There was an accident in the garage. Wires got caught in the ladder and—" There was a sudden outbreak of pique among Ariadne's little gruntlings and the television volume was turned up "—got electrocuted. Dad may have to go—" Ariadne dropped the receiver, charged over to the set and switched it off. Instant outcry, mutiny in the ranks, set turned back on, lower volume.

"Sorry, Amy. A bit of a riot going on here. Who did you say was electrocuted?"

"Trigger, no, Tiger, no, Tigger, you know their hairy cat. They had it over 14 years."

"And Dad?"

"Oh he's alright. You know what he's like. He's had electric shocks before now. But he told me about a lump—"

Ariadne was not listening. She was thinking. Did her heart jump with filial joy at the news that her father's heart had survived the shock of the patricide device? There was a certain smug pleasure expressed in the thought, 'So, cock-of-the-walk Alex, with your cocksure plan, you've made a cock-up of it.'

Was Ariadne a wholehearted conspirator? We will evade the

answer by reminding one and all that Ariadne was supposed to have a conscience.

She sighed and turned away from thoughts of death. To make the Anton Piller raid legal, it was essential to have the warrant processed by a solicitor. She had spoken to the CARMAD organiser, Shirley, about obtaining one but the woman curtly told her to see the Citizens' Advice Bureau – "If there's any of them bloody well still in operation."

The solution to the problem came about in a coincidental manner only to be found in novels of a particular genre.

The disillusioned Marxist with the fly-blown beard rang up to tell Ariadne that the 21st Century Committee had the same name as an estate agent, a trade association too odious for any right-thinking left-winger to contemplate. He had spoken to the cyclist, who would be away for a week or two seeing the widow in Essex about selling antique bikes. "Bet he's after a cut one way or the other." Perhaps Ariadne could see the schoolmaster, who lived three streets away, about the matter. He added in a disgruntled tone that perhaps they should think of dissolving the committee.

The retired schoolmaster lived in a one-bedroomed flat on the top floor of a distressed town house.

"Come in, my dear, come in." He ushered the fatly panting Ariadne into his gloomy den. "What a pleasure it is to see you. May I offer you some refreshment? I am afraid it's only instant coffee. Do sit down. Yes, just wait a moment till I clear these newspapers."

When he had stopped fussing and doddering, Ariadne told him about the name problem. When she repeated the suggestion about dissolving the committee, he was quite devastated.

"Oh no, no, not really." He sat on the edge of the bed and stared bleakly out of the window at the bleak horizon of roof tops. "I did so like going around to your nice warm apartment and meeting those nice people. It was something for me to look forward to every week and my only chance to have a stimulating conversation. I wanted to feel useful, even at my age."

Ariadne thought it best to divert the conversation into another channel. "Is that magazine I showed you really a collector's item? How much do you think it's worth?"

"Aesthetically or financially?"
"Both."
"Aesthetically, it's mostly rubbish. Financially, if you can find a very keen collector of suchlike trivia, and there are some with less discrimination than sense, I'd say a pound, may be two pounds, at best perhaps five pounds."

So her hoped-for windfall was a rotten apple. She tried a different tack.

"I wasn't actually thinking of the value of the magazine in that manner. You see, some years ago my mother put a lot of money into helping to start the magazine and I'm trying to get some of it back for her. The trouble is, I need a solicitor but the cost—"

"A solicitor!" A tiny spark flickered in his rheumy eyes. "Then look no further. I'm a qualified solicitor."

"But I thought you were a schoolmaster—"

With a certain amount of repetition, he explained that, yes, he had practised law for many years until he had decided – he mumbled something about a messy divorce case – to take up teaching. More socially useful, he added as a justification.

"Ha ha," he cackled. "There's no age limit in law and solicitors, like judges, can continue even if they're a hundred-and-one, ha ha, as I was saying to old what's-his-name, he's seventy-eight if he's a day and still sending them down, when we were having lunch at the Garrick – now when was that? – but never mind all that for the moment, my dear. Do tell me, how may I help you?"

Chapter eighteen

Ivan was very restless. He turned to push cold knees against Sally's calves but this left the rear of his exposed rear overhanging the valance. Five minutes later, he rolled over the roughened sheets and lay on his right. Sally grumbled, followed his movement, shoved him another half-inch towards the edge and murmured, "How'd you get those spots on your back, Jack?" It was not unusual for her to ask gnomic questions of strange men in her sleep and the next day vehemently deny any knowledge of the named person.

Ivan tried to focus on the blinking red figures of the digital clock-cum-radio but since the device had been inadvertently baptised with cold coffee six months ago, it had developed most incontinent behavioural problems. Occasionally the radio would awake and run neurotically through all the stations. As for the flashing numbers, the byte was worse in the dark and the telling of accurate time was capricious rather than chronometrical.

Ivan lay on his back while Sally gently snored. The famous Chinese philosopher, Thai Saih, held that a sturdy mental jog through the open park of the mind was a sure cure for insomnia. But which exercise path should he take? Last week he had calculated the first two hundred prime numbers and had wound up wide awake and wind-blown with utter stupor. An astral body flickered between the curtain-parting. How about listing famous quotes with 'stars' in them. "What is the stars." Now that was his favourite. "The night was in gloom, with no stars in the sky." Ivan softly hummed the tune and sang the end of the quatrain. "Except for the few that were – dum dei dummity – there in your eye." Hold hard there. Does that mean the female of the romantic party was monocular?

Sally nudged him and drowsily asked, "Is that you singing, darling?"

"Sorry. Didn't mean to disturb you."

"It was you, then. I thought it was Harry."

There was nothing for it. He would have to get up, go to the lavatory and have a drink in the kitchen. He was always surprised how the vacant streets in the dead hour of the morning seemed lightly muffled by the winding sheets of cerecloth. Even the night animals, like the vixen he had seen crossing the road once at 3.30am, appeared to be padded in silence.

A battered transit van slid down the road, hesitated for a second outside their house and then crept to a halt beyond a neighbour's laburnum tree. A second or two later a gas-guzzling rust bucket of a once-white car wheezed to a stop just behind the van. "People are always getting lost around here." Just then a 2CV came around the corner, hesitated and continued on.

"Anything to report, Mister Christian?" the voice from the bed imperiously asked.

"Everything's shipshape and Bristol fashion, Captain."

"Very good, Mister Christian, haul up the mainbrace. Nothing to report then, ha ha."

Tomorrow he would ask her about this sub-conscious interest in the mutinous deep. And who the hell were/are Harry and Jack?

REPORTS ON THE EVENTS IMMEDIATELY LEADING UP TO THE SO-CALLED PILLER RAID.

Report No 1. Given by she who is known as Ariadne, self-styled prime organiser of the above incident as she unravels the thread that took the wrong turning down the maze.

'It nearly didn't happen. Everything was against it. I mean, I was up to my eyes in the CARMAD campaign, the Charter committee was falling apart, for instance, the cyclist had decided to stay in Essex with the widow – well, I won't go into that now.

'Anyway, imagine how ghasted was my flabber when Ron the schoolmaster revealed that he was a qualified lawyer. When I told him that I was trying to recover some of my mother's money from my father, who was living with a younger woman, Ron was more than willing to help. And he wouldn't accept a penny for his trouble. "It's something to occupy my mind," he said.

'He knew this ga-ga judge who counter-signed the documents and soon there was the warrant ready for execution. As quick as a shot, I got in contact with Amy's husband Bob to help out with the raid.'

Report No 2.

(Due to certain circumstances, this report is incomplete.)

'I, Ronald Jasper Pharfetch, solicitor, late of McVoid, Nullity, Klause & Kassation firm of solicitors, Old Holborn, specialist in divorce and also Headmaster (rtd) of Scrooge Hall private school in the county of Berkshire, do hereby affirm that on the dates hereunder, under the instructions of my client (space for name) .... and guided by the information supplied to me by the aforesaid client did contact Mr Justice Bumblebee, c/o Garrick Club, on the matter of a warrant to execute—'

Report No 3. Given by Robert Flathead, police constable presently attached to Outer Cheam police station, Surrey.

'Appertaining to the incidents above and below, it is necessary for me to state here and now that my participation was in the nature of a family obligation and, as I was off-duty at the time, could not be regarded as part of my official work as a police officer. It is true I was in uniform at the time in question but I disguised the fact by wearing a trenchcoat and in mitigation, I should add that if a breach of the peace occurred or words said or actions taken which could cause a breach of the peace, which no police officer should condone, I was prepared to unbutton my trenchcoat and reveal my authority.

'Be that as it may, when I was apprised that a warrant had been legally drawn up I made arrangements with Fred Ottermole (Slogan: You are safe in the hands of Ottermole.), licensed bailiffs and poll tax collectors, to rendezvous with certain parties at 0500 hours outside the designated premises.

'I did regret at the time that I could not induce WPC Wendy to be in attendance, a woman's touch is very important in domestic situations, but on reflection it was just as well she had taken a few days' leave to be with a sick friend in Bournemouth.'

Report No 1. Cont'd. (Ariadne). Part 2.

'Of course, I had to take old Ron with us, after all he was the solicitor in charge and he clutched the warrant in his palsied claws for dear life. Funny, I still think of him as the schoolmaster. I didn't fancy dragging him out of his flat at such an ungodly hour and anyway I thought it would be better to keep an eye on him myself, so he stayed the night in my place on one of the children's mattresses. Not that I got a moment's sleep with him wandering in and out of the toilet and then coming over to where I lay to complain of the cold. God, 70-plus with a shrivelled winkler and he was still after a grope. A case of the spirit was willing but the flesh was well past its flashing days.

'I recruited my eldest to come with us. Actually he didn't need any urging once I told him what we were up to. He thought there might be a bit of head-bashing to be done. And to think I named him after Bob Dylan because he was conceived on the Isle of Wight. He was the only one of my children to be expelled from the Woodcraft Folk.

'Anyway, we bundled Ron Pharfetch into the car, wrapped him up in several blankets and off we went while he coughed, gargled and grumbled in the back seat. Bob's van arrived just before us and him and his friend – I wouldn't like to meet that mighty hulk on a dark night – got out and Ottermole had a quick glance at the warrant to make sure it was in order – Ron wouldn't let it out of his hand – and Bob said they were going to effect an entry at the rear. I thought I saw Angelica's car going up the road but I could have been mistaken. I insisted that I should go with them because only I knew what to look for but Bob said I better wait in the car in case of trouble and they would call me when the door was opened, forced was the word he used. My Robert went with them and I saw them stop at the corner under the street lamp, look at the warrant and then count the houses. Ottermole, Ron and my Robert disappeared around the corner and Bob returned to the car. "What's the number of your father's house, Arry?" he asked. I told him. "Jeesus!" he shouted – I didn't know he was religious – and dashed after the other three. '

Ivan's star-quote count had subdued his troubled body. "Catch a falling star and put it in your pocket. Go, and catch a falling star. Get with child a mandrake root. I am undone says your man Donne. And yes, earth is but a star, that once had shone. Hitch your wagon to a star, starry starry night."

Estella slumbered, Sally turned. "Why don't you go to sleep, dear. You're keeping me awake."

"I heard you snoring."

"Don't be a big lump, Joe."

"And then there's the dog star Sirius, Alpha Canis Majoris. You cannot be Sirius."

Muffled sound of dogs barking through the secondary glazing. Who is Joe and why did she have to remind him of the cause of his restlessness. "You'll be the star turn at the hospital when they inspect your lump," she had said as one would speak to a fretful child. And it was to be today. To sleep, perchance to dream and in that dream to see masked monsters, swathed in green plastic, smelling of ether, basilisk eyes staring like dark stars as gloved hands brandish knives of retribution.

As if from a distant planet (could it be Pluto, woofing hound companion of Mickey Mouse?) and through the swirling nebula came the turmoil of angry voices and the agitation of yapping curs. Sally fiercely nudged Ivan. "Do something about that radio." His hand scythed across the cabinet and swept the device to the floor. It squeaked and its red eyes shifted into oblivion. But still the cries of havoc came. Sally sat up. "It's Corgi-and-Beth at the end of the road. I'll never go to sleep again. See what's happening."

The off-white gas-guzzler was revving up with hacking coughs of odorous clouds spewing from its shaking exhaust pipe, its two nearside doors swinging open. A burly youth half-carried, half-dragged what appeared to be a decrepit bundle of rags with legs towards the vehicle. As the car began to reverse, he flung his burden into the rear and then leaped into the passenger seat. The car made a wheel-screeching 180 degree turn across the road onto the pavement and then roared away into the crepuscular haze. Meanwhile two other men came around the corner, their trotting gait hampered by a squad of trouser-tearing corgis. They had just reached the laburnum tree and their van when Corgi-and-Beth's husband thundered towards them, his chest and feet bare, his pants hastily pulled up to full mast.

Ivan slid back the secondary glazing and thumped open a obdurate window to get the full flavour of the altercation. During a full and frank exchange of opinions, a few frictive words associated with violent sexual activity and the male genitalia were instantly recognised by the auditors, though none could quite connect such phrases as "warrant taken out", "wrong information given" and "stuff it up yours". The yapping low-slung animals and the screeching Mrs Corgi-and-Beth kept up an insistent chorus. The bulky man vigorously shook two dogs off his legs while the second man undid his trenchcoat to reveal a policeman's uniform ("Is this an Old Billogram caper?"). Then they jumped back into the van and drove off as if pursued by the hounds of hell. Five minutes later two panda cars screamed up and stayed for over an hour.

The next day the couple toured the immediate neighbourhood, seeking possible witnesses to the affray and confirming descriptions of the assailants and vehicles. Remarkably enough, most people asserted that they had taken sleeping pills and were only hauled from their drug-induced slumbers by the noise of the panda cars. One cantankerous old biddy launched into an acerbic diatribe against the dogs and insisted that the filthy defecating animals be put down forthwith. Neighbourly harmony was hardly helped by Corgi-and-Beth's assertion that if they had their way, aged battleaxes would be put down and save the tax payers a shit-cart load of money. Sally and Ivan had gone to the hospital – see later – and missed the inquisition.

At Ariadne's insistence, an emergency meeting of the plotters was convened on the night normally reserved for the now-defunct 21st Century Committee. With the desertion of the cyclist to the flat fields of Essex and the feathery bed of a recycled widow, the defection of the disillusioned Marxist to a shaven-headed religious cult and the comatose state of the schoolmaster, Ariadne's diary had an unexpected gap.

It had not been an easy day for her. To begin with, there was the problem of Ron. As he rolled on the back seat on the way home from the fiasco of the 5am raid, gasping and gagging sounds came from his throat, his mouth agape and his pallid face luminous with fear. They drove into the forecourt of Saint Jankers and after at least one hour's arguments with an assortment of nurses, receptionists and bleary-eyed interns, he was admitted into one of the few wards open. Ariadne pretended to be his niece but now she had to find out if he had any real relatives living. The caretaker of the block was most stroppy about letting her into

Ron's flat, but when they did enter the suffocatingly musty apartment, all she could find was a crumpled notebook with scribbled names and addresses. To make her effort worthwhile, she took the battered suitcase full of alleged collectors' items. "And to think that a man could live so long," she mused, "and all he possesses is a bag of manky booklets."

When she rang Saint Jankers, she was warned that Ron had not long to live. They advised her to start preparing for his disposal. Disposal?

She had a stand-up row with Robert Allen when he came in to show off his new security-firm uniform and truncheon. He left in a huff to have a jar with his mates. There was a near-riot when she banned a video (The children had pooled their money for its hire) that promised to show an excessive amount of female flesh and robust attendant activities. "What about the inalienable rights of the individual to the freedom of choice?" pertly asked an articulate one who had read a draft of the proposed charter.

Then she had an irate call from Shirley of CARMAD who wanted to know when those bleeding stuffed envelopes would be bleeding well ready. Next Bob rang to say that Ottermole was anxious about the pay for his services. "I mean, it wasn't his fault it was the wrong address and besides, there's the cost of his torn trousers. Ottermole can be a hard man when he wants to be." He added ominously that he would be round later to discuss these matters further.

Ariadne hid in the kitchen while her enraptured children stared at threshing limbs in a deep-pile shag carpet. She had just put the coffee pot on and shakily lit a cigarette when Alex arrived.

"Well then, how did it go?" he asked. Ariadne blustered about waiting until Angelica arrived. "Let's hope she makes it soon," he retorted with a pout as he glanced at his satellite-seeking watch. "I've got things to do, you know, letters to write, matters to sort out." He struck a sullen pose for a few seconds and then began to expostulate about SHE, his ex-wife, and her demands for more money and her threats to deny him access to Michelle and Darren. He was halfway through his secondary anxiety – the wedding, cost of thereof – when Angelica appeared.

She seemed to be slightly distracted. This could be attributed to her fleeting view (head quickly averted) of the flashing flesh on the television. "What's this? A kitchen cabinet?" she quipped as she laid her briefcase on the breakfast bar. "Those cardboard boxes out there—"

"You mean the CARMAD campaign. What about them?"

"Do you know that one is addressed to Dad?"

"And talking of which—" Ariadne and Alex said together.

"Okay, you say what you have to say, Ari."

Ariadne deleted most of the embarrassing details of the failed raid. Alex was incandescent with malice. "You mean to say you trusted a half-deaf, decrepit geriatic to – to, God, words fail me."

"And what about your cock-up?" hissed Ariadne like a stepped-on snake.

To sum up. Results of patricide exercises. Alex: One electrocuted hairy cat and several ditto goldfishes. Ariadne: One comatose ancient on the brink of handing in his final brief and one pair of shredded trousers. Angelica (her part was still in the experimental stage): Demise of one 'dear friend' and one ditto scraggy hound known to his bereaved owner as Jackson Pollock. As yet not ascertained, effects of anon letters to Ivan.

"Let us recapitulate, right," orated Alex. Angelica switched on the secret tape recorder. "Our father ("Who art in Surrey," Angelica murmured) is wilfully neglecting the welfare of his children, right. There's the danger that what is rightfully ours could be left to HER, right. Now, we have reasons to believe that dad had acute heart trouble and—"

"Get on with it, Alex," Ariadne muttered impatiently then, glancing out to the other room, signalled to the others to be silent.

"Hello, hello, family gathering, is it?" Bob stood in the kitchen doorway, his hands behind his back. "Didn't mean to intrude. Just want a private word with Ari."

"That's okay, Bob. Ange and Alex are in on this."

"In that case then – (Pause) – thought I'd mention it but do you know your children are watching a SEX film?"

"It's not a sex film, Bob. It's an educational film about the Third World."

"Oh, educational, did you say. Well, without beating about the bush, Ari, about our phone conversation and (Ariadne rummaged in her handbag) the cost of our (Ariadne began to write out a cheque) our little business, oh, make it out to me and I'll settle with Fred." Ariadne handed him the completed cheque. "What's this? Twenty pounds? If I give this to Fred, he'll go spare."

"That's all I have in the bank. (This was a tiny fibette. She had recently received £50 from the twin's father, along with a curt note announcing that he was commencing court procedures to adopt them.) He'll just have to wait for the rest. How much more does he want?"

"Another twenty might just about cover it. Fred's a business man, not a charity worker. You wouldn't like him to come knocking at your door, would you now?"

"Alex, can you help?"

"I've only got my credit cards with me."

"I'll write you a cheque." Angelica opened her briefcase and laid pens, pencils, chequebook and the brown plastic bottle of tablets on the breakfast bar.

"Hello,what's this?" Bob lurched across the kitchen, picked up the bottle and looked closely at the label. "Where did you find it? No, don't tell me, she left it behind when she was here. She's always doing that. God knows how many times she had to go back to the clinic for a new prescription. Wouldn't mind so much but it cost an arm and a leg for every renewal. If her head wasn't screwed on, though I think there is a screw loose anyway, she'd leave that behind as well."

"Those belong to Amy?"

"Didn't you know then? I thought she told you everything. Her condition was diagnosed after we had the last nipper."

"What condition?"

"High blood pressure, palpitating heart. That's why she has these tablets. The doctor warned her that any excessive exercise or sudden shock and she could drop down dead at our feet."

Chapter nineteen

There comes a point in novels of a certain kind, usually when the author has galloped seven-eighths of the way over the course and is running out of breath for the finish, when a dramatic and startling announcement, denouncement or revelation is made to general consternation.

Examples:

a) Announcement. Enters butler. "Lord Squelch is unable to grant you a divorce, your ladyship. He is lying stone dead in the library."

b) Denouncement: Stern-faced private detective: "Lady Squelch, to hide your guilty secret that the gamekeeper is your illegitimate son by the French pastry cook and knowing that your husband had a weak heart, you crept up behind him in the library and shouted 'Vote Labour'."

c) Revelation: Lady Squelch rises to her feet and rips off bodice to display a hairy chest. "Ha ha, how wrong you are, big Dick. The gamekeeper is the real Lord Squelch as you will see by the family strawberry mark on his right buttock. I am the real gamekeeper begat by the first Lord Squelch and the good plain cook. The body in the library, the so-called second Lord Squelch, was a minor actress of radical lesbian tendencies who once had a part in Prisoner Cell Block H until she staged a riot."

Of course, you may be intrigued by the above playlet and be anxious to know how the resting actress came to her final rest. 'A great loss to the profession.' The Stage. 'A wonderful character actor and a wonderful character to be with.' Elderly actor who could not quite remember her name. 'End of an aura.' Obit in the Guardian. She drank from a poisoned chalice.

But to return to our plot-clotted tale and the revelation that it was Amy's faltering heart at fault. Her siblings immediately made loud protestations of concern for their sister's enfeebled state, urged her stolid husband to take special care of her and vehemently asserted that they, her nearest and dearest, should have been told everything.

Bob was somewhat surprised and a little embarrassed by their reactions and had the sneaking feeling that he was being implicitly blamed. He was not too far off the mark.

After he had left with a smug smile on his phiz and the two cheques – one for him and one for me – snug in his wallet, they sneered at his greed, his mental calibre, his lack of moral integrity, his overweening macho ego and his alleged Panda-car philandering with WPC Wendy.

Alex did advance a modicum of justification for the last mentioned. "Don't suppose Amy's condition has done much for their sex life. Well, just think of it, no sooner has he raised his truncheon than—" Since the date of their wedding was anounced, his affianced had not revealed so much as a bra strap to him. "I want to keep myself pure for you," Dawn had whispered with a becoming blush.

The conclave was interrupted by one of the older children asking Ariadne where she had hidden Chicago Cops V as they had watched the sex video twice and they were absolutely bored with all the bonking. After that, each one of the kitchen trio dwelt on his or her inner thoughts.

Ariadne's inner thoughts: Desolation, desperation, because everything, but nobody special, was getting on top of her. Was she getting too old for all this? And, anyway, what was it all for? The life force was ebbing, great causes were turning to dust and ashes and the centre did not hold. Who said that? Did she really really care about new roadways, old forests, thick-lipped tribes in Patagonia, recycled tin cans, her father's house, her mother's lonely life in Eastbourne? Gawd help me, what if the old biddy came to live here?

Alex's inner thoughts: What a waste of time and effort. Our plans are really and truly scuppered. Now how can I get some money for the wedding? If only Dad wasn't such a tight wad. If only he hadn't got HER watching his every move. I knew right from the beginning that this stupid idea of frightening him to death was a no-hoper – I mean, who thought of it in the first place? Not me. I just went along with it. I'll work out something on my own without these females putting their oars in.

Angelica's inner thoughts: It's imperative for me to take the initiative now. I don't need their total cooperation but I must have their compliance. If they hesitate, I'll tell them they've been recorded.

She was the first to break the silence.

"So, what's our next step?"

Puzzled gazes. "Next step? What do you mean? To do what?"

"To do what we set out to do. To expedite, to execute, to eliminate."

Alex: Well, it's all up the spout now, isn't it? (Thinks: She's all words but no action.)

Ariadne: I don't know, Ange. Perhaps we should wait a while to see how things work out. (Thinks: So far all that this has cost her is money but my nerves are in tatters.)

Angelica: Do I take it then that both of you wish to abandon the scheme, regardless of the fact that you, Amy and Mum would benefit to a great degree from its success— (Thinks: As I expected. One has been made cowardly by conscience and the other by consequences.)

Sister and brother protested their fidelity to the concept but—but!

Angelica: And in spite of what you said? (Thinks as she clicks switch on hidden tape recorder.)

Tinny voice of Ariadne. Startled sister cries, "What's this? What's this. Turn it up. I can't hear a word."

The phone rings, stops, child calls out, "Mum, it's for you from the hospital. Says your uncle is in a bad way."

Ariadne hurtles out of the kitchen. Angelica follows her and returns within seconds with a CARMAD box. Alex is leaning over the briefcase. "Have you got a cassette in that? Bloody hell, I didn't think even you would go as far as that."

"I'll go as far as necessary to finish what we promised and if needs must and the devil drives I'll drag you both behind me on the trail."

There was an unsprung tension in her thin body and an intensity in her dilated eyes. From where Alex was standing, they looked like Catherine Wheels. He was lost for an immediate response, either banal, which was his wont, or profound, in which he was usually found wanting. He had made an uncomfortable discovery about his 'little sister'. She was possessed in her obsession with a charged force beyond his comprehension or control. This frightened him. The bustling return of the fretting Ariadne might be the diversion he required to reassert his masculine prerogative.

"What am I going to do, I ask you, what am I going to do?" Her hand shook as she prodded a cigarette into her mouth. "Where's those effing matches? Why, why, did I say I was his niece? I must have been mad to start this whole Piller thing, mad to recruit that dodderer."

"Get a hold on yourself, Ari," Alex ordered, ever ready with an off-the-peg cliche in a crisis. "What are you on about?"

"Him. Ron. The old fool of a so-called solicitor. The hospital said he's fading and they want me over there to sign this and that and God only knows what else. Where's that address book? He must have some real relatives living somewhere." She began to root in her capacious and overflowing shoulder bag. "I must have put it into the box with all those manky booklets he had under his bed.I had to throw his stinking suitcase on the skip. Now where did I leave the box?"

With a tight condescending smile for female foibles, Alex began, "Quite frankly, Ari, you should have done a feasibility study before you—" but his distracted sister was not paying attention to his lecture. "What's that doing here?" she asked, pointing to the CARMAD box now resting on Angelica's briefcase.

"I am taking this home," said Angelica indifferently.

"But you can't. Shirley will be around tomorrow – no, damn it – if I've got to go to the hospital – wait, she said it'll be tomorrow evening or the next day. Are the leaflets with the envelopes?" She flipped back the cover. "Yes, they're there. If Shirley comes tomorrow—"

"Tomorrow, tomorrow, tomorrow. I'll bring it back tomorrow evening."

"But why, why are you taking it?"

"Have you seen who'll be getting this bundle of agitation?

Who'll be the licker of envelopes and paster-on of labels? Our father who art in Surrey."

"I don't quite understand what you intend to do."

"I intend to do what you and Alex have singularly failed to do. I intend to score a direct hit."

Angelica strode through the main room with her double burden. The sounds of crashing cars and zinging of ricocheting bullets from that much-beloved classic Chicago Cops V overrode Ariadne's call, "But, Angie, I haven't heard your tape."

"You wouldn't want to hear what's on the tape, Ari."

"Why? It's only us talking and—" She stared hard at her brother. "You mean she's recorded us— the bitch!"

"Exactly. She thinks she has a hold on us now. Just to go along with whatever smart-arse scheme she's concocting. Well, I'll show her who's the real brains of this outfit." Without another word of fond farewell, he marched out, leaped into his car and drove home at an inordinate speed, all the time muttering, "I'll show her, I will, I'll show her who's the real brains of this family."

Angelica laid briefcase and cardboard box on the table, slid Faure's Requiem into the CD player, stripped, went into the shower and as the scalding water doused her body, cried out, "Tomorrow, tomorrow and yet, tomorrow."

Chapter twenty

"Tomorrow is another day," Sally sang with less trill than tune and no thought to compete with the chirruping sparrows squabbling on the food table. The cautious cats watched the avian marital conflicts and their tails twitched with dreams of crushed bones and scattered feathers.

She remembered the correct adjective and resang the verse, "Tomorrow is a lurverly day," then sighed, looked in the mirror and quoted, "I have forgot much, Cynara! gone with the wind, flung roses, roses, riotously, with the throng." But wasn't Cynara a blowzy barmaid with a capacious bosom? Tomorrow, but yes, lovely tomorrow and tomorrow must be another day that creeps in this petty pace.Yet, what if it was announced on radio, television, in brazen headlines, that tomorrow would not be another day?

"It has been officially confirmed that as from midnight tonight recorded time will cease to be recorded and tomorrow is not another day. We are now going over to Downing Street where our reporter, Gavin Galeworthy, is waiting to bring to us the latest news on this untimely event."

Tomorrow and tomorrow will be blank, the contours bleached to shadeless and shapeless hours. Tomorrow Ivan was to go into hospital for his underarm op, the extirpation of his lump, the removal of his cancerous – no, change that – rancorous malignity. Then why warble instead of being woebegone? Perhaps it was a way of fighting back the tears? Perhaps it was the smile on the face of the clown while his/her heart was breaking? Perhaps we are running out of cliches. Perhaps we should sing another song.

"On with the (prolonged note) motley." Multicoloured dress from the Next line of floppy wear heaved over head and shoulders and stretched over wriggling hips. "The paint and the powder." Outline rim of blinking lid. Flip-flop downstairs to smile benignly at grousy-faced husband.

Brightly. "Tomorrow is another day."

Morose visage turns as mind stops contemplating the last days of Socrates. The apt, though amended, quote, "Tomorrow I will say, but already it is time to depart, for me to die, for you to go on living," was swallowed with the bitter drink. (Suddy Guinness stout drained from a gas-exploding canister.) Instead, the reply was a whimsical, "If you had a tune, you could sing that."

Choral commencement of cantata BWV 12 (Not to be confused with BMW 12), mixed polyphonic harmonies with the themes of separate emotions. 'Weinen, Klagen,/Sorgen, Zagen,/Angst und Not (Rough neo-Gothic translation. 'Weeping, Lamenting,/ Worrying, Fearing,/ Anxiety and Distress.')

"Does he know," thought Sally fatuously, "that the spectral shape of Mister Hodgkins might be standing by the hospital bed with the sickle of his namesake disease grasped in his phantom hand?"

Last week they had gone to Saint Jankers with the re-sealed letter to see Cucumber's designated specialist. After 20 minutes of mis-directions from clipboard-clutching women with curt accents, traipsing along tiled passages, hurrying through cluttered corridors (time was running short) panting up and down stairs, their progress impeded by the limping, the halting and the decrepit, they met a surly West Indian woman swabbing the flags. She indicated, with a wave of her hand, their ultimate destination. It was five yards from their starting point.

Halfway through their ill-guided tour of the labyrinth, Sally caught a glimpse of a vaguely familar form. "Perhaps I'm mistaken. The world is full of fat women."

The large waiting-room was crowded with park benches and the afflicted of all ages. "Take a seat. You'll be called in five minutes," the receptionist told them crisply. An ancient man with a red dribbling nose and a yapping cough moved up to give them room. "Lungs full of soot, they say, 'cos of the fags," he said, "but I says it's me weak chest on account of lifting them hods in all weathers all me life. What do they know, I ask you.If you stop us smoking, what's left for the working man these days with the price of beer as it is."

When the hod-carrier was called, Sally and Ivan sat close

together hand in hand. "We're like Thomas Hardy's pair of lovers sitting on a seat near Tooting Common," Sally said.

"Remember – 'Two linked loiterers, wan and downcast;/ Some heavy thought constrained each face,/ And blinded them to time and place.' "

"They did not sit. They were walking slowly, whispering sadly."

As call followed call, those summoned rose wearily and walked slowly towards a curtained alcove. Some whispered sadly to their waiting companion on their return.

Thirty minutes later, Ivan was called. A rotund woman of middling years took his place. "I don't know, I just don't know," she beamed at Sally. "If it's not one thing, it's another. It was about a month ago – no, I tell a lie – it was the day after Jack, that's my husband, went back to work after being six months out on account of his gall stones. I started to have rheumatoid arthritis in my arms, shoulders, hands, you know I couldn't put a thing to my mouth. It could've been the worry—" The woman listed an alphabetical list of complaints from arthritis to ulcers.

A man with a scaffolding structure round his torso lowered himself carefully on the seat and detailed his ten-year history of stomach operations. "I'll tell you for nothing, it's like bleeding Clapham Junction."

An Egyptian mummy sat on a wheelchair opposite Sally. Bandages covered everything except his yellow face. He smiled shyly and began to unravel the windings around his head.

"Excuse me," Sally said to the chatterer, "I must catch a breath of air" and quickly walked outside.

The cleaner slapped the wet mophead on the slabs and glared at a portly young woman dashing by.

"Ariadne!" Sally called out. A startled face turned towards her and then, as if damnation was imminent, the quarry disappeared round the side of a building. "Wait, I've something to say to you." But what? A few blistering words about anonymous letters of poisonous import and malevolent phone calls? Whatever Sally said would be relayed back to her Medusa-faced sister, a great loss to M15.

"That Missy come messing my floor," the elderly cleaner grumbled.

"Is she visiting somebody?"

"Unless she's the angel of death. She's come out of Intensive."

"Sally, there you are." Ivan was standing in the doorway. "They said you were out here." When they re-entered, the multi-afflicted woman grinned. "You found her, then. I knew she couldn't have gone far."

A tousled-haired young man and an close-cropped young woman, both wearing white coats and carrying clipboards like driving examiners, stood behind the desk, watching the receptionist pound the computer terminal."Just working out when we can fit your husband in."

"Is it something serious?"

"No, no, shouldn't be," said the young man cheerfully. "A little problem with the lymph gland (That should please Cucumber), more than likely cat-scratch fever, you do have a few moggies, easier to get rid of them than your husband, ha ha. A snick here, a snip there, zip him up again and then it's a matter of waiting for the lab report."

"It looks as if we haven't got a bed available at this moment in time," said the receptionist, "but—"

"Three Caesarians tomorrow, chop-chop, quick and cost-effective, two varicoses can be decanted, at least one terminal due to expire, so, in total that clears six items, our present client is an in-and-out item, two-three days at the most, no complications—"

The admins went into a huddle and a minute later Sally and Ivan left with a chit for his admittance in a week's time.

Sally said nothing about seeing Ariadne; nor did she mention a third anon letter received, and now hidden in her knickers, this morning.

On that very day on the other side of London, an obnoxious stew had been brewed and was gently cooling in the miniscule bathroom behind the shower curtain while the potion's acidic whiff was being smothered by sprays (ecologically sound and ozone-friendly) of lavender essence. Then the concocter of this mixture cleared the debris into the waste bin and decided to relax for five minutes with a cup of caffeine-free coffee and the sonority of Brahms' Requiem.

Imperative knock-knock. Angelica frowns, forgets chain lock and opens door fully. Two men in large raincoats stand on the threshold. We have met them before.

Olly: (Plump going on for obese. Age approx 45.) Afternoon, Miss.

Stan: (Thin going on for scrawny. Age approx 35.) Afternoon, Miss.

Olly: We were passing by this way, miss, and I said to Stan, let's call in and see if the young woman is at home and save us a second journey. Isn't that right, Stan?

Stan: Yes, Olly, that's what you said and I said, she'll be at work, on account of being a career woman with executive responsibilities. (He hissed slightly on the last word.)

Olly: And you were wrong, weren't you, Stan. That is, wrong about her being at work. We all must have a day off now and then, just to get away from the stress and strain. A change is good as a rest.

Angelica: What do you want?

Stan: We don't want anything, miss.

Olly: But before we answer let's ask you a question. Do you often do that?

Angelica: Do?

Stan: Yes, miss, do you often open your door to strange men?

Olly: Because if you do, take my word as a policeman, you shouldn't, the way things are. And in the long run, it's us who's left to clear up the mess.

Stan: And if it's all the same to you, miss, it's better we talk behind closed doors.

(As on the first occasion, Stan peeped into the kitchenette, gawped at the CD player and the books and then looked closely at the glass figurines. Olly stood by the desk and slowly withdrew a notebook as if it were a penis at a hen party.)

Olly: (Slowly as he reads from the notebook.) Enquiries

appertaining to the unfortunate demise of miss mumble mumble. It has now been ascertained that the said young woman suffered her untimely death as a consequence of ingesting a noxious substance, nature unknown as no trace of any noxious substance was found among her belongings.

Angelica: I know.

Stan: (Sharply) You know what, miss? The nature of the substance?

Angelica: (Slightly flustered) No, no, not that. I know that my friend – that is – she was an acquaintance, we went to the theatre – that is, I know she died as you said.

Olly: Oh, and how do you know?

Angelica: (Pertly) Because you told me.

(Both men seemed a bit crestfallen.)

Olly: (Returning notebook to pocket) In that case, miss, there's nothing more to say. Just thought it best to keep you fully informed on the progress of our enquiries.

Stan: Seeing as how she was a close friend of yours.

(Angelica opens door for them to depart.)

Olly: (Sniffs) Been cooking, Miss? I can smell the vinegar. My missus can't stand vinegar.

Stan: (In doorway. Takes out crumpled letter) I think this belongs to you, miss. We must have picked it by mistake the last time we were here.

Angelica: (Takes letter) Oh, yes. It's from my ex-husband, Kevin.

Olly: Funny name for a dog, Jackson Pollock. Seems it was poisoned.

Stan: I wouldn't be surprised if it wasn't one of them animal libbers.

Olly: Dare say you're right. Funny old world. We'll let you know, miss, if there's any more progress.

Scene from another time in two parts. Part one. "Angelica dear, will you be a darling and see that everything is alright in the kitchen while I have a little chat with Cedric." (Or Harry or Stephen or Fred or Bill.)

Cedric: (or clammy-handed Harry or leering Fred or tobaccostinkard Fred or after-shaved Bill) "No need to hurry, young lady, ha ha."

Part two: Almost near the end of the meal. "Cedric (or Harry or et al), what is the matter? You looked flushed (or deadly pale). Are you alright?"

Distraught man staggers to feet: "Don't worry. It's nothing. A bit queasy, that's all. Food too rich for me. Where's your—" Exit in haste.

Discomfited hostess blames wine brought by guest. "It did taste vinegary to me. Trust him to buy some cheap plonk."

Angelica now made her coffee, slid Brahms' Requiem into the player, placed the CARMAD box under the desk, brought the pan of obnoxious brew – now cool and viscous – from the shower, slipped rubber gloves on her hands and, with a small water- colour brush, painted the sticky part of each envelope with a daub of the concoction.

Ariadne's crowded place had been invaded by the bulky presence of the CARMAD commissar, Shirley, who, in between pantingly orating on the absolute necessity of total involvement in this absolutely vital campaign, inspected each box and commanded the traffic of reluctant volunteers (the children) taking the passed boxes down to her station-wagon. "Ah, let me see that one. Yes, you shouldn't have bothered bringing it up. It's for the Southern region. Should have put it straight into my car. Are we absolutely clear now?

"Absolutely."

"Excellent, absolutely excellent. You've been an absolute brick, Ariadne. Helped us no end. No time to stand and talk. Have to get this show on the road, ha ha, no pun intended. Must dash before the evening build-up. Absolutely horrendous. What we need is a unified transport policy. Ta ra for now."

Rather than being run down in the doorway by the departing Shirley at full throttle, Alex sidled into the landing lay-by to let her pass unimpeded. Freed of the necessity to stand on ceremony, Ariadne merely greeted her brother with, "Didn't expect to see you, Alex," as she harried her brood into preparing for the evening meal.

"How many times have I told you, not there, you clot. Bridgy, it's your turn to butter the bread, yes, it is. Duane, wipe your sister's nose. No, no, no telly while you're eating. I don't care if you do miss Star Trek or whatever. Well, it's not my fault we're late. That bloody woman would call at this hour. Easy to tell she's got no kids."

Alex stood beside Angelica at the window. "Are you recording all this?" he asked. "Makes a difference to tape a family at tea, doesn't it, instead of selected bits you can use for blackmail."

"Blackmail!" It was on the tip of her tongue to add the cliche "is an ugly word" but she refrained, knowing he was void of any humour, subtle or black. "Don't be such a pompous ass, Alex."

He sucked his lower lip in between his teeth. "Our little sister has certainly changed for the worse," he thought to himself. "And no wonder. She hasn't had a proper man since that wimp, Kev. I suppose that's why she's taken up with them dykes. It's not natural." Ariadne bustled over to them. "Well, that's got them settled down to their scoffing. Wish I could get them silent as well. It looks as if I'm going to lose two of them, the twins, anyhow. Their father is trying to adopt them legally. Perhaps they'll be better off." A passing cloud of weariness shaded her face. "If I miss them too badly, I'll just go ahead and find others to take their place." She shrugged her shoulders as if to unload the present cares from her back." Let's have a cup of coffee. I'm dying for a fag and a few minutes' peace and quiet."

As the conspiratorial kitchen cabinet had no agenda or even agendum, Ariadne led off with a generalised question to Alex. "It's rare to see you more than twice in any one week. To what do we owe the pleasure?"

"I – er – that is, I wanted to know what Angie intended to do with that box of envelopes. Also I – er – (Hesitation) where can I find Shamus?'

"Shamus?" both sisters exclaimed. They had very different reasons for their startled responses.

"God only knows where Bridgy's father is at any one time," said Ariadne, "but if he is in town you'll more than likely find in him at the Cuchulain Catholic Youth Club. What on earth do you want to see him for?"

Angelica's reason, if you can call it reasonable, was a sharply suppressed and fiercely self-denied inner lurch at the mention of the Celtic charmer's name. She said nothing of this to the others.

Alex implied that he wished to talk with Shamus about computer technology.

"Are you kidding? Computer technology?" Scornful Ariadne obviously did not believe him. "That bog-trotter wouldn't know how to switch on an electric light even if he was caught in the dark without a box of matches."

"Women don't understand these things," said Alex loftily and then adroitly turned the spotlight on Angelica by asserting that as they were all party to the conspiracy – "And you made sure of that by taping our conversations" (Tight-lipped Ariadne threw a wary glance at the black briefcase.) – she should tell them how exactly she intended to execute her plan to execute their father.

Angelica's original half-formed plan was to paste the sticky part of a stamped addressed envelope with a vile substance and then, by some means not yet worked out, have the hapless Ivan lick-seal it. The beauty of the idea was that the returned letter would take with it all traces of the vile substance. Her dear departed friend and Kev's lurcher Jackson Pollock were the unfortunate laboratory rats in the initial experiment, hence the ominous visit of Stan and Olly. She was annoyed with herself for the drastic results of the overdose. She was a very precise person and had only intended to create an interesting tummy-bug with the first operation.

The idea had come to Angelica when she read a Freeman Wills Croft crime novel in which a naughty nephew sent digitalis smeared s.a.e to his wealthy aunt. She did not think it relevant to mention this, nor did she think it necessary to reveal the prescription to her siblings. It might give them ideas and she would be most suspicious if she started to get s.a.e.s herself.

And what is the formula? you may ask. For the sake of all wealthy aunts with dicky hearts, troublesome ex-husbands and ex-wives and others for whom someone out there nurses a stubborn grudge, we shall refrain from explaining the ingredients. If you are really interested in forensic science, an armful of specialist books should repay your studies.

Alex declared that the scheme was too clever by half and he was full of objections. "What if Dad used a sponge instead of licking the envelopes?" Answer: He was a great nibbler of biscuits and the substance would be transferred from damp fingers to food. "What if he didn't bother sending off the envelopes?" Answer: If he had promised to do it for one of his interminable worthy causes, he would keep his word. He spends more time with bleeding hearts than he ever did with his children. And so on.

"When shall we know it has succeeded?" Ariadne asked.

"You mean, if it succeeds?"

"It will."

"And then – what?"

Alex puffed out his chest to display his leadership qualities. "And then, if this is successful, we shall, all of us, be around to their place like a shot and be fully prepared to check and counter-check everything and I mean everything, there's a lot there that's rightfully ours, and I for one will not put up with any of HER nonsense." He inspected his satellite-seeking watch. "But if it's not successful, well, all I'll say for now is that there's more than one way to kill a goose. I'm off now. I've other things to see to. Where did you say this youth club is?"

"Just off the Kilburn Road near the Tricycle Theatre. Ask anybody with an Irish accent. Are you going to see Shamus?" But he was going through the main door by then. "The idiot thinks sliddery Shamus is hand and glove with the IRA. He'll have quite a surprise, he will."

"I must go as well, Ariadne. I've a few letters to write."

"What do we do now, Angie?"

"We wait. That's what we'll do."

Chapter twenty-one

"We've been waiting here for hours." It was not quite true but the tension stretched every second into a minute and every minute into an age."Have you everything you need? Books? What did you bring? The Catastrophe Theory! Oh, Ivan, do you really think this is bed-time reading? Sorry, darling, didn't mean to nag. It's your warped sense of humour. Look, I bought you a new pair of pyjamas. I can't have you wearing those institutional long johns. They make you look like an old—"

A young nurse approached them. "Will you come this way, please."

"She's pretty. Don't you dare flirt with her. Some men really fancy women in uniforms. It must be the starch."

"I'm afraid you can't come in with (looks hard at Sally and then glances at pink form) your husband. If you'd like to wait until he's settled, you'll be let into the ward for a few minutes to say goodbye."

Say goodbye.

Goodbye.

"Hello there. Is it yourself, Alexander?" It was years since Alex's full name had been used. If the speaker had not been standing right in front of him, smiling like a sweaty Puck garbed in garish shorts and emerald green vest, Alex would have looked around for the other Alexander.

The smile was replaced by a frown of concern. "Is Bridgit all right then? There's nothing the matter with your sister, is there? She's a big-hearted woman, God bless her, always doing something for somebody and wearing herself down to the bone. I've said to her myself, time and time again, the poor and the pitiful—"

As if adrift on the Liffey at full spate, Alex clung to the small raft of consciousness and waited till the garrulous flow slowed to an eddy. "Bridgit is as fit as a fiddle," he replied to the first question. And as there was no evidence of his big sister being worn down to the bone, quite the contrary, he added helpfully, "Ari, I mean, Ariadne is gameball." He had never heard the expression till tonight when he was passing the Biddy Mulligan pub. One enormous Paddy shouted to another potato-eater, "And tell me, how's the udder man?" and the second bawled back, "Ah, yer man's gameball, gameball."

The word was not foreign to Shamus. He uttered a pious platitude of thanks to the Almighty for keeping a divine eye on his two favourite females and then, with a slight hint of suspicious hardness, asked Alex why he had called into the youth club.

"I was on my way to somewhere else and as I was passing the Tricycle Theatre (he had passed the theatre twice and missed it both times) I thought I'd pop into the youth club, Arry told me you might be here, and ask you out for a jar."

"A jar, is it? Now that's a lovely thought on a hot sticky night. If you'll hang on here I'll go and make myself decent and put on my walking-out clothes."

To while away the waiting-time, Alex strolled along the right-hand aisle of the long hall. The centre floor was occupied by several ping-pong tables where energetic youths slammed the white plastic balls back and forth, a large, very battered billiard table and a pool table. The last two were surrounded by hustlers bellowing encouragement or disparagement at each other in unecclesiastical language. Those who were not displaying their sportsmanship were sitting by the walls. Apart from two nubile girls, who giggled when he smiled at them (Jail bait, thought man-of-the-world Alex), none took any notice of him.

"Of course, this could be just a front for the IRA where they do their recruiting. Perhaps the posters around the walls will give a clue." Excursions to Lourdes. Special rates for senior citizens, students and unwaged. Excursions to Knock. Ditto special rates. Grand ceilidh and old-tyme dance on Saturday at the National. Car boot sale. Rose of Tralee beauty contest. Back from their whirlwind world tour, The O'Flathery Singers and McNamara's famous band. Ah ha, perhaps there is a coded message in that last one.

"Are you fit to face the night air, Alexander?" Shamus called from beneath the exit sign and then turned to have a few words with a pair of bulky men lounging in the doorway. Dressed as he was in a dark navy blue raincoat, black trousers and black shoes, he was a different man entirely from the laughing-boy image he usually presented. Alex wondered why he had the collar of his coat turned up around his neck. Outside the hall he took Alex's arm and guided him away from Kilburn High Street towards a narrow street and into a dingy public house. "It's a bit quieter in here with none of that loudspeaker music blasting the senses out of your head."

It was also gloomy and nearly empty, apart from a couple of ancients muddling through their half-pints in a corner.They had no bother finding a secluded alcove though they had a little local difficulty in urging the sullen barman to stop washing glasses and take their order. When their drinks were on the table, a lager for Alex and a pint of stout for Shamus, the latter asked, again with hardness in his tone, "What is your problem, Alexander?"

Alex had not expected such directness. "Problem, Shamus? I didn't say I had a problem."

"I'd dearly love to believe, Alexander, that you were on your way to an unknown destination when it came to your mind to have a convivial evening with a man who could have been, if God had not willed it otherwise, a relative of yours by marriage but—"

"I often wondered why Ariadne and you didn't—I mean, with Bridgit—"

"The truth of it is that your sister, a woman who's full of love for all humanity, a love she gives generously with her body and soul (Is he talking about Ariadne or Mary Magdalene?), declined my offer and left me free to find my true vocation. Has she told you, but no, she couldn't because I haven't asked her yet, that I'm thinking of giving Bridgit a long holiday on my brother's farm near Ballymoe? It'll give the little girl a taste for the old country."

"Talking of which, I mean the old country, I suppose you're very much involved in the Cause."

"The Cause? The cause of what?"

"You know, Ulster, Troops Out, the Troubles, the shooting, the bombing, all that sort of thing," explained Alex laboriously.

"The poet was wrong. It wasn't a terrible beauty but a terrible tragedy that was born."

"There's some who'd say the end justifies the means," said Alex hopefully.

Shamus laughed but there was no mirth in it. "Every tin-pot tyrant and demagogue trots out that little misquotation when they're starting their devilment and—"

They both looked up with startled surprise. "They told me I would find you here," said Angelica.

Shamus hastily rose, his face beaming as he reached out to lay a hand on the new arrival's arm. She will pull away from him, thought Alex, and give him one of her man-hating glares. But she did neither and produced what was to her brother's eyes a sickly-sweet smile.

"Alexander and I were firing the first shots, if you'll excuse the bellicose metaphor, of what could prove to be a most interesting philosophical debate with theological overtones."

Baffled Alex wonders, "Why is he mouthing all those big words? Is he trying to impress her? Holy cow, she looks as if she is impressed."

"And what is the theme of this discussion?"

"The inapt phrase ineptly used and misused – ha, but hold hard, what must you think of me not offering you a sweet drop to add to your honey. What will you have?"

"A glass of dry white wine."

"Well now, we might be disappointed there. The only wine they ever stock in this place is some dreadful red biddy but – " He leaned over, winked and touched Angelica's hand " – let me tell you, they've stowed a few bottles of the finest brandy in their sanctum sanctorum for the local clergy who call in after a dry hour or two of hearing confessions. I'll go and give old sourpuss a holy order."

When Shamus went up to the bar, Alex clacked his teeth together like a snapping turtle, poked his snout at Angelica and hissed,"What the hell are you doing here?"

"I'd ask the same of you but I have my suspicions and I think they're well founded. You think he's involved with—"

"This is my pitch and I'll handle it my way without any interference from you or any other busybody."

"And you imagine, and this is about the only time you've ever used your imagination, that he'll obtain explosives—"

"Who said so?"

Angelica tapped her briefcase. "You did. Would you like me to replay the relevant section? Listen to me, Alex,I don't want him involved."

"Oh, why not? Gone a bit soft on him, have you? Bit of a turn-up for the books, isn't it?"

"And what books would they be?" Shamus stood by the table, a balloon glass of the finest brandy in one hand and a half of lager in the other. "Kant's Critique of Pure Reason or the collected works of Saint Ignatius Loyola?"

Alex wished that the blathering Irishman, if he must talk about books, would at least stick to those that were reviewed in The Sun or The Star. Angelica asked, half in jest, whether Shamus had read Kant.

"Why, my dear girl, it was a categorical imperative that I should cut my wisdom teeth on both Kant and Hegel. Now, where were we? Ah yes, Alexander was about to expound on the causes that would justify the unjust phrase, the end justifies the means. Am I not right, Alexander?"

Alex had the same panicky pant-wetting feeling he used to have when called upon by the teacher to face the class and read out his essay on what he did during his holidays. He glanced sharply at Shamus and then Angelica. The first had a benign smile and the second fixed him with an unremitting stare.

"Well, for instance, and this is off the top of my head, suppose there was a man of property who neglected his children, refused to ever give them a penny no matter how unfortunate their circumstances and suppose, just for the sake of argument, late in his life he marries a young woman with the full intention of depriving his children of everything—"

Shamus raised his right hand as if to give a papal blessing. "Is your father an evil man then, Alexander? Is he, Angelica?"

"Well, not exactly. That is to say—"

"Then why are you contemplating evil? Even the worse among us is not beyond redemption."

Alex wriggled uncomfortably in his seat. The least of his contemplation was redemption. And this peculiar talk, this God-slot-on-Sunday waffle, was most unnatural in a well-established drinking den. "Well, Shamus, as They Say—"

"So you are also familiar with the famous Chinese philosopher, Thai Sai?"

"No, Shamus, yes, Shamus. (What was he on about?) I was just about to say that it's better to choose the lesser of two evils."

"Ah, yes, but the response to that was given by the blessed Hannah Arendt herself when she remarked that even if you choose the lesser, you still choose evil. Which brings us back in one fell swipe to the teleological implication of your a priori thesis, that is, the end justifies the means."

The sullen barman, who was busy wiping glasses and quietly humming the opening choral of Bach's Cantata No.140 (he had difficulties with the German words), stopped both activities to lean on the counter and lend an ear to the discussion. The ancients turned to peer at the group. Alex began to have a headache and looked to his sister to save him from this barrage of big words, but she seemed lost in reflective thoughts.

Angelica's reflective thoughts: It's not every day you would find a philosopher sitting in a back-street pub off the Kilburn Road, particularly one who's young, articulate and knowledgeable in the names of the sages. Would he be versed in the poets? Be wise to writers? Harmonise with the musicians? Not in a month of Sundays would the likes of him be found in an accountancy office. Those louts, with their beery breaths, sweaty armpits barely smothered by lashing of pungent aftershave, loud braggart boasting – none could compare with him – can I compare thee to a summer day in Academe. Perhaps! Perhaps when the family affair has been laid to rest – no pun intended – an arrangement could be made, something of a Platonic nature, of course, more of an intellectual companion, by which they would enjoy a night here, a night there, the theatre, say, or a concert, is he fond of chamber music? And afterwards, a quiet meal, conversation, explore post-existentialism, exchange books, and then? Then there will never again be the need to sit on hard benches in a gloomy, smelly Fringe community centre to watch mawkish "women's" plays and listen to strident arguments among the converted and the committed.

"What do you think, Angie?"

"I think your ideas, Alex, are either criminally stupid or dangerously insane and—"

"Have you gone deaf or something? I'm not asking your opinion on my ideas. You've made that clear enough already. What do you think of what Shamus was saying?"

"I'm sorry, Shamus. I let my attention wander."

"And who can blame you, my dear girl, when a couple of old gasbags are blathering away with their teleology here and their sophistry there, not to mention a touch of solipsism—"

"And not forgetting Socrates," the barman called out.

"Ah yes, Mister Crito, there is the irony in the soul to be remembered and there's no escaping that."

"You never said a truer word."

"Please accept my apologies, Shamus, and—"

"No apologies needed, Angelica, but an apologia shall be given."

There was the same flicker of a wink, the gentle tap on the hand, the inclination of the head. A slight smother of dampness shone on his face. Why does he sit there muffled up to the chin?

"As I was saying to your dear brother." The dear brother raised his arm to scrutinise his satellite-seeking watch in the manner of one whose next phrase, when a breathing space was available, would be an apology for a hasty departure.

Shamus gave the gesture a time-lapse of a second's attention and then continued, "The Jesuits were unjustly condemned for coining the maxim, the end justified the means, but that coin was not of their making and what is presented as the currency of politics and false doctrines is a base forgery. The statement itself is preposterous and defies logic for the morality of the methods taken to achieve a goal is determined by the purity or impurity of the ultimate purpose. If that is evil then the means, no matter how sanctified by received morality, are evil; but if the end transcends man's moral truths, the means used are a matter of indifference. Take a modern instance when a policeman strangled a mad dog that was attacking children. Was he not morally correct to use that means to save lives? But if he had done so because killing gave him joy, then his joy was evil and the means were evil. Or consider a more literary example: Hamlet's dithering about killing his father – " Both Angelica and Alex stiffened – "or should I say, stepfather, when he discovered the man at prayer. Obviously, being well-read people, you are familiar with the drama and there's no need—"

There was a need for Alex, made categorically imperative by the throbbing pain to his over-taxed brain, to seek familiar territory of banality away from this preaching Paddy. "This is all very interesting, Shamus, but I didn't come here for a debating society—" He pushed back his chair.

"Hold hard there, Alex old son. I take your point of order and as chairman of this debating society I declare a natural break. Will you have the same again or would you like a drop of the hard stuff? Persuade him to stay, Angelica."

"Another five minutes of your time, Alex, wouldn't go amiss."

"You're a darling girl, Angelica. I'm beginning to feel the heat of the argument."

"Why don't you take off your coat, Shamus."

"I suppose it's better to divest than be defrocked. Did you hear the joke about the pub in Dublin where the literati go for a jar? It's said to be full of defrocked Prousts."

"You argue like a Jesuit priest yourself, Shamus."

"And why not, why not indeed." Shamus stood up, turned towards the bar and began to undo his overcoat. "The same again, Mister Crito."

"I anticipated you there, Father (Father??) and the Guinness was slithering into the glass before you could say three Hail Marys and a Glory Be To The Father. (Father again?) And a half of leeched bog water for the udder man and a schooner of ecclesiastical caprice at full sail for the young lady, is it then?"

"I'll see to it you have a soft penance for your sins when you care to give us a call, Mister Crito."

The old ones cackled as Shamus went up to the counter.

Alex growled. "It's been a waste of a night, a bloody waste, that's what, and it wasn't helped by you interfering."

"More fool you, thinking Shamus could supply you with explosives. Apart from the utter idiocy of the idea, not to mention the danger, what possessed you to imagine he would do such a thing?"

"He's Irish, isn't he?"

"He's an intellectual, for Christ's sake," said Angelica fastidiously.

"Oh, hark at you. I suppose you fancy him. What would Arry say?"

A glass of brandy was placed on the table in front of Angelica, a half-pint of yellowish liquid before Alex and a dark overcoat was draped across the back of the chair.

"As the great Chinese philosopher Thai Sai remarked, a little drop of what you fancy can't do you any harm. But I think we've had enough philosophers for the night. It's time to talk of frivolous themes and cabbages and kings."

Angelica and Alex directed their gazes at the undone black jacket and continued upwards till they came to the gleaming white stiff collar beneath the smiling face of Father Shamus, priest of this parish.

Chapter twenty-two

There are several homecomings to record. The last will be obliquely dealt with when the occasion arises. We shall begin with Alex.

To say he was raging with curiosity would be overstating the case; but his headache did not help to soothe his bile. Did Ariadne know that her erstwhile lover and father of her daughter Bridgit was now addressed by the hung-over denizens of the Kilburn Republic as Father Shamus? Was the squeaky-clean clergyman, in his wild seed-sowing days, her fourth, fifth or tenth? The order of his coming and going was irrelevant now and his holy order could be regarded as darkly irreverent. And if she did know, why hadn't she told Alex? Was it her sly way of pricking his pomposity? Well, she's the expert on pricks. Think of all the wallies, wets and wimps she's had over the years. As for pomposity: Who? Me?

After ten minutes of half-listening to inconsequential chatter, Alex growled, "See you again sometime, Shamus," (Sub-text, never) and left the pub to march up Kilburn High Road; preoccupied with his failed tactics, shattered strategies and the inconstancy of fate and females. At Shoot-Up Hill he remembered that his car was left in a side street at the other end. Thirty minutes later he entered his flat, switched on the television and the radio in the kitchen, made a weak cup of instant coffee – he had lost all appetite for food – swallowed two Paracetamol tablets and returned to the main room to slump on the settee. With the remote control held like a ray gun, he spent what was left of the night channel-hopping.

Did he, one may wonder, reflect on the nature of good and evil? Alas, the answer is not since Sunday school. Alex even had difficulty in grasping that the good guys in Westerns wore white hats. "We might as well give up here and now," he muttered as he lingered on the opening titles of an old black and white film. A man with a pug face stood behind a desk in a cluttered book-lined room, a folder in his hand. "When Harvey Hardlock's body was found in the library of his palatial Surrey home, clutching a begging letter from his spendthrift son, the immediate diagnosis was that he had died of heart failure. But at the inquest, arsenic poison was found in his stomach. Was it self-administered or was he murdered? And if the latter, by whom?" Flick, flick to Sports Round-Up and two boxers pounding each other's brains to jelly.

There were two messages on the answering-machine. Number one was from Dawn. "Mum says when you come over on Sunday (Unsaid, for a free meal) will you make sure to bring your guest list. (Voice wobbles.) A terrible thing has happened, the wedding-dress shop in Wimbledon has gone bankrupt and we may not get our money back. Please ring, Alex. I'm reelly upset, I thought you might know what to do."

"In other words, Alex, you poor old sod, you need to find even more money than you thought. Angelica's cock-eyed scheme will have to succeed or I'm sunk without a trace. And talking of trace, what if Tracy brings a court case to milk me for more maintenance? Now that is evil."

The second message was from Ariadne. It began with a moan about the cost of all the phone calls she'd have to make to find relatives of the old fool of a schoolmaster. "And I forgot to mention it in the hurry, but guess who I saw at the hospital? HER! Is she pregnant? Think of the implication of that, Alex."

He did not think of the implication of that till the next day when he was having eggs and chips in a City cafe. Of course! Another mouth for the will to feed; another claimant for the inheritance.

Though Alex's contribution to the clerical pub's merry chatter had been limited to grumpy grunts, his rapid departure had the effect of drying up Shamus's loquacious flow. He rose to go, muffling his neck and saying, in a shy, almost embarrassed manner, "Nunc dimittis servum tuum, Domine."

Angelica tried a jest to breach what seemed to be a widening spiritual gap. "If you had a tune you could sing that."

He replied with a wry smile: "So could the tinker, tailor and candlestick maker."

Angelica was not too surprised that the pub was called The Meditating Monk; it was sufficiently tenebrous for any cloistered matins and lauds; but she was somewhat taken aback to see that the two old boys were also clergymen. "I suppose you're going to tell me, Shamus (it felt fatuous to call him Father), that the grousy barman is also a priest? Perhaps he's in training to be a Trappist?"

"I'll have you know, my dear girl, that in Ireland a bar-tender is called a curate. Tell me now, did you come by car, carriage or coracle?"

"I've parked down the road."

He took her arm in a soft grip as they hurried over the pedestrian crossing but let go as soon as their feet touched the opposite pavement. It seemed to her that he was keeping a discreet distance between them.

"You're not worried what the gossips might say if they saw you in the company of a blonde?" she asked rather boldly.

"If they did, I'd give them a hard penance that would keep them on their bony knees for the telling of twenty rosaries." Once again he took her arm. "I've traipsed these streets many times in delectable company and not a single eyebrow has been raised. It's the privilege of my calling."

"And what privilege is that?"

"The privilege of eunuchs."

Did she detect a tinge of bitter regret?

As she was fitting the key into the car, he asked, "Have you ever read The Tragic Sense Of Life by Miguel de Unamuno? It's a darling book."

She had never heard of book or author. "Perhaps you've a copy I could borrow."

"Perhaps and then perhaps not."

"What's its theme?"

"That's a short question for a long answer." She stepped inside and he leaned against the open door as he bent his body to look at her. "But to give you a flavour of the long and short of it, Unamuno writes that man – and woman, I should add – is constantly searching for the joys of eternal love but mistakes the carnal for the spiritual. The brief temporal ecstasy is followed by arid desolation."

"I don't understand that at all, Shamus."

He stood back from the car. "Neither do I."

When she entered the monastic cell of her small flat, she stripped off for a shower and stood for nearly a minute under the downpour. Then she inspected her thin, naked body in the long mirror, cupped her slight breasts with her hands and shivered. What price must be paid for brief temporal ecstasy when neither carnal or spiritual love intrudes this arid joylessness?

The two glasses of sanctified brandy had given her a taste for something more sinful than a mug of warm cocoa. She poured out a creme liqueur. There was a message on the machine from a spitting Ariadne, full of spurious outrage that a man of Ivan's age should even think of starting another family when he so wilfully neglected the one he already had.

What form would this offspring take as it hatched from the viper's egg?

Did Angelica, as she sipped the liqueur and listened to the opening Credo of Beethoven's Missa Solemnis (was it heretical for a Catholic priest to listen to a Protestant Mass?), reflect on good and evil, the misused maxim that the end justified the means and the nature of eternal love? The night was late and lonely, the music sonorous, the drink sweet in temporal joy. It was too late to change the tune, the chalice of sweet revenge had not yet been drained and there were too many lonely nights left before the end justified the evil.

But tomorrow? Confess? "Bless me, Father, for I have sinned in thoughts, words and deeds and the greatest sin of all, Father, is the wish I harboured, the will I enjoyed and the ways I worked to avenge myself on HER who had deprived me of my father. In mitigation, Father, I plead the tragic sense of life and the desolation of death." Then in a soft whisper. "Have you read about Heloise and Abelard? You may borrow my copy, Father."

Tomorrow and tomorrow and tomorrow.

"I'll see you tomorrow, dear. Don't worry. (Who's worrying?) The doctor said it's only a minor operation." Another minute of fussing concern, a wan smile at the pale man in the next bed, a quick glance around the ward, cough-cough in one corner, skinhead wrapped in bandages in another, a dirigible in the opposite bed with plastic tubes stuck in the nostrils. "At least you'll have company for the night. Tomorrow then."

Sally was still moist-eyed when she drove into their road and nearly collided with a station wagon that pulled up by their house. "Bloody hell, why didn't he signal?" When she parked the car in the garage around the back, she hesitated on the path. "Suppose we've been burgled again? Maybe there's someone already in there just waiting for me. Suppose you get a grip on yourself." The back door was not hanging off its hinges, the drawers were not spilled onto the floor and the house echoed with a spectral emptiness. The mewing cats filed after her into the lounge and butted their heads against her as she crouched on the sofa. As she went to feed them, someone banged brutally on the front door. "Alright, alright, be with you in a minute."

The large rotund figure of Shirley, commissar of the CARMAD campaign, prodder and pricker of bureaucrats, scourge of clipboard planners, stood on the doorstep, a big prosthetic cardboard box clutched to her expansive chest. "Ah, there you are. I did ring the bell but it doesn't seem to be working, you must have it seen to, and I thought, oh no, nobody's in and I have a dozen more deliveries to do (What was she? A midwife?), not that I mind making a second journey, nothing is too much for a good cause, I always say—" The box is thrust into Sally's arms. "It's absolutely imperative that these are sent out as soon as possible. Tell (Quick look at name on lid) tell Ivan that all he has to do is seal the envelopes and put on the address labels. Sorry that they're not self-sealed but those cost a mint and it's absolutely necessary to keep expenses to the minimum. Anyway, everything in the box is on recycled paper. Nobody can accuse our campaign of not being ecologically sound, can they?"

"But Ivan is not here. He is—"

"When he comes home then. I remember you, don't I, from George's party? Yes, of course. Poor George, he doesn't deserve all this trouble, does he. You have heard, haven't you? Wish I could stop and tell you all but I must dash. Tat-ta for now."

Shirley swept down the path like a Saracen-armoured car exploring the Falls Road and, with a final wave of her hand, boarded her station-wagon.

Sally laid the box on the table and took out an envelope. "What am I going to do with these? Nothing. Absolutely nothing." She drifted into the kitchen, set up the coffee machine, saw with some annoyance that the cats had ignored the stinky food on their tray and switched on the radio. A man barked, "Now, Missus Rover of Perth, it's not unusual for a 12-year old Pekinese like your Ruby to eat its own defecation". Quavering voice, "I know, but her breath smells."

"Oh shit," said Sally and switched off the radio. The silent house held its odorous breath. "Well, what can I do? I must go on living. We shall go on living, Ivan. Do I quote? I do. How many words are there for the doldrums? Lacuna? That hollow pit. Hiatus? What shall I do?"

When she returned to the lounge with the coffee, one of the cats was making a nest in the box and another was licking the sticky part of the envelope. "Out, damn spot," she said to them. "I'll get on with some work, that's what I'll do. There's that feature to be finished and—"

She piddled around for half-an-hour and then went into the study to switch on the word processor. "And what was the stupid woman saying about George and his troubles? What troubles? I wish he'd trouble to contact us about the wills."

The wish was answered though the troubles were not willed. The phone rang insistently. "If it's that bitch again with her bloody music, I'll give her a real mouthful," said Sally, who believed in direct hits.

"Hello, Sally. Richard here. I was wondering if you'd like to have supper with me some time this week. I'd like to talk over that proposition I put to you, you remember, about doing features on conferences. As I told you I have a flat in Eastbourne which you are free to use—"

"Sorry, Richard, but I'm busy this week. Ivan is in hospital and – "

"Really. Nothing serious, I hope. Still, it shouldn't stop you from dining out. After all, you must be lonely not having a man about the place. Shall we say Thursday?"

"I don't want to upset other people."

"Upset? Who? Prunella knows I have business lunches."

"I was thinking of Deirdre," said Sally insolently.

"Deirdre!" Pause. Sharply. "That's my affair, not yours." Receiver slammed down on cradle.

"God, I wish I had a man about the place." A second wish. Touch wood, throw salt over your shoulder while facing east, turn three times and make a third wish. "I wish I didn't feel so lonely."

Knock knock on the door.

"George, what a surprise. Do come in. I'm afraid that Ivan isn't here."

Pale face behind glistening glasses. Apologetic smile. Shuffles over threshold into lounge. Shoulders stooped. "I hope I'm not intruding. Interrupting anything important. I was passing this way and decided to call in with these." Flourishes large brown envelope. "The wills. So you can look them over and make any amendments. Of course, you both will have to come into the office to have them witnessed. Did you say Ivan's not here? I hope you don't think I'm guilty of dereliction but—" Long sigh.

"Would you like coffee, George? Have you eaten? I was about to make myself a meal."

Almost cringing. "I don't want to be any bother. I hate being a bother to people. I always try to be accommodating, tolerant, forgiving, perhaps too much—"

"You're no bother at all, George. I'll slip two supermarket specials in the oven, Mark 5, 25 minutes. Lasagne okay for you?" Sally began to feel cheerful. This was exactly the diversion she needed.

He stood in the kitchen doorway as she stripped off the Cellopane, put the packets on the top shelf of the oven and made more coffee. "I'm afraid I may have misled you, Sally. I wasn't really passing by. I'll go into more details – but no – why should I—where is Ivan?"

When she told him – "Only a minor operation. Should be out and about in a few days' time" – his moon face crinkled with worry.

"Oh dear, dear. I wish him well. Perhaps I shouldn't be here. I mean—"

"Is Deirdre expecting you?"

"Deirdre? Deirdre expects every man to do his duty."

"Give her a ring to tell her where you are."

"No! No!" It was very nearly a shout. He vanished into the lounge and when Sally brought in the coffee, he was pacing past the bookshelves. "You have a very fine selection, you and Ivan, quite a catholic taste. You don't mind me browsing, do you? Libraries are so personal."

While Sally read through the documents, he plucked out a book here and there, read a page or two, carefully replaced the volume and muttered, "I'm not disturbing you, am I? Please ignore me. Many people do."

"These seem to be in order, George, but, of course, Ivan must read them and—"

"Of course, of course, no question about that." He came over and looked miserably at her. "Sally, I have a request and a pertinent question."

"Can they keep for a minute or two. The meal should be ready now. I'll open a bottle of Liebfraumilch to celebrate the occasion. If you move that box—" She dashed in and out of the kitchen with plates, glasses, cutlery and the food.

George was staring morosely at the box which he laid on the floor. "I should be more active, more involved. And yet, I am. I have been. Was this the cause, the reason? Am I at fault?"

"Sit down, George. Bon appetit." Clatter of forks on plates as steaming pasta is raised to lips. "So, what shall we have first? The request or the pertinent question?"

"Please don't think my question is more impertinent than pertinent but I must ask you this. Are you having an affair with Richard?"

There was that knickerful of letters from Miss Anon (And we all know who that was) intended for the eyes of Ivan only, plus one signed with venom in the name of his wife. Still, even the implication was perversely flattering.

"The answer to that is no. Who told you such crap?"

"I knew it must be wrong. The truth is—" And the truth was, as it now came out in spurts and gasps, that the enraged Deirdre, in between furious sobs of jealousy, had confessed her involvement with Richard and had accused Sally of being the 'other woman'.

"And the request, George?"

"Could I – would you consider – could I hope?" (Surely not a second proposition in one night?) "That is, I would have asked Andrew and Zena but they have their own troubles, their house is small and they have children, but would you consider letting me stay here for the night. I could sleep on the sofa."

(Ah well, though the answer would certainly have been no, it would have been nice to be asked.)

When Sally came down after fixing up the bed in the spare room, George had emptied the box on the table and was busy sticking the labels on the envelopes.

"I must keep busy. Do something banal, something tedious, something to stop me thinking. We must work for today and for generations to come (Was he quoting?)."

"Why don't you phone Deirdre and tell her where you are?"

"I'll tell her I'm staying with friends." He dialled, waited and then replaced the receiver. "She's not at home. Who is she with now, I ask?"

Chapter twenty-three

What did Sally do next? Did she sally forth to greet the sallow sky with rheumy eyes or did she sully her chaste sleep with sultry dreams? Actually she excused herself in the politest of terms to her unexpected guest, assured him that though she would love to discuss the ways of the world and wayward spouses, she did have an urgent feature to finish. She then went into the study, switched on the word processor and began to type like a weary woodpecker.

At 11.30pm, hypnotised by the blinking cursor, she sat in a daze and at midnight, she gave up and went into the lounge. Like a good party hostess, she hid her fatigue behind a bared-teeth smile. George was huddled on the wild cat's favourite chair – the dispossessed feline stood a few feet away, its tail lashing in snake-winds – and seemed to be intently listening to a Wagnerian Doom and Drag CD. Ivan was a man of firmly held prejudices, though not in the least bigoted, and compared Wagner's operas to Nazi caterwauling; but one of his minor weaknesses was competitions and he had won a boxed set of Storm Troopers' Delight in a 'Fit-the-nose-to-the-composer' contest.

George was very still and quiet, all blubbering spent. His apparent deafness could have been caused by the strident female prop-forward bawling out a Rheinish rant, but he did not move when Sally leaned over and turned down the volume. It usually worked with Ivan. "Oh, my Gawd, what if he's dead?"

Imagine the headlines in the News Of The Screws. 'Prominent solicitor collapses in love-nest. Anguish of forsaken wife. Mistress's husband in hospital. Police investigate. Archbishop writes.' Sally tittered at her bad-taste joke.

"George, George, are you alright?" His eyes were extraordinarily pale and slightly out of alignment. "Who? What?" He struggled out of his coma. "Ah, Sally, it's you. I thought it was— What time is it? Goodness, is it that hour? Felt a bit queasy. Must have been all the excitement.(Nice of him not to blame the wine.) You are very kind to me, Sally."

He went upstairs very slowly. Sally gave him 20 minutes to do whatever men do in bathrooms before following. "Well," she said to herself as she lay in the half-empty bed, "the company, if you can call it that, was better than being lonely." She drifted into unconsciousness.

Brrr, brrr. "Hello, who's that?"

"George. Is he there? Tell him I wish to speak to him."

"George? George who? I'm afraid you've got the wrong number."

Sally turned to the phantom by her side for a cuddle and embraced an empty space. "Ivan, where are you? Oh no, I remember, I remember. And who was that biddy ringing up at this hour? What time is it? Seven?!!"

Eight o'clock. Hauled out of a doze. Brrr. Brrr. "Hello, who's that?" No reply. Sound of moaning cello in the background. Irate Sally sits up, receiver clutched to ear. "Listen, you long-haired streak of misery, I don't care from what fetid mire your coprohagous body crawled from to make these calls but I warn you: fuck off or else."

In the short space of time between the last word and the satisfactory slamming down of the receiver, a thin voice could be heard. "Please will you—"

On the other side of London the voice continued, "—try to stop Ivan handling those envelopes." The phone was slowly replaced. "Too late. Too late. But then, if it is to be done, let it be well done and make an end of it."

Sally was quite pleased with her instant fiery response but the heat of the moment was not sufficient to ward off the chill creeping over the half-empty bed. "There's nothing for it, Sally old girl. You're sans fleshy hot water bottle and sans coffee-making servitor. Arise, as morning breaks the bowel of night – is that right? – and talking of bowels and bladders—" She leaped out of bed and dashed into the bathroom.

"Is that you, Sally?"

Her guest had just finished sloshing water on his face and turned to stare blindly in her direction.

Gasp suppressed shriek, protective hand shot up to cover bouncing boobs and second protective hand shot down to hide her private parts. "Sorry, George, didn't realise—" Step backward three paces out of viewing angle of doorway and then turn to dive into bedroom, shouting as action hastens, "I'll wait till you're finished." Mutter-mutter. "Shit, I forgot all about him. Bet he's had more of an eyeful this morning than any time in the recent past."

He called out, "Alright, Sally, I'm finished now." He was still as pallid as he was last night and his large glasses gave him the appearance of a sickly snowy owl. As they passed on the landing – Sally now chastely clad in a sky-blue nightgown – he nodded towards the towel draped over his arm and the toilet bag (simulated leather) clutched in his fist. "Had them in my car. It's parked around the corner. Nobody will know I stayed the night with you."

Sally slammed the bathroom door and shot the bolt over. "Oh terrific! More of that and I'll have enough anon letters to paper the front room."

One minute later. Tap tap on the door. "Sorry to disturb you, Sally but is it alright if I make myself—"

"Yes, yes. Help yourself."

Another minute passes. Tap tap. "I don't mean to be a nuisance, Sally, but can you tell how the coffee machine works."

Groans of exasperation. Unbolts door and trots downstairs with mumbling guest ("Deirdre is quite good with these domestic devices but I'm really hopeless") bumbling in the rear.

Sally whizzed round the kitchen. Filled perforated cup with fine-grain coffee, filled centre cylinder with water, filled nodding guest's ears with terse instructions and filled importuning cats' tray with dry biscuits. Picks newspapers and four letters off the mat, ignores reproachful look from biscuit-hating cat and quickly returns to bathroom. Turns on shower tap, switches on plastic waterproof radio and sits on lavatory seat to read letters and papers.

Letters one and two: You could be the lucky person to walk away with our first prize of £10,000/ Drive away in our super super car. Chance would be a fine thing. Into bin. Letter three: A special invitation to a private viewing of The Art of Aural Decoration Down the Ages. Ear, ear. Letter four: Addressed to Ivan but the sender has not changed her scent. Another one for the exclusive knicker collection.

Guardian front page: (EC and UN in near accord on PPC with OPC at Cairo MES conference.), Mail (Duchess of Windsor dies without seeing a single episode of EastEnders. Man killed in Princess Di's village. Last night in the main street of Little Compost, by-standers and women and children were horrified to see Fred Mucker fall off his tractor dead-drunk. Little Compost is just 100 miles from Princess Di's residence and news of the tragedy was kept from her because she is still recovering from the trauma of a broken fingernail.)

There were at least two more tap-taps on the bathroom door but Sally made sure to keep the radio volume high – lots of loud pop with sound-bites of breathless babble – to protect her decorative aurals from outside interference.

Ten minutes later she emerged. "Is that you, Sally?" (Of course, it's me.) I'm, er, I'm off now and, er, just want to thank you—"

He held the CARMAD box in his arms, his towel and toilet bag on top. "I hope you don't mind me using your phone – tried to ask you but the radio was on – anyway, I had a chat with Deirdre, a long chat and—"

(Thinks Sally: "Who gets the phone bill when a solicitor talks to his wife? Will he discount this from our legal costs?")

"—we decided to give it another go, to try and resolve our – and she wants to thank you for looking after me – and – do tell Ivan not to worry about these envelopes. I'll do the necessary and give him my best wishes and – thank you very much, Sally, you're very kind—"

Sally in her blue gown stood in the front doorway and watched his short figure waddling down the path. She gave him a shy wave of her hand and shut the door.

Three days later Deirdre rang Sally to tell her George had died in his sleep. "Old Doctor Thoroughgood, he's our family doctor, you know (Even in sorrow, she's a snob), and has been for nearly forty years now, and he said that George was under a terrible strain with all the work he does – did – not only in his practice but also all that extra FREE legal advice he gave to feckless people. I've said to George over and over again, why don't you—" And so on and on in a similar vein concluding with a request. "Please, please, Sally, don't mention to anybody he stayed the night with you – oh dear, that sounds awful but you know what I mean (mini-sob mini-sob). I just don't know how to thank you for being so kind and—"

But we jump ahead of ourselves. Sally rang the hospital to ask about Ivan's operation. To innocent and inexperienced people, this would seem to be a simple matter of picking up the phone, dialling a number and within seconds receiving a direct answer to your question. But no. First attempt – engaged signal. Second try – engaged signal. Search directory to make sure you have the right number – yes, you're not blind and bothered or a daft old bat just yet. Third go. Success. Tired female voice, "Ello, Saint Jankers." Breath sigh of relief. "I'm enquiring about a patient who—" "You want Enquries. Hold on and I'll put you through."

One minute ticked by. Enquiries send call to Reception, Reception pass it on to Section A who put through to Section B. Next in line were Casualty/ Intensive/ Surgical/ Out-Patients/ In-Patients and finally back to the first person Sally had spoken to. Tired female voice, "Are you a relative? Oh, wife. Can't be too careful. All sorts of oddballs ring up. What did you say his name is? Don't seem to have it here. What was the ward again? Oh, yes. Hold on, I'll put you through to the ward."

Perky Irish accent. "Yes, your husband's had his op. He's sitting up in his bed as frisky as a two-year old and he'll be ready for a canter over the fields and far away."

"Next time I'll ring the vet first," thought Sally. That evening she was first through the door at visiting time. He wagged the empty sleeve of his pyjamas. "I'm afraid they had to cut my arm off," he said and for a horrible second she believed him. The skinhead swathed in bandages reluctantly rose from the bedside seat, scowled at her and carefully carried away a chessboard. "Finish the game later, uh, okay," he gloomed.

Sally and Ivan stared at each other. Hospital wards killed the art of conversation. It was by no means the only thing they killed, either.

"Are you feeling alright now? Are you getting enough food? Did you tell them you're a non-meat eater? I miss you. I think the cats do as well. So-and-so sends you their best regards. I finished that feature. God knows when it'll get in."

Sally did not tell him about her unexpected guest, about the CARMAD box of agit-prop or the early morning non-speaking phone call. "Don't want to worry the invalid," she said to herself.

At the exit doors, she looked back.The skinhead and Ivan were bent over the chessboard. As she was fitting the car key into the lock, a dilapidated off-white gas-guzzler whizzed by and Sally caught sight of a familar grumpy face leaning over the wheel.

Ariadne had a lot to be grousy about and the last thing she wanted to do was to trudge right across London, but the hospital administrators had insisted that she make the journey to give interminable details about her 'uncle'. Ariadne heartily wished he would do the decent thing and die. But who would pay for the funeral?

Back home, blow had followed blow. Robert Allen, her first-born, he whom she had named after her hero of heroes, had decamped to live with an older woman in outer Hendon, the twins' father had started court proceedings to have them placed under his care, citing her disorderly lifestyle as sufficient cause, Shamus, in his civilian guise, had taken Bridgit to Ireland – "A little holiday," he said but Ariadne had her doubts – she had been voted off two committees and her bank had sent her a nasty letter about her overdraft. Her deepest fear was that Mum might find out she now had a spare room and abandon Eastbourne to its easterly winds.

As for the great conspiracy, she did not dare to ask what had passed between Shamus and Alex. As for Angelica's scheme, her little sister had not said a word since the doctored envelopes were sent off. After much deep thought and stertorous breathing, Ariadne resolved to ask Amy, the only one still in contact with Ivan, to enquire after his health.

But first she had to listen to the flow of Amy's frets before wading in and fishing for information. "By the way, Amy, I've heard from someone who lives over there that Dad is ill. (Gasp from other end. "Oh dear, if it's not one thing, it's another.") I'd ring up myself but you know HER, she'd just tell me nothing, but after all he is my Dad and—"

"She can be a bit stand-offish but that doesn't bother me," said the valorous Amy. "I'll give them a ring and then let you know."

Sally was somewhat surprised to get a phone call from Amy. "Hello, Sally, it's me, Amy. It's been such a long time since we, that is, the kids and I came to see you and is Dad alright, only I heard he's ill."

"Who told you?"

"Oh well, really, it was a friend of a friend if you know what I mean. Is he sick then?"

"He did have to go into hospital but—" (Sound of rough male voice shouting into Amy's shell-like: "Bleeding hell, you're not on the phone again.")

"Had to go to hospital, did you say? (Male voice: "Where's me tea?") I must go now, Sally. I'll call you again."

10.30 the following morning: "Ari, it's me, Amy. I'm afraid I've some bad news for you. Dad's in hospital. She didn't say what for but she sounded upset. Do you think it's serious? I mean, I don't think I can stand any more shocks the way my health is—"

And answering-machine shall speak unto answering-machine.

Message: "Alex/Angie. Ariadne here. We must have an urgent meeting tonight. Dad has been taken to hospital. Sounds serious."

5.15pm. Return call from Angelica. Promises to be over by 7.30pm.

6.05pm. Return call from Alex. Grumble, grumble, just got in, just made a cup of coffee, just didn't feel like going out again, just about to put his supper on. Ariadne promises to give him supper (Thinks Alex with inward groan: Why does she insist on cooking in pots and pans instead of shoving a package in the oven like normal people?). Eventually and grudgingly agrees to come.

7.31pm. Angelica arrives. Notes that the children are strangely subdued and watching The Sleeping Beauty. "They're very quiet," she says. Ariadne replies,"That's because I told them if they didn't behave they'd be sent away as well. You know Robert has gone to live with a scrawny biddy nearly twice his age, Bridgit's gone to Ireland and I expect the twins are next."

"Bridgit gone? With Shamus?" Angelica sits by the table. "Is

Alex coming? We'd better wait then." Opens briefcase, takes out paperback book and begins to read.

7.45pm Alex arrives. Expresses fervent hope that this is not a waste of time and wonders why it could not be discussed over the phone. Complains about the skip outside the house. Glares suspiciously at Angelica's briefcase and asks her what old rubbish she's reading now. Snorts with disdain when she tells him that it's The Tragic Sense Of Life by Miguel Unamuno. "If you really want a good read, try Alistair Maclean."

8.05pm. Ariadne lays deep bowls and a steaming casserole in earthenware pot on table. Angelica declines food because she does not eat corpses. Alex tucks in.

8.06 to 8.35pm. Sounds of chewing and chomping from Alex and Ariadne. No sound from Angelica. Background noise of The Sleeping Beauty. None seemed willing to mention the 'situation'. Why this reticence? Surely now, with the possibility of success in sight, they would rally their teeming thoughts for the final charge towards the shattered lines of the enemy: HER.

Could it be that the worm of guilt was turning in their conscience? Or that one, or two, or three had fallen to contemplating the nature of good and evil and whether the ends tainted the means? We shall never know.

8.36pm. Ariadne opened her mouth first. She always did, impulsive to the last. First a mopping-up operation on all doubts. Was Amy quite quite sure? How serious did she say? Was Angelica really confident that her formula (the word 'poison' was avoided like – well – poison) would really work? Nod of the head. No need to go into previous experiments.

8.55pm. Discussions on options. Option one. If – well, we all know what we mean – and after the funeral we all return to the house, then we shall have to tell HER in no uncertain terms where we stand and what are our legal rights.

From Angelica: "We shall have to secure our entitlements, that is, we must be prepared to take an inventory of the house and be allowed to investigate bank accounts and building society deposits."

"Yes, yes," said Alex testily, "I was coming to that. As for the bank accounts and such, that's more your line of country."

Option two: If we are not invited to the funeral (Outraged cry from Ariadne: "She would not dare keep us away from our father's funeral"), we must, all of us, and that includes Amy, visit HER and do what we intended to do in the first place.

But if? If the situation was not what it seemed to be? If the hospital cured the afflicted man? Well then, we are back where we started. Was there a secret wish in each that those ifs might prove to be true?

The next day Ariadne had a bit of luck while going through the schoolmaster's grubby notebook in her search for his relatives. She tried five of the phone numbers – two were sex bookshops, two no longer existed and the last was a snooty men's club – but on the sixth, a woman with a languid high-faluting accent said, "Oh yes, I do believe Julian, my husband, has an uncle with that name. I'll ask him to speak to you when he arrives home. Thank you for calling." In the evening, Julian called. "Yes, your description does fit my uncle. Ill, did you say? Thought the old chap had passed away years ago. Mind you, we haven't spoken for yonks. Do you know if he has made a will? Could be complicated if he dies intestate." They made arrangements to meet and visit the old man in a few days' time.

When Ariadne entered the hospital foyer, a tall, trim man in a very expensive suit was talking to the receptionist. He turned and gave Ariadne a frosty look. "You must be my uncle's – for want of a better word – friend. I have been informed by this lady that you've claimed to be his niece. Is that correct?"

"You know what these bureaucrats are like. They're always getting hold of the wrong end of the stick."

"Be that as it may, it could prove to be a serious matter. If you'd care to wait, I'd like to discuss this further."

"I'll go up with you." But the receptionist cried out, "You can't go in. You're not a relative."

Ariadne went outside and lit a cigarette. We will not dwell on her thoughts at this moment. Other visitors were arriving and among them was Sally, dressed in sombre clothes, carrying a small suitcase and looking very downcast, in fact, almost distraught. Ariadne watched her speak to the receptionist and then go through the ward doors. "Well, who the hell can tell if she's pregnant with all that fat she's put on."

Ariadne re-entered the foyer. "Tell that man, the one I was speaking to, I have to go but if he wants to speak to me he has my phone number." She paused. "That woman who came in, she looks upset." The receptionist did not reply but a nearby cleaning woman piped up. "She's had a tragedy, poor dear. It comes to us all in the end."

When Ariadne arrived home, she made two phone calls.

Chapter twenty-four

It was the fourth phone call of the day. "Good afternoon, madam. I'm speaking to YOU on behalf of the Acme double-glazing company and I'm taking this opportunity to inform YOU of our new line in conservatories and, of course, to tell YOU of our special discount offer to selected customers and this means YOU." Though the words were carefully enunciated, there was something familar to Sally in the way certain phonemes were slurred.

"I'm sorry but I'm not interested—" (Hell, why should I apologise to these cold-caller creeps?)

"Ah, Madam, that's what they all say till they see our brochure and read our astounding discount offer. One of our highly trained surveyors will be in your area today, in fact he is calling into a near-neighbour of yours—"

"Don't you understand plain English. I don't want anybody calling, I don't want a conservatory."

"But Madam, our highly trained surveyor will just need a few minutes of your time without any obligations on your part."

"Listen, you insolent weasel, the last thing I want to hear is you—" (Why don't I just put the phone down?) Sally drew in her breath and then spoke in the measured tones of one speaking to a half-deaf idiot. "I have no wish to speak to any caller today, tomorrow, next week or ever. I have just returned from a funeral and—"

"Ah, Madam, you have just lost a loved one. Please accept our sincere consolation (Consolation?? He's not just a creep, he is a semi-literate creep) for your distress. But may I beg you to consider, even in this moment of sorrow, that if you are selling your house, a conservatory would certainly enhance the value—" He was still talking when Sally put the receiver back in the cradle. She then pressed the 'ready' button on the answering-machine.

Less than a minute afterwards the phone rang in a North

London flat. "It's happened," the caller announced. "She's just come back from the funeral."

"The conniving bitch, and not a word to us. Well, we'll show her."

"We'll go there tomorrow then?"

"Tomorrow? No, tomorrow's Saturday and I'm helping out with a car boot sale."

"Come on, they won't miss one body."

"I can't let them down. I'm secretary of the co-ordinating committee. It's a joint effort organised by Help the Aged, Save the Children and other good causes."

"Sunday then. Let's say for now, eleven o'clock outside the house. I'll let the others know."

When the caller laid down the phone, he said, "Co-ordinating committee. She couldn't co-ordinate a bag of oven-chips."

At five minutes past eleven on Sunday morning, Sally had begun to run the bath when the front door bell went DING. "That's funny," she thought, "it hasn't gone ding for ages." She waited a few seconds for the DONG but it did not come. The bell went DING again. She pulled the dressing-gown over her nightdress, wriggled her toes in the fluffy slippers, turned off the taps and, with her footwear slip-slapping on every step, descended the stairs. DING. "Won't be a sec," she called out as she removed the keys from the hook above the kitchen worktop. The cats emerged from their hiding holes, circled her, rubbed against her shins and the youngest nipped her ankle. "You'll just have to wait. Can't see to you all at once." She had turned the tubular lock and was about to fit the key into the mortice when a sense of caution stopped her. "Who could be calling at this hour on a Sunday morning?" She shuffled into the front room, pulled the heavy drape back an inch and peered out.

A middle-aged man wearing a dull brown suit accompanied by a slightly younger, sharp-nosed woman dressed in uniformly dull brown clothes stood facing the door. They both carried briefcases and the man held the newspapers against his chest. "Oh no, not them." Sally groaned. "They can go and God-bother elsewhere." At that moment she thought she saw Alex standing at the bottom of the path and pulled the drape back for a better view. Yes, it is he, frowning importantly at his super, anti-magnetic watch. Chugging towards him, like a naval corvette steaming toward an illegal fishing boat, came Ariadne.

Sally dashed into the hall, struggled with the obdurate mortice and then tugged at the sticky door. "What do you want?" she shouted. Ariadne stared blankly at her and Alex raised his arm slightly like a half-committed fascist. "With you in a minute," he replied.

"We bring you Good News," the middle-aged man said.

"What? What?" Sally asked in bewilderment. This was to be the first of many bewildered questions. A 2CV pulled up and Alex went over to talk to the driver, tapping his watchface as he did.

The middle-aged man triumphantly brandished the newspapers just beyond Sally's reach. "But you won't find the Good News in these organs of Satanic perversion. No, the Good News all men expect can only be found in the Bible."

Angelica emerged from the 2CV, an executive briefcase in one hand and a clutch of clipboards in the other. A transit van stopped behind her car and she and Alex went over to talk to the occupants. Ariadne stood foursquare at the bottom of the path, her arms folded as she stared at the doorway.

"And who has been ordained to show the way to the truth and bring the Good News to those who seek in vain among the false books of Satan, you may ask."

"I didn't ask," Sally replied with increasing irritation, "and, if you don't mind, get off my doorstep or I'll—"

"Many have spoken to us in wrath till we delivered unto them the Good News."

"Praise be to God for his infinite wisdom and mercy," the man and woman intoned in unison.

Alex was the first to reach the doorway. Behind him, in single file, came Ariadne, Angelica, Robert and, almost invisible behind him, Amelia. "Excuse me, excuse me," Alex said politely and firmly to the man and woman. They parted to let him pass but Sally stood in his way. The small crowd bunched up behind him.

"What are you doing here, Alex?"

"We have every right to be here. In case you've forgotten, let me remind you that we're Ivan's children."

"You don't need to remind me of that. And Robert? He's not one of Ivan's mistakes. He's some other benighted person's error."

Robert pushed to the front. "If I was you, young woman, I'd be very careful about what you say. I am here as an officer of the law to make sure there isn't a breach of the peace and in my book obstruction is an indictable offence."

"So, whether you like it or not, we are exercising our legal right to enter this house."

"This is my house!"

"That is something which will have to be determined by a court of law, that is, if you want matters to go that far." Alex pushed past the now-flabbergasted Sally, followed closely by Ariadne who snorted, "Your house!" as she went by.

"Just a minute, just a minute." Sally's frantic attempt to fly after the intruders was hampered by her fluffy slippers and a cat brushing against her legs. She stumbled into the see-through lounge and, with claws extended, tried to grab Ariadne; but Robert suddenly came between her and her quarry.

"It is my duty to warn you that the use of force or unnecessary violence to impede the execution of a legal enactment can warrant a charge of first-degree assault and grievous bodily harm."

"Grievous bodily balderdash! It's no wonder you're still plain constable Plod with all that gobbledegook. I was only thinking of necessary violence to clear this rabble from my house." 'This rabble' now consisted of the three sisters, their brother, the brother-in-law and the two God-botherers. They all stood in an intimidating ring around Sally.

"Your house!" Ariadne repeated with the same disdainful snort.

"I hope I don't have to add insulting language to the list of offences," Robert said sternly.

"And what are they doing here?" Sally pointed to the God-botherers.

"I invited them in to comply with the letter of the law," said Robert. "In view of the attempts to obstruct, to commit violence on a member of this party and the use of abusive and insulting language likely to cause a breach of the peace, I felt it was my duty to call in a person or persons unattached to the case in question to act as independent observers to prevent future allegations of a malicious nature. I therefore asked this gentleman and lady to be our witnesses.

"But we are Witnesses," they both cried. "We are Witnesses to the coming of the Lord God!"

Ariadne's mouth dropped open, Angelica turned slightly away and Amelia twittered, "Oh, that's nice. We're not really church-goers ourselves."

"Oh God!" Sally's desperate cry was louder than the Trump of Doom. She had gone past the point of explosive outrage and was trying to convince herself that this was some dream. "I'll wake up soon," she half-whispered and closed her eyes. "Then I'll come downstairs, put on the coffee pot and feed the cats." She opened her eyes but they were still there. Alex stood directly in front of her, holding up his left arm to frown importantly at his satellite-seeking watch. Even though he wore specially raised shoes and Sally was in her slippers, she could still see the crown of his head. "He's got a bald patch," she noted with daft irrelevancy

"We've wasted enough time as it is," Alex said in his best officious tone. "We wouldn't have had to come to this extremity if you had bothered to keep us informed."

"Typical!" Ariadne declared. "Tried to keep it all to herself, she did, and not say a word to us who've got a moral as well as a legal right to be here."

Alex clicked his fingers and, like a well trained troupe of performing poodles, the three sisters stepped smartly up to the table and Bob stood stolidly to attention by the door. At a second signal, a curt nod from the ringmaster Alex, Angelica laid the executive briefcase on the table, opened it, took out lined sheets of paper which she clipped on the boards and then handed one each, plus pen, to her brother and sisters. She offered another to Robert but he refused, asserting that as he was here as an officer of the law to prevent a breach of the peace, he could not participate.

"What about them?" Angelica asked, pointing to the man and woman.

"Oh no, they must remain impartial. They're witnesses."

"Yes, we are Witnesses to the coming of the Lord." The man took out a handful of magazines from his battered brown briefcase. "Would you care to read the Truth?"

"Not now. Not now." Alex nodded towards the sofa. "Why don't you sit down and watch."

"We shall watch, as if it were the tower of a beleaguered city," the woman said as she and her companion flopped down on the puffed-up cushions.

Sally spoke slowly and carefully but loud enough for none to miss a word. "I object strongly to everyone of you barging into my house." She looked sharply at Ariadne. "I repeat, my house. Before I ask you to leave, no, before I demand that you leave, tell me exactly what you think you are doing."

"I should imagine, even to you, that that is obvious." Alex replied scornfully. "We are taking an inventory of the contents of this house, which includes whatever is in the garage, the garden shed, and, of course, the loft. Now, if it's all the same to you, we'll make a start. I'll begin with the garage. Is the back door locked?" He snapped the dangling keys from Sally's hand. "Which one opens the back door? Never mind, I'll sort it out for myself."

"What in hell's name gives you the authority to do this?" said Sally.

"Authority? By the authority invested in us as the rightful heirs of our father. What else?"

"But your father—"

"I'll do the kitchen," Ariadne said as she and Alex went out. Within seconds, there came the clatter of pots and pans being hauled out on to the floor.

Sally felt both dizzy and confused and slumped down on the sofa between the witnesses. The man dropped a magazine on her lap. "You are troubled, dear lady, with the weight of worldly goods but if you turn from this dross to God, he will erase all temporal trouble from your heart. Read the words of Truth."

"Praise be to God's words of Truth," the woman intoned.

Angelica took a tape measure from her case and directed Amelia to count a section of books. "You do have a lot of books," Amy said to Sally. "However do you find the time to read them all? But then, of course, you haven't any children, have you? I thought to myself, I did, when I saw you in your dressing-gown at eleven o'clock on a Sunday morning, how lucky some people are."

"Who's looking after your children now?" Sally was surprised at herself for asking such a trite question so calmly.

Robert, on point duty by the door, supplied the answer. "A colleague, WPC Wendy, kindly offered to sacrifice her morning rest period to oblige me."

Amy muttered under her breath, "WPC Wendy is after what she can get." Aloud she said, "Angie, I've counted these in this section. Shall I count the rest?"

"No, I'll just measure the length." Angelica ran the tape along the shelves. "Twenty-two inches in that section. Sixteen sections. How many did you say? Twenty. Averaging out, that is 320 assorted hardback books, an approximate value of – let me see – " She looked at a typed piece of paper. "How much is that per yard? No, I'll have to convert it to metres."

"Yards! Metres!" Sally exclaimed. "That's your father's collection of Tolstoy, Marlowe, Eliot, Pound, not to mention the art books. You can't measure culture by the yard."

Angelica was now counting a section of records. She spoke without turning around. "No, that's true. New EEC regulations have banned the yardstick but then, when culture is a commodity, it must be counted, weighed and measured in the appropriate commercial units. As for secondhand books, they are normally bought and sold in bulk."

Sally was at a loss how to make a valued reply to the accountancy weighed-and-measured statement and did not even react when the man beside her leaped to his feet and cried, "There is but one true book, the Holy Bible, and all other books should be consigned to the flames of perdition."

"I must ask you, sir, to be silent," Robert said.

Alex marched in. "That's the garage done. There's a scratch on the nearside of the car and the lawn mower hasn't been properly maintained. These things tend to lower the re-sell value. How are we doing ?"

"Angie seems to be in control here, Alex," said Amelia. "I'm only in her way. What would you like me to do?"

"Why don't you go upstairs and begin with the bathroom."

"It's not advisable to go upstairs." For the first time in this whole episode, Sally began to feel self-possessed.

"Why not?"

"Oh, go upstairs if you want to. I won't stop you."

"I hope you've realised by now that it's not in your power to stop us." Alex spoke with the aggression of an office boy left in charge of other unruly office boys.

"Shall I go then, Alex? The bathroom, did you say?" "Yes, Amy, go on then. You know what to do. Angie, don't bother with the hi-fi. I'll check out all the technical equipment. I'm going to tally what's in the study. As far as I can remember, there should be the word processor, printer, typewriter, tape recorders." He turned to Sally. "I hope nothing's been moved."

"Moved? Why should anything be moved? While you're in there, dust down the printer and give the screen a wipe. I'd ask you to do a spot of hoovering as well but the machine has been playing up lately."

Her coolness irritated him. His upper lip curled and his nose wrinkled in an effort to simulate a nasty sneer. "I suppose you think we should be sorry for you. I suppose you imagine we should be offering you our sincere consolation (Consolation??) for your loss. Well, let me tell you, you're badly mistaken—"

"How's business with the Acme double-glazing company?"

"Don't know what you're talking about. You should know that I'm a national expert and—"

"Then why don't you finish your inventory as quickly as possible. I want to get dressed, have breakfast and give the place a thorough spraying of air-freshener. And before you all shake the dust of My House from your heels, which I hope will be very soon, please leave your stock-taking sheets behind. I've always wanted to find out exactly what we possess but I've never got around to doing the job."

There had always been a surrogate sibling rivalry between Sally and Alex. His cheeks turned ruby-red and he stormed out of the room, shouting as he went, "We'll see about that, we will. We'll see about that."

"I'm glad for your sake, young woman, that you're taking things a lot calmer now." Robert rocked on his heels and put his hands behind his back. "Under the circumstances, I think we can forget about the abusive language and the obstruction, yes. Heat of the moment, you could say."

"It's the grace of God," said the man. "He turneth away wrath."

"Praise be to the grace of God in the moment of wrath," intoned the woman.

For a few seconds Sally almost felt benign and wondered if, when she made some coffee, she should offer all these busy people a cup each, perhaps with a few plain biscuits. Angelica was now counting the CDs. She picked out one and looked at the picture on the jewel case cover. "I see you have Berlioz' Symphonie Fantastique."

Benignity be damned. "Put it back where you found it," Sally snapped.

Amelia shouted downstairs. "The bathroom is locked."

"Never mind that, Amy," Robert shouted back. "Start in the next room."

"I've looked in there. It's full of tools and such."

Alex appeared in the doorway. "Never mind them, Amy. I'll check out the tools." He pushed the coffee table to one side and towered over the sitting woman. "Where are the keys to the desk?"

"Why?"

"Why?" His voice grew louder with every word. "Why? Because I want to see what's in it, that's why. And another thing, where's the car logbook and where are the deeds for the house? Where do you keep them?"

"In the top drawer of the bureau," Angelica said.

All past mysteries were falling into place for Sally and in that second or two, time expanded to allow her to recall events as if she were rewinding a tape in slow motion.

Alex strode down the room and nearly bumped against Ariadne as she steamed in.

"In all my born life, I've never seen an oven so filthy," exclaimed Ariadne. "Half the pots are rusty and as for that manky Welsh dresser with those cracked plates—"

"It's locked. It's locked." Alex was frantically pulling at the top drawer. His enraged voice hit a falsetto note. "Where's the effing key?"

Enough was enough. Sally brushed the accumulated holy magazines off her lap and stood up. The man and woman also stood up.

"Are you very anxious to have the keys?"

"We have the key to the truth," the man and woman said together.

"Of course, we bloody well want the keys."

"Then why don't you ask your father for them?"

All eyes were fixed on Sally and several mouths fell open. From upstairs came the sounds of a cistern flushing and then a door opening. "Hello, Amy. What are you doing here?" Ivan asked

In quick succession, there came a scream, a gurgle, a rasping gasp and then the soft thump of a plump body hitting the floor.

Chapter twenty-five

At the successive sounds of the scream, the gurgle, the rasping gasp and the soft thump of a plump body hitting the floor, all turned towards the doorway and froze as if captured in a still photograph.

(The stage is darkened, the watchers stir uneasly in their seats, rustle papers, fumble with coats and handbags. "Is this the end?" some ask. Others whisper anxiously to their partners, "But I don't understand. What happens next?" A scatter of applause rattles down the aisles from the rear – where friends of the actors are sitting – and, row by row, increases in a drum-roll crescendo. The stage-lights come on to reveal an empty room.)

Robert was first out of the door and up the stairs, followed closely by Alex and Ariadne. The voices grew louder on the landing with Ariadne's the highest as she demanded to be let through. "I have medical training, you know." (Her six months behind Boots' counter.) Angelica replaced the CD and, in almost a conversational tone as if there was no hubbub elsewhere, said, "I have the LSO version of the Symphonie Fantastique."

Sally was equally calm. "Yes, we know. We've heard it on the phone, that and other dire dirges."

"Oh, you have. Then perhaps I should leave." She picked up her briefcase.

"No, not perhaps you should. You will leave. You all will leave."

"First, I'll see—" She went out of the room, hesitated and then tip-toed up the stairs.

Sally gripped the middle-aged man's right arm just above his elbow – thumb and index finger pressed hard against the bones – and his female companion's left arm on the same spot. "All includes you two." She then held her arms out in front, as if pushing a shopping trolley, and propelled the pair through the lounge doorway into the hall where she released her hold, pulled the sticky front door open and stepped behind them. "In these times of domestic turmoil God's consoling words—" the man began. Sally placed the flat of her right hand against his spine and the flat of her left against the woman's, pushed them both stumbling over the threshold and slammed the door.

(For a second nothing happens on stage and then, two by two, beginning with the very minor characters, the actors enter upstage, walk towards the front, bow – all smiling with hopeful expectation of good reviews and something more than a ripple of applause – and each pair separate to stand to the right or left. When the obligatory noises of appreciation fade, the house lights come on and the audience shuffle up the aisles towards the exits. "But what happens next?" A persistent woman asks. Is she wondering whether her companion has booked a table at a posh restaurant or will whisk her back to his Barbican flat or hurry her through the litter-strewn, crowded streets where the car is parked half a mile away? Or is she emotionally and/or intellectually affected by the drama/ dark comedy she has witnessed?)

But what happened next? That is a vext question.

The mourners sat, heads bowed and faces stiff and stern, eyes fixed on the tiled floor by their feet,while the preacher tediously spoke the platitudes of his calling and only one emitted a sob when he, looking at the card in his hand, talked of 'our beloved daughter, Amelia, loving wife and mother.' At the rasping sounds of There Is A Green Hill Far Away (Words written on a hillside, now known as Bogside, overlooking the walled city of Derry) the congregation rose to their feet, and each, clutching a hymn book, sang and stumbled through the unfamiliar words in reluctant harmony.

When the ceremony was finished, the preacher came down from the podium, said a few words to the chief mourner, patted the heads of the bewildered children and hurried to an adjoining room. "When's the next due?" he asked his assistant. "15 minutes. Time enough for a coffee, yes." While the assistant poured hot water into two mugs, the preacher lit a cigarette."Funny crowd, this lot. Have you noticed? None of them spoke to one another. Wouldn't think they were a family."

A coffin's length from the ionic-pillared portico of the Chapel of Rest, the adult members of the congregation stood, separated by a palisade of silence like dark-clad strangers on a bleak railway station platform. For a short while nobody spoke or stirred, not even as much as to stare with curiosity when a second cortege crunched to a halt on the gravelled lane fifty yards away. Then a child whimpered, "Dad, I wanna go – I do. Badly." The chapel weeper emitted another sob and cried, "Ah, the poor, poor orphaned children. What is to become of you?" The child's father looked blankly at the sobber. "We better make a move then," he said.

One by one, the mourners trudged in single file down between the linear cypresses and none but the chief mourner spoke a word to or threw a glance at the man who had stood apart from the gathering, his face turned away like one who did not wish to be party to their public show of grief.

Alex stood at his door, the keys jangling in his hand. There was something wrong. Yes, he could feel it, something indefinable, an intrusive sense of unease. Intrusive? Intruder? He quickly inspected the windows and the beadings around the door but there was no broken glass, no tell-tale marks of a jemmy.

He turned the keys in the three locks, pushed the door in, waited for two seconds, then entered his cold flat, switched on the main light, picked up the mail and, slowly turning in the middle of the floor, made a visual check to see that all he held precious were still in their places. Yes, the list was complete. Precious items in their proper places: the television set, the video machine, the midi-HiFi system with its continuous loop tape section, the record collection (Beatles, Freddie and the Dreamers, Cliff Richard, early Elton John, Gloria Gaynor, Shirley Bassey, three box sets of select Classics for Lovers), the ornamental silver-plated chess pieces (A Christmas present from his fiance: "You told me so much about how you used to beat your father at the game three times out of four") and, of course, the cat's-cradle executive toys.

Then all was for the best in this best of all small worlds and the best way to secure this domain and better still, to off-load the worries, the fretting tensions, the numbing sense of guilt engendered by this preceding worst week of all possible worst weeks, was to snap back into mindless routine. Switch on the television, switch on the kitchen radio, make coffee, put a package in the oven – no, not the last. He had no appetite after the funeral feast.

Funeral Feast! "I've made a cold collation for your guests, Bob, is that alright," a busy neighbour had said as she directed the mourners towards the plates of sliced meat, potato salad and shredded lettuce. Angie had muttered to him – it was the only time she spoke to him all day – "Thrift, thrift, Horatio. The Sunday joint does coldly furnish forth the funeral table." He did not understand her remark, something snide without a doubt, and pretended not to have heard her. And who was Horatio? Wait, wait. What about, 'I knew him, Horatio.'? Or, 'There's more things in heaven and earth, Horatio.'? Could it be the same person?

Bob stood like a stunned ox at one end, talking in low tones to two other men, obviously coppers. Where was WPC Wendy in his hour of need? Apparently had asked for and obtained a transfer to Manchester, of all places, to be near her mother.

Of course, Our Mum, in between putting on short performances of her bereaved-mother act – gushing tears on tap, muffled sobs, cries of "My lovely daughter" – bustled in and out of the kitchen and so hustled the helpful neighbour that the woman took off her apron and left without another word. "I thought HE (Ivan) would have made an effort to come here," she said in turn to her surviving children, "if nothing else, at least to have a few words of support for poor Bob." Poor Bob, indeed. "Amy married beneath herself." As did Alex and Angelica. Ariadne's countless men did not count.

Later she announced that, "She owed it to her lovely daughter (muffled sob) to abandon, nay, sacrifice her sea-view apartment in Eastbourne to come and live in this house and give back to the dear little ones some of the love and attention that had been so dreadfully snatched from them."

The hours dragged by till only the immediate family remained and though the conversations were desultory and the space between every sentence was a two- to three-minute gap, none of those who had homes elsewhere seemed willing to be the first to depart. Why? Could it be that each one feared a conspiracy by the others to burden him or her with the blame?

Alex was the one to take that risk. "Let them for all I care. I know what they'll say. If Alex hadn't asked Bob and Amy to lend support that morning none of this would have happened. How was I to know, I ask you? Typical, isn't it.I always get the blame, no matter how innocent I am. But life must go on, that's my motto, and there's no point brooding over what has happened. It has happened and that's that." There was a knock on the door and the woman from downstairs stood on the mat. "It's only me," she said and handed him an envelope. "Your children and their mum were here earlier and asked me to give you this. Tar ra for now."

"Wants more money, I bet. Read it when I've looked through the rest." There was only one real letter among the heap of junk mail.

'Dear Alexander,

(It's from Dawn's mother. Why doesn't Dawn write to me?)

'We were terribly upset to hear your sad news and—(At least twenty more lines of polite condolence)

'Of course, under the circumstances, there's no question but the marriage will have to be put back. We have given up all hope of recovering any of the money from that Wimbledon Bridal shop. (Skip this section. Bound to be heavy suggestions that he should make extra contributions. Turn over page.)

'—but then we, that is Dawn, her father and me, have had a long talk about it and we have come to the conclusion that this delay does give everyone time to reconsider. You see, Alexander, the problem is you are much older than Dawn and—'

He crumbled up the letter, re-smoothed it, read it again then threw it on the floor and stamped on it. "Too old, is it, too old," he shouted at the television. "Let me tell you my Dad is—" A dreadful thought struck him. "What if, in years to come, Michelle and Darren were to conspire against me,their own father—no, they wouldn't." He tore open the other envelope.

(A scrawl from Tracy.)

'I got sick and tired waiting for you to come to a des (crossed out) make up your mind about them pots and things my granny gave me for a wedding present theyr rightfully mine the solliciter said and we came around today to get them but as your not in Shel knew a way to open your window and she and Dar got through and handed them out to me. Dont take it out of them they only did what I told them to.

'Tracy.'

What a liar. Of course she knew I would not be at home today. And how did Michelle undo the latch-locks from the outside? A sudden recollection. Three days ago, when he had the children over for the afternoon, they were standing on chairs by the window, giggling. Up to some little child-like game, he had thought. Gawd, anybody, just anybody could have got in that way and stolen his Beatles' records, knowing full well that they are collector's items.

A man with a muddy face glared out of the television screen and shouted, "I was not angry since I came to France until this instant."

"My feelings exactly, mate," said Alex. He allowed the anger to well up within himself. It was the first time in this week of numbed sensibility that he had indulged in any primal emotion.

After the funeral, Ariadne had tried to return to normal, to be her old self again, to pick up the threads but, as for the last, the skein had become unravelled. She had rung around to various groups, even those who had voted her off the committee – just to see how things were going – but the replies were a variation of, "We're all very sorry to hear about your sister and we agreed that for the next few months, we shouldn't really bother you." Even CARMAD Shirley was not interested in this willing volunteer ('What else have I to do?') " I really think, my dear, you should absolutely get over your sad loss first—I know what it's like. Dear friend and helper died days after he had handled some of those envelopes (Ariadne felt a sudden chill)—Thank you very much for offering your valuable help—we'll keep in contact."

Whenever the phone rang, she pretended indifference and snapped at one of the children to 'answer it. Can't you see I'm busy?' Busy? As the song went, busy doing nothing. But her heart did leap with expectation. Someone, somewhere would surely be saying, 'Let's ask Ariadne.' None of the calls were for her. Perhaps she should ring Alex, Angelica – she had not heard a word from them since that day – or Bob, just to see how he was coping. But no, no to the last. She would only get Mum. Of course, there was Dad. Why not? She rehearsed her opening remarks. "Hello Dad, it's me, Ariadne. I was wondering about the outcome of your operation. Have you had the results of the test yet?" But what if the call was answered by HER? Alternative opening remarks. "Hello, Sally, it's me, Ariadne. How are you? I've been terribly worried about Dad's operation."

Three days and nights went by before she plucked up the courage to dial Ivan's number. "Hello, who's that?" It was HER. For a second the rehearsed words stuck in Ariadne's throat. "Bloody hell," the other voice continued, "I thought I told you to stop these calls."

"Sally, hello, Sally." It was hard to use that name. "It's me, Ari, I mean, Ariadne. How are you? I've been –" Click, buzz as the phone at the far end was put down. Four minutes later Ariadne's phone rang. 'I know what's happened. Dad asked HER who called and when he was told he said, "She's my daughter after all. I'll talk to her." '

A man's voice. "Am I speaking to Ariadne?" Framed in the mouth for gushing leap over the lips, 'Dad! How lovely to hear from you.' Phrases sink back as voice continues, "This is Julian, Ron Pharfetch's nephew. Extremely sorry to hear about your sister." In brief, the brief message was that smoothy chops wished to discuss 'certain matters' relating to her posing as the Schoolmaster's niece and would like to see her at some convenient time. A convenient time – "I am up to my eyes at this moment, but" – was fixed for the following week.

This reminded Ariadne of the cardboard box-full of 'collector's items' and after searching through the yellow pages, she found a book dealer in Hampstead who might be interested. It was a dusty, grubby shop and the man had a dribbly nose. "Well, it's a pretty grotty lot, nothing of real value. Tell you what, I'll give you a fiver. Alright then, I'll make it a tenner to take them off your hands. Okay, let's say fifteen, the extra to cover your fare. That's my final offer. Suit yourself, but if you change your mind – let me have your number just in case a genuine collector comes in."

When Julian called, he seemed ill at ease, looked nervously at the children as if afraid they might bite his ankles and, at first, refused a coffee. "Uncle Ron has passed away," he announced. She showed him the box of booklets and papers – "didn't want any jobsworth flinging them in the incinerator" – and he replied that he knew a man (He would), an old chum from Oxford, who was in the antique business and could assess their worth. Then he relaxed, did not mention her 'niece' pretence and talked in general terms about how people like him in high-powered executive positions found it difficult to meet 'real' people. As they say in the best novels, their eyes met across the table. Just then the phone rang.

"If you'll excuse me, Julian." Maybe when they were on more familiar footings she could call him Jules. Hey Jules

"Why, hello, Mum. How are you getting on with—oh, I see, I mean, you're not imagining—he can be a bit abrupt—"

While she listened and said "Yes, no, I see" at suitable intervals Julian inspected the contents of the box and when, five minutes later, she put down the phone, he was standing up.

"I'm sorry about all that, Julian, Mum's having a difficult time with her son-in-law, my dead sister's husband. He is—"

"I really must dash, Ariadne. Thank you for everything. Very nice coffee." He and the cardboard box disappeared out of the door. A week later he sent her a cheque for twenty-five pounds, 'to cover her expenses' (Was this a parting gift?) he wrote in the accompanying note. He also added that his chum had said the booklets etc. were of very minor literary interest. The same day the book dealer rang to offer her fifty. One month after all this there was a news item in the Guardian about a James Joyce handwritten manuscript, a sequel to Finnegan's Wake, discovered among a pile of fairly useless pamphlets. The lucky (unnamed) finder told the reporter that he had already been offered £30000 for this extraordinary literary artefact by a Japanese university.

For two days Angelica did not stir from her flat, put the answering machine on – nobody rang – and laid her mail to one side unopened. For two days and nights she listened to music, requiem following requiem, and read, re-read and contemplated The Tragic Sense Of Life. On the third day she rose, removed the secret cassette tape from the briefcase and cut the ribbon into one-inch pieces. Then she went into the bathroom, turned on the shower, stripped and stared at her naked reflection in the mirror. She held the long pointed scissors in her left hand and stared at the blue branching veins on her right wrist.

"To die, to sleep – but this is irrational, against nature – who am I to talk of nature or what is natural. I exist, I am, I live, I think, breathe. I have my own contained world, this place, my music, my books, myself and I need none to intrude into my private space."

She changed the scissors into her right hand, lifted up a hank of her blonde tresses and cut. Snip. Snip. Snip.

The doorbell rang. She hastily flung on a gown, turned off the shower and opened the door.

"Mumsie, what are you doing here?"

"That's a fine question to ask your mother after she's traipsed all over London to be with you. Didn't you get my letter? I would have phoned but anytime I did, he started on about the cost and of course his brats spied on my every move. That's the thanks you get for doing your best."

"But, Mumsie, are you not looking after Bob's children?"

"Would I be here if I was? I just couldn't stay there another minute. Complaints, arguments, and to cap it all, his divorced sister and her brood came down from God knows where in the North. I've told you all this in my letter."

"What are you going to do now?"

A man, breathing heavily, stood outside the door, two large suitcases at his feet.

"Will you pay him, Angelica dear, oh, and give him a bit extra for bringing up the cases. What am I going to do now, you ask? Well, I thought you looked a bit scrawny, anorexia is the word, when I saw you at the funeral and I decided you needed a mother's care. What have you done to your hair? So that's what I'm going to do. I'm coming to take care of you, of course."

Sally did not ask Ivan anything at all about the funeral. What was there to ask? Anyway, he would tell her when he was ready. When he did return home, he looked tired, fretful and (she tried to brush this from her mind) aged. Of course, he may have been anxious about the results of the test. A week went by with one reluctant to mention the past events and the other too sunk in inner reflections.

Two things happened to breach the wall of silence. The results arrived, Sally opened the letter, her heart in her mouth. He had had what the laboratory people termed cat-scratch fever, not the dreaded big C. Ivan brightened and began to talk about the second cortege on the day. It was, apparently, for the mother of two leading members of a South London gang.

The second event was Ariadne's foreshortened phone call. All that Sally had kept suppressed now surged up and smothered her with a feeling of utter distaste. When Ivan came in that night, she was standing in the middle of the lounge with a large plastic bag at her feet. It was half-filled with torn paper, the anon letters somewhere near the bottom.

"Why are you doing that?"

"Because—" she opened a grey cardboard box and ripped up old receipts, delivery notes and guarantee forms. She had always been so careful to keep these, though many went back several years. "Because I am leaving—"

"Leaving?" He hesitated to add 'me'

"I am leaving this house. It has been invaded, mauled, soiled, tainted with envy, jealousy, greed, and – yes – death and hatred. Those people, your evil children, my wicked stepchildren, have brought their sickness into my home and everything I touch is smeared with the sweat of their diseases."

"So they've won, then?"

(The theatre is empty. The cleaners and the ushers are in the foyer, laughing, telling rude jokes. The manager unlocks the door and calls out, 'Goodnight, sweet ladies, goodnight.'

A wraith crosses to centre stage, stands and speaks to the depleted seats. 'If we shadows have offended, think but this, and all is mended: That you have but slumbered here while these visions did appear. And this weak and idle theme no more yielding but a dream.')